Donna A

Christmas
in the
Scottish
Highlands

bookouture

Published by Bookouture in 2021

An imprint of Storyfire Ltd.
Carmelite House
50 Victoria Embankment
London EC4Y 0DZ

www.bookouture.com

ISBN: 978-1-80019-351-2
eBook ISBN: 978-1-80019-350-5

Christmas
in the
Scottish
Highlands

BOOKS BY DONNA ASHCROFT

Summer at the Castle Cafe
The Little Christmas Teashop of Second Chances
The Little Guesthouse of New Beginnings
The Christmas Countdown
The Little Village of New Starts
If Every Day Was Christmas
Summer in the Scottish Highlands

To Nick Cook
An amazing teacher

Chapter One

Belle Albany slowly pedalled her red bicycle out of Christmas Village Primary School and swung right onto the main high street. Her breath caught as she took in the imposing mountain ranges that flanked the edges of the valley where Christmas Village was located. Despite living in the small Scottish district since she was eight, she was still in awe of the stunning views. It was only four o'clock but the sun had already started to set behind one of the highland peaks – and the globe-shaped street lamps and white Christmas lights that adorned the street she was cycling along suddenly flicked on, making the thin layer of snow on the ground sparkle. Belle knew she probably shouldn't be riding her bike in this weather, but it had been a long day teaching the ten over-excited kids in her primary two class, and she just wanted to get home. She had a long evening ahead of her. She'd been trying to find temporary accommodation for Clyde and Isla MacGavin, the parents of little Adam, one of her students. The whole family were about to be evicted from their home – and despite helping them for the last week, she'd found nothing and time was running out.

The street was empty of people, and Belle pedalled past The Corner Shop where Tavish Doherty was polishing the insides of the front windows with his usual military precision. She knew that signalled he'd be closing soon. The post office next door had shut hours before, but a smattering of people were sitting in Rowan's Cafe which was further up the high street. Belle could see slivers of steam rising from customers' mugs and disappearing into the gold and red tinsel that had been strewn across the ceiling. She toyed with the idea of stopping at The Workshop, the small hair and beauty salon situated at the far end of the quaint row of high street shops, so she could pass the time with her best friend Kenzy Campbell. But as she approached her legs refused to stop pedalling; perhaps they were afraid that if they did, they wouldn't be able to restart?

As Belle drew closer to the T-junction at the end of the high street, beside the old spruce tree laden with mounds of icy snow, her mind began to rehash the conversation she'd had a few hours earlier.

'Lassie, I'm so sorry to ask but I need your help and there's no one else who can do it.' Robina Sinclair, headmistress of Christmas Village's small primary school, had wrinkled her mouth as she'd cornered Belle in the playground at lunchtime. 'I desperately need someone to take on the school nativity – if I can't find a volunteer we may have to cancel. I'm already teaching extra classes and don't have time. I've spoken to the other teachers, but they either live too far out of the village or they've got other things on. If it doesn't go ahead, the wee ones in your class will be devastated. You know the bairns in primary two always get the big parts, and your lads and lassies love dressing up.' Robina's whole face had drooped and her wrinkles had deepened into crevices.

'What's happened to Benji Nevis?' Belle had asked. Benji taught the youngest children in the school and organised the nativity every year.

'Ach, he's been called away until the New Year because his da's recovering from a heart attack – his family farm won't run itself.' Robina had raised a bushy eyebrow and Belle had nodded even as her head had filled with the million things she already had on her to-do list. Could she really find the time to help?

'Of course I'll take on organising the nativity, it's no problem,' she'd promised. It wasn't like she had a social life to give up. Her boyfriend of two years had emigrated to Australia five months ago without a backward glance so she was young, free and single again. If she had to stay at school for a few more hours over the next weeks, it would be worth it for the look on the children's faces. She could tell her da all about it the next time he called – perhaps this time he'd pay attention.

'Aye, I knew I could rely on you, lassie. I always can. There's no one in Christmas Village who's more reliable, or as willing to help out.' The old headmistress had tapped Belle affectionately on the shoulder. 'Come to my office before you leave today and I'll give you Benji's notes. You know he organises the props, the set and everything. His plans for this year were *very* ambitious.' She'd had a bounce in her step as she turned and trotted down the long corridor.

Heavy snowflakes began to fall from the sky, melting on Belle's cheeks as she puffed out another breath, speeding up as she approached the T-junction at the top of the high street, ready to take a right. The wind was freezing now and the flakes were starting to thicken, settling on the ground into something deeper than a mere smatter. But she'd be home in less than ten minutes if she pedalled faster. A soft flake landed in Belle's eye and she blinked it away, catching sight of a blur at the edge of the pavement a few metres ahead. She pressed gently on her brakes, intending to dodge whatever it was, at the exact moment a mountain of ice slid off one of the lower branches of the spruce tree, falling just as Belle drew up beside it. The huge lump of snow splatted across her face, temporarily blinding her. She squeezed hard on the brakes, letting out a surprised screech as the bike refused to cooperate and instead slid on the layers of ice. Belle held on for dear life, blindly steering herself in what she hoped was a straight line.

'Stop, ya wee devil!' Belle shrieked as she skidded further along the road. Then the bike jerked to an abrupt halt as it hit something with an ominously fleshy thud – and she launched off the seat, landing on the metal frame and handlebars which jabbed painfully into her stomach and inner thighs.

'Ouch!' Someone moaned, and Belle swiped frantically at her eyes until she could see. An elderly woman was lying prone on the snow in front of her.

'Mrs Lachlan?' Belle asked, hurling the bike to one side and dislodging her bulging backpack from her shoulders, throwing it onto the pavement. She scrambled forwards and crouched next to the woman, her heart beating wildly, ignoring the cold which was now seeping through her trousers. Then Belle took her arm, helping to ease her into a sitting position, righting the chunky ruby tiara that was tucked into the woman's tartan cap. Who wore a tiara unless they were going to the opera?

'Call me Edina, lass,' the woman croaked, squinting through the snowflakes floating between them.

'I'm so sorry, I shouldn't have been cycling.' A ball of guilt lodged in Belle's throat as she frantically checked for injuries.

'Ach, lassie, don't you worry,' Edina murmured, scraping a globule of ice from her cheek and beaming. 'I saw the snow hit you, nothing you could have done. I couldn't stop myself from stepping out.' She glanced back at the pavement. 'I was halfway onto the road before I saw you coming and realised you couldn't stop.'

Aside from the tiara, Edina was wearing dark trousers, snow boots and a long tartan coat. Belle knew the woman was a spritely seventy-seven. A widow, she lived alone in Evergreen Castle – a six-bedroomed fortress, complete with high curtain walls and a small round turret, which was located at the far edge of Christmas Village – but rarely strayed from its grounds. 'I just posted some cards and was encouraging my pet donkey Bob to follow me home – he likes to go on walkabouts when he feels like company,' Edina confessed. She winked at Belle before grabbing a carrot from her pocket and waving it at the small grey donkey who was crouching underneath the spruce tree, seemingly shielding from the snow which was now coming down in thick droves. Edina swiped at her trousers and put her gloved hand on the ground.

'Ouch!' She groaned as she tried to straighten one leg and ease herself upwards. 'That hurts.' She slumped back onto her bottom and grimaced, clamping a hand to her left ankle. 'I may have bruised it, what an eejit.' She let out a slow breath as she took in their surroundings. 'I dinnae think I can walk just now, lassie. You may have to get some help before we both turn into wee snowmen.' Her attention caught on the bike lying in the snow behind them. 'Unless you can get me onto that. If you can, perhaps you could wheel me back to Evergreen Castle?'

'What's happened here?' a gruff voice barked from behind them, making both Belle and Edina jump.

'Ach, Tavish!' Edina declared, her cheeks flushing a becoming shade of pink as Belle stood and whirled around, before grabbing the shopkeeper's arm and leading him forwards. The older man was dressed in a thick Aran jumper with a dark navy overcoat. He peered at Edina as his small black Scottie dog came trotting over to sniff her legs.

'Iver!' Tavish ordered, sounding like the ex-sergeant major he was, and the dog shot back to his heels.

'I accidentally knocked Mrs Lachlan over with my bike – she's hurt her leg, I dinnae know how we're going to get her home.' The ball of guilt had expanded while they were speaking and Belle tried to push it back down her throat. She was supposed to be all about helping people like her da did, not wounding pensioners out for a stroll.

'I'll carry her,' Tavish snapped, pushing his blue beanie hat up and off his forehead. He had silver-grey hair, matching stubble, and sharp green eyes which belied his seventy-five years.

Edina gave Belle a delighted wink as Tavish knelt and swung her into his arms. She looped an elbow around his neck and let out a soft chuckle. 'If I'd known it was this easy to get you to visit the castle, Tavish Doherty, I'd have thrown myself in the road a year ago. Do you think you'll show me that tattoo now we're better acquainted? We both know it's not the first time I've asked.' The sturdy old man ignored her and instead began to march along the main road which would lead them left – in the opposite direction to Belle's house – towards Evergreen Castle.

Belle sighed and grabbed Edina's handbag, scooping up her bike and the soggy backpack before turning to look at the donkey, who was eyeing her suspiciously. 'You coming?' she asked, and the creature let out a loud honk before trotting out from underneath the tree, leaving Belle to bring up the rear.

Belle had lived in Christmas Village for twenty-two years but had never entered the grounds of Evergreen Castle. She wasn't a friend of the family and Edina's husband, Reilly Lachlan, had been a surly curmudgeon who'd abhorred company, so villagers had tended to avoid the castle when he was alive. As Edina still kept herself to herself, nothing had changed in the five years since he'd died. For the first time, Belle wondered if the elderly woman was happy spending so much time alone.

As Belle followed Tavish up the long, wide drive flanked with fir trees, she took a moment to scan the grounds, which were covered in a lush layer of thick snow. In the distance, not too far now, she could see the small castle which had multiple windows dotted across the right side. Every room was brightly lit and more lights shimmered across the edges of the turret at the far corner of the building, before trailing up and down the high walls. The donkey let out another loud honk as they got closer to the main building and trotted off into the field to Belle's left, no doubt seeking shelter in a shed or barn.

When Belle got to the main doorway, which was huge, arched and crafted from oak, she leaned her bike against the outside wall and pushed the door so she could enter the main hall – Tavish had left it ajar when he'd carried Edina inside a few moments before. Lights glared down from the ceiling, highlighting walls covered in dark panelled oak and lavishly framed paintings of men, women, horses and donkeys that a historian could probably trace back to centuries before. She swiftly shut the door and patted her arms, wondering if it was colder inside than it had been in the snow, then followed the sound of voices. She walked past a curved arch that led to a turnpike staircase into an enormous room with a vaulted ceiling, more bright lights and a long oak dining table that could have easily seated all ten children in Belle's class. To the right of it, in front of a vast fireplace, was a long leather sofa draped with a tartan blanket, a round footstool and two comfortable-looking high-back chairs. A large portrait with a gilt frame of a man Belle suspected was Edina's late husband in his youth glowered at them from above the fireplace. There were two empty brass candlesticks on the mantelpiece, a framed photo of a dark-haired woman, and another of a man standing in a stark office with his arms folded. Next to that was one lonely card which seemed to represent the sum total of the Christmas decorations in the castle.

'Let's take a look a ye.' Tavish lifted Edina's left foot onto the footstool and gently eased off her boot. Iver moved closer to the fireplace and sat on the fluffy rug, staring soulfully into the empty grate.

'It's just sore,' she grumbled, frowning at Tavish. 'I'm fine, man. Nothing a wee dram and a good night's sleep won't put right.'

'Aye, well I'll be the judge of that.' Tavish whipped off his beanie hat, dislodging a torrent of snowflakes, and placed it on one of the high-back chairs, then took off his coat and folded it carefully, before putting it in the same place. He knelt and gently prodded

Edina's ankle, giving her a knowing glare when she drew in a sharp breath. 'I suspect a break or fracture.' He shook his head, frowning accusingly at Belle.

'I'm so sorry,' Belle murmured, feeling awful as Edina waved her hand.

'Not your fault, lassie, I was the one who walked into the road.'

'I can drive you to the hospital,' Tavish offered.

'Not now!' Edina snapped.

'Then at dawn,' Tavish growled, as he searched the room and grabbed a gorgeous handmade appliqué cushion from one of the chairs at the dining table. He placed it under Edina's leg, his movements surprisingly graceful for such a large man.

'You can visit in the morning when you drop off my newspaper. Come in for a cup of Scottish Blend.' Edina sucked in her cheeks when Tavish tried to ease her foot from side to side. 'You'll see then this is nothing more than a wee bump.'

Tavish's thick eyebrows drew together. 'Aye, well I served as a medic for thirty-plus years in the Royal Regiment of Scotland and I'll tell ye now, that's no bump.'

Edina folded her arms but her small frame gave off an air of amusement. 'I'm sure you'll have a few bandages and a cane in your wee shop. That'll be all I need. I dinnae want to go to a hospital.'

Tavish let out a long-suffering sigh as he scanned their surroundings before his attention rested on the grate and empty log holder beside the large fireplace. Belle was surprised there wasn't a fire roaring in the centre; it didn't look as though the castle had any other form of heating and the cavernous room was cold. 'It's frigid, lass,' Tavish said. 'Where do you keep wood for the fire?'

'I need to chop some.' Edina jerked her chin. 'My gardener usually does it but he's been away for a couple of weeks and I've used it all up – and I've nae had time to cut more.'

'I'll do it before I go.' Tavish looked around the stark room, again muttering under his breath about cantankerous old women who didn't take care of themselves. 'You can't stay here by yourself until that ankle's fixed.'

'I'll be fine,' Edina said sharply without looking at him. She tried to move her leg from the stool but winced and lay back on the sofa, clasping her gloved hands in her lap. Belle's chest tightened with guilt.

'You need someone here to fetch and carry,' Tavish said stubbornly.

'There's no one to ask.' Edina's voice held a tinge of sadness but she jerked her chin again, meeting the old man's eyes.

'Um.' Belle tentatively lifted a hand, feeling like one of the kids from her class.

'What about your wee girl and grandson?' Tavish asked. Belle had heard the Lachlans had a daughter, but word was she didn't live close. She knew nothing about grandchildren – as far as she was aware, Edina had none.

The elderly woman shook her head. 'Tara's got her donkey sanctuary in Skye; she'll nae be free to visit just now and I definitely won't be worrying her. And neither will you.' She fixed Tavish with a stern glare. 'The laddie has his work in London. I'll not be bothering him with some sob story about a bruised foot. I'm a Lachlan, I can take care of myself. I just need a night to rest and I'll be grand.' Her face crinkled with pain as she tried to lift her foot off the stool. 'I can look after myself,' she repeated, but this time the words carried a smatter of uncertainty.

'Aye?' Tavish's mouth tightened as he glared towards the exit. 'You won't be able to get up those turnpike stairs, lass, let alone feed yourself or light a fire.' He marched into the far corner of the large room and swung one of the doors open, closing it again before opening the door next to it. 'Aye. There's a bed in here, it's a big enough room – we can move your things in now.' He nodded at Belle, jerking his head towards the arch that led to the staircase meaningfully. She nodded and hopped up from the sofa where she'd been perched.

'I'll not be leaving my bedroom.' Edina's lips thinned into an obstinate slash. 'I've slept in that bed for over fifty years – it's seen me through a marriage, the birth of a daughter and the death of my husband. I'll not have some wee bump on the ankle forcing me out of it now.'

Tavish put his hands on his hips. 'Then you've got to find someone to move in, lass, because I'll not be leaving you here alone. I can carry you to your room at night, bring you down in the morning, but you'll need more help than that – I've got my shop to run so I've nae got time for more.' He pulled his mobile out of his pocket and frowned at it. 'I could organise a carer... someone from the village.'

'I'll not impose on a stranger.' Edina's face paled as she pushed herself up, leaning forwards. Belle suspected she was about to get to her feet so she could shake her fist at Tavish, and moved so she could stand between them.

'I'm happy to move in for a week or two,' she said slowly as an idea began to form in her mind. It would help ease her guilt at hurting the pensioner, and at the same time solve one of her biggest problems. 'I know I'm a stranger, but you've met me now.'

'Won't your family miss you?' Edina asked.

Belle frowned. 'My da's settled in Kenya. I used to live with my godmother, Annie Gilbraith, but she died of cancer in January.' She cleared her throat as a lump formed inside. 'I live in her house now – *my* house, I mean.' Belle winced. 'But I'm by myself so no one will know if I'm gone.' What a sad indictment of her life.

'You don't want to move in with a boring old woman.' Edina looked sadly around the huge room.

'In truth, you'd be doing me a favour.' Belle sensed Edina might be more inclined to listen if the person in need wasn't herself.

Edina cocked her head, still frowning. 'Go on, lass.'

'There's a family of a wee bairn in my class at the primary school where I teach who need a place to stay for a while. They're about to be evicted from their house because the owner needs the property. I've tried to fight it but there's nothing to be done. I've been looking for temporary accommodation, but there's nowt available unless they move to Lockton – and that's a long way from school for the lad.'

Edina pursed her lips. 'Lockton is a forty-minute drive.'

'If I could lodge here with you, they could move into Annie's—' She stopped. '*My* house for a while.' It would give them time to find a decent place without the threat of eviction hanging over them. Okay, so she'd have to move in with a stranger, but compared to the things her parents had given up in their lives, it was nothing. 'Just until you get on your feet. I can cook, chop wood, light the fire.' Belle looked around the room, wondering when it had last been cleaned properly. It could be beautiful, with a little love. She could find some Christmas decorations in the loft at home to brighten the place up, or get the children in her class to make something. 'I wouldn't be here that much – I teach all day at the primary school and I'm organising the nativity. But I'd be able to cook for you in the evenings, shop, do the washing, all the essentials.'

'I'm not used to company,' Edina said, as Tavish let out a loud huff. 'Do you have a boyfriend?'

'Not anymore.' Belle felt her cheeks flush, a little taken aback by the abrupt enquiry. 'He moved to Australia.'

'He broke your heart?' Edina asked, and Belle swallowed.

'Well… we weren't serious.' Which had been part of the problem, at least as far as he was concerned.

Edina stared at her for a few moments, her gaze penetrating. 'Any pets?'

'Um…' Sensing this might be a deal breaker, Belle grimaced. 'I've got a cat, Jinx, he used to belong to Annie. He's house trained and very friendly. The lad in my class is allergic to cats, so Jinx would have to move in too.'

Edina pushed out her bottom lip, considering, but instead of shaking her head, which Belle had expected, she leaned further forwards. 'Does the cat like donkeys?' Her tone was serious.

Belle's eyes widened. 'I dinnae know – but he's very laid back so I'm sure he would.'

Edina looked thoughtful. 'Bob likes cats – he's been going for more walkabouts recently, and it would be good for him to have company of the four-legged kind. The poor wee lad is bored of me.' She patted a hand on her chin and glared at Tavish who was still holding the mobile, poised to dial. 'Aye, I suppose we could try it for a week or so. Bruise or not, my ankle is sure to be on the mend after that.'

'Great,' Belle said. 'I'll go home and grab a few things now – move in tonight if that works for you?' She could fit most of the essentials – including Jinx – into her old car. But as Belle said her goodbyes and hopped back on her bike so she could pedal out into the snow and down Evergreen Castle's driveway, she wondered if her latest attempt to do good might just be one step too far.

Chapter Two

Belle dusted the mantelpiece as Edina took a slow loop around the sitting room, testing the cane Tavish had brought over on his visit this morning. It had been five days since the accident and Edina's ankle now sported a navy boot-shaped cast. Tavish had insisted on making a trip to A&E in Morridon on the morning after Edina had been hurt. The doctor had taken X-rays and declared she'd fractured her ankle and needed at least six weeks' rest along with a programme of exercises she could do at home. Which meant Belle had assured Edina she would stay in the castle until after Christmas.

The MacGavin family had been ecstatic when Belle had offered them her house. They'd been terrified they'd be homeless or have to move out of the area before Christmas. So Belle was happy she'd been able to help everyone, even if she did miss having time to herself.

'Ach, things are a lot easier with the cane, but it's still frustrating,' Edina said, making her way over to the high-back chair by the fire so she could slump onto it and rest her leg. Belle had made breakfast this morning and put it on the table beside her, but Edina still didn't have much of an appetite. 'I worry I'm getting too old to live in the castle.' She glanced around the large room, frowning.

'Why?' Belle asked, skimming the duster over a couple of the pictures on the walls.

Edina waved a hand at her leg. 'Just look at me, lass, Tavish is right about the castle not being practical. At the moment I can't do a thing for myself. But I don't want to leave this place – it's my home.'

'You don't need to though, do you?' Belle asked, turning to look at Edina who was now glaring at her foot. 'I mean… no one's pressuring you to move?' she added, careful to keep her tone light.

Edina let out a long exhale. 'Ach, ignore me, lass, I'm just being maudlin. Could you pass me that cushion please?' She pointed to the appliqué pillow Tavish had tucked under her foot when she'd first been injured, wincing as she tried to make herself comfortable.

Belle grabbed it from the sofa, wanting to ask more. Why hadn't Edina answered the question? It was obvious from the set of her shoulders that she no longer wanted to discuss any potential move. Perhaps she'd find a way to come back to the subject later. 'This is beautiful.' Belle traced a fingertip over the textures and patterns sewn into the cushion fabric before handing it to Edina. 'Who made it?'

'Me,' Edina said, blushing. 'I used to do a lot of needlework when I was younger, but I don't get much of a chance now. I've no one to make anything for.' She placed the cushion on the chair and adjusted her leg. 'When are you off to work?'

'In half an hour.' Belle checked her watch. She'd got up extra early so she could make breakfast and do some dusting, but time was getting away from her. She picked up a walnut frame from the mantlepiece and swiped the cloth over the photo of a dark-haired woman, unsettling a cloud of dust.

'That's my daughter, Tara,' Edina said, picking up her coffee and leaning back in the chair.

'Did you mention she runs a donkey sanctuary in Skye?' Belle asked, carefully putting the picture back.

Edina nodded. 'Tara's lived there for over thirty years.'

'Do you see her often?' Belle asked. 'I mean…' She cleared her throat as she tried to think of a subtle way of asking why her daughter hadn't visited.

'Aye.' Edina smiled, then pointed to the blue boot. 'You mean why hasn't she come since I hurt myself?' She waited until Belle nodded. 'Tavish was asking the same last night. The lass runs the sanctuary alone. If I told her, she'd be here like a shot, but she'd have to turn her life upside down to do it. I don't expect that. Tara calls or texts every week to check up on me.' She shrugged. 'But I haven't mentioned the accident. By the time I do, I'll be fine.'

'Right,' Belle said, not really understanding. Surely Edina's daughter would welcome the chance to help? The silver frame propped next to the picture of Tara displayed a photo of a tall, broad-shouldered man – he had an angular face and Belle spent a bit of extra time wiping the cloth over it so she could study him. He was gorgeous and there was something haunting about those blue eyes…

'That's my grandson, Jack Hamilton-Kirk,' Edina said proudly. 'And no, I haven't told him either – he's got enough to worry about with his work to be bothering about me. He's a very successful lawyer.' She beamed.

'Does he visit often?' Belle asked, dragging her eyes away from the photo.

'He's not been yet. He's estranged from Tara unfortunately. Long story, no time to go into it now…' Edina added when Belle began to ask. 'Last time we saw him, the lad was only five – but he got in touch recently. He's handsome – single too.' She winked and Belle quickly put the frame down and took a seat on the sofa, ignoring the lingering hum of attraction.

'What made him contact you?' Belle furtively checked her watch. She'd need to leave for school soon but suspected Edina got lonely. They'd had a few conversations since she'd moved in, though while Edina was friendly, she held herself back. This was the first time the elderly woman had volunteered any information about her life. The first hint that she might want to open up and perhaps even make friends.

'Ach.' Edina shook her head. 'Jack's da died six months ago and he found some letters I'd written when he was clearing things out.'

'He didn't know about them?' Belle asked, surprised.

Edina frowned. 'Jack's father hadn't told him. Once my grandson read the letters, and realised who I was, he replied.' She smiled, her face suddenly animated. 'We talk on the computer every week. Jack's been so busy at work he hasn't had a chance to visit yet, but he's promised he will soon…'

'He's not been up here at all?' Belle asked, fighting disappointment. What could possibly be so important it would stop a man from visiting his long-lost grandmother?

Edina shook her head firmly. 'The lad's got more important things to worry about. He's a good boy.' She looked at the frame wistfully. 'He'll come up to see me when he can. There are a lot of memories here; I suspect he might not be ready to face them so soon after his da…' She blew out a breath. 'What are you up to at school today?'

The change of subject was abrupt, and Belle took a moment to respond as her mind tracked through the million things she'd promised to get done. 'We're making Christmas decorations. The children will be writing Christmas lists on Monday and I've got to get some things organised.' Belle picked up the duster and stood. 'I'm sorry I have to go. But I'll be back at noon to organise lunch.'

'You're a good lass.' Edina's expression didn't change but Belle could see a hint of longing in her eyes. 'It's a shame I can't join you.' She nodded at her ankle. 'I do so enjoy spending time with wee bairns and it's been so long since I have…'

'Well, you'll be more than welcome to come to school when you're better,' Belle said, wishing she could think of a way to brighten up Edina's life before that.

Angus Ferguson squeezed Belle's hand and let out the kind of excited gasp only a six-year-old could muster as Belle led him into the huge dining room at Evergreen Castle. She'd put up a lot of decorations last night, and a wave of pride radiated through her when the rest of her class gasped as they were guided in by a couple of parent helpers who'd offered to assist for the morning; probably because they were desperate to see inside the building. A large Christmas tree sat to the right of the vast fireplace in which a fire roared – courtesy of Tavish. Belle had stayed up late decorating the tree with baubles and tinsel and making a large golden star for the top. There were fairy lights trailed around the mantelpiece and across one of the far walls. The long dining table had been laid with a red tablecloth ready for today's lesson.

Edina sat at the top of the table, looking like a queen. She wore a velvety red cape which Belle had found in her wardrobe, a pair of tartan trousers and a thick white woollen sweater. The outfit was completed by a pair of extravagant earrings and a beautiful diamond tiara – the sixth Belle had seen her wear since moving in. Edina had spent extra time on her hair and make-up this morning, shooing Belle out of her bedroom so she could get ready before Tavish arrived to carry her down the stairs. Belle had set out a stool under the table so Edina could rest her leg.

Edina beamed as a few of the children tentatively approached, waving a hand at Bonnie McGregor as she bravely pulled up a chair a couple of seats down from the top. The child's light blue eyes were like saucers as she gazed up at the vaulted ceiling before surveying the contents of the table.

'Are you a princess?' Lara Smith asked Edina, pointing to her tiara.

'Aye,' Edina murmured, putting a fingertip to her lips. 'But don't tell, lass.' She shushed, and Lara giggled and put a hand over her mouth.

'Sparkles,' Bonnie murmured, taking in the pots Belle had laid out, along with glue sticks, Christmassy stickers and stars. There were coloured pencils and a large sheet of crisp white paper set at each of the places on the table, along with a square red envelope that each of the children would write Santa's address on later. Edina had her own paper and coloured pencils and she beamed as the children slowly approached.

'Say hello to Ms Lachlan, class,' Belle said as each of the ten children chose a chair to pull out, a few of the braver kids vying for the spaces at the top of the table closest to Edina.

'Aye, don't be shy.' The elderly woman beamed, her cheeks rosy with excitement. She waved her hands, encouraging the children to sit as they chorused a loud hello.

'As I told you earlier, we're here to write and decorate our Christmas lists for Santa. It's the fifth of December already so we need to make sure they have plenty of time to reach the North Pole. Ms Lachlan was so excited when I told her what we had planned that I asked if we could come here so she could join in and write a Christmas list too,' Belle explained.

'Aye, I haven't written to Santa for years!' Edina said, grinning at the children as they sat.

Belle had had the idea of moving the lesson to the castle after their conversation a few days before. She'd been determined to do something to brighten up the older woman's life. In the last week she'd seen how lonely Edina was. While she spent some time in the village, most of her days were spent alone within these four walls. So Belle had arranged a last-minute trip to the castle, delivering the consent forms to each of the children's parents herself over the weekend. She yawned and rolled her shoulders, wondering when she'd last slept for more than five hours. 'We practised writing letters last week so you should know what to do. Can anyone tell me what we should put first?' Belle supressed a grin when Bonnie and Lennie McGregor, the blonde, blue-eyed twins, both bounced up and down, waving their hands in the air and grinning at Edina when she put hers up too. 'Lennie?' Belle asked, promising herself she'd pick Bonnie next when the little girl's smile dimmed.

'Dear Santa Cause!' Lennie shouted at the top of his voice.

'That's almost right, it's Santa Claus, C.L.A.U.S.' Belle spelled out the last word slowly as she encouraged both of the parent helpers to join the children at the table. 'Remember, you need to think carefully about what it is you'd most like for Christmas. I'm sure you've all got ideas for toys, which is great. But remember, you can add other things to your list. They don't all have to be physical things – something you can touch or feel – you might want to ask for something you'd like to see happen in the village, at school, your home or even to someone else.' For a brief moment Belle's mind was whisked back to when she was eight, when she lived in Kenya with her mam and da. Her mam had always insisted they write to Father Christmas on the first of December, to give the letters plenty of time to arrive. But while Belle remembered once asking for the latest Lego truck she'd seen in a magazine and for some blue princess shoes to go with her sparkly dressing-up dress, her mam had written about the children in the orphanage where she volunteered, detailing their need for medicine, writing equipment and nutritious food. Belle frowned; she could still remember feeling guilty when she'd found out.

'I want a sister,' Bonnie declared, her eyes narrowing as her brother began to write slowly, taking care with the letter 'D', probably so he could earn extra brownie points with Belle. The twins constantly competed for her attention and keeping them both happy was a juggling act.

'Aye, I always wanted a sister, or a brother would have been grand.' Edina grinned and picked up a red pencil. 'But I think it might be a bit late to ask for one now.' The older woman had bloomed in the short time the children had been in the castle. This morning at breakfast, after Tavish had carried her into the kitchen and Belle had made her tea and toast, Edina had looked pale and she'd glanced around the room as if she wasn't sure if she should be there at all. Belle wondered again exactly how many visitors Edina usually received. How many hours she must have spent alone in the huge cavernous rooms since her husband had passed. And why was her grandson taking so long to visit? Belle had been here for a week now and Jack hadn't called once. Belle suspected Edina lived a lonely life. Her mantelpiece was hardly filled with Christmas cards – she'd only received one, and that had come from Morag Dooley who ran the post office in Lockton.

'Are you writing a list, Miss?' Nessa MacLeod pushed her long blonde hair out of her face as she leaned on the table and Belle shrugged. She hadn't written one in twenty-two years – not since her mam had died.

'Aye.' Belle nodded and sat in one of the empty chairs at the opposite end of the table to Edina. She stared at the piece of paper, before picking up a pencil.

Dear Santa, she wrote.

I'm sorry I haven't written for such a long time, but I hope everything is good with you, Mrs Claus, all the elves and reindeer at the North Pole.

She looked up as Nessa nudged her arm. 'If I ask Santa to make me Mary in our school nativity, do you think he could?' Her blue eyes were clear and Belle swallowed. She'd done nothing about organising the Christmas play for the school yet and time was running out. She'd avoided Robina for most of last week, aware the headmistress would demand an update, but she hadn't even had a chance to read Benji's notes. There were just so many things to do. She'd promised Kenzy she'd go for a drink with her in the pub this evening and wondered if she could get out of it before dismissing the thought. She'd find a way to fit it all in, she always did.

'Aye, there's no harm in asking,' Belle said softly. Nessa would be a good choice for Mary; she made a mental note. 'We all know Santa may not give us everything on our Christmas list, so think carefully about what you most want,' she advised the class.

'You know where Santa lives?' Nessa asked, pouting as she leaned over to read Belle's letter.

'Aye.' The post office gave out an address each year and Belle knew if she posted the cards in plenty of time, Santa would also reply. 'Don't forget to put your name and the school's address in the top-left corner of your letter like I showed you on Friday.' She raised her voice above the chattering children. 'I've written it on some cards which you'll find in the centre of the table – just copy it and that way Santa can reply.'

'He writes back?' Edina glanced up from her letter.

'Aye,' Belle assured her. 'Be sure to include the address though. You can put Evergreen Castle on yours if you like.'

'What do I write next?' Doug Wallace, one of the shyest children in Belle's class, went scarlet as everyone turned to stare at him.

'There's a certain order to these things,' Belle said.

'Aye,' Edina jumped in. 'Start by telling Santa your name and age,' she explained loudly, as Belle nodded at her to continue. 'Tell him if you've been good; perhaps you could even let him know some of the nice things you've done. For example' – she tapped the red pencil against the white paper set in front of her – 'I've told Santa that I'm seventy-seven. I have a donkey called Bob who I usually visit every day, because he enjoys the company. Recently I've been trying to find Bob a friend – I'm worried he gets lonely in his barn all by himself.' Her lips pursed.

'I'm six,' Lennie said loudly, shoving his sister away as she tried to read his letter. 'Bonnie is too. We have the same birthday.' He pulled a face. 'I made my nana a card when she was in hospital and when she came home, she brought it with her. She told me it helped make her better.'

'I made a card too.' Bonnie frowned at her brother. 'Mine had glitter on it and a picture of a princess. She told me it made her feel happy inside.'

Edina nodded seriously. 'Then you should tell Santa about your cards. Those sound like very good deeds to me.' The older woman went back to writing her list and Belle wondered what she might be asking for. More visitors perhaps? She obviously adored having the children here and she was great with them.

'You haven't told Santa about any of the good things you've done,' Nessa whispered to Belle. 'Or told him how old you are. Did you forget?' Her brow furrowed as she stabbed a finger at Belle's letter.

'Oh.' Belle picked up her pencil again and wrote, *I am thirty years old*, adding the school's address onto the top-left of the white paper. She tapped the pencil against her chin before writing.

This year I: raised over six hundred pounds so the village play-ground could be repaired; organised the spring and summer school fete; helped my best friend repaint her beauty salon; knitted twelve blankets for premature babies in Morridon Hospital; gave blood; adopted a penguin, mountain gorilla, donkey and a polar bear.

She paused, trying to remember if she'd forgotten anything. The list of good deeds seemed inadequate compared to all the life-saving work her da did.

'Wow!' Nessa gasped. 'Santa will definitely give you a lot of presents. Now you need to tell him what you want. I asked for a pink canopy to go over my bed, like Bonnie has.' She stabbed her pencil at her list. 'How do you spell giraffe?'

Belle told her before turning back to her letter. She stared at the page for a few minutes. *My Christmas list is*, she wrote before looking up; Edina was scribbling something onto her paper. The children were quiet now, a few thinking, some asking the parent helpers for ideas or assistance with spellings. Belle watched them, feeling her insides warm. Her life was already full enough; aside from wanting to see more of her da, there wasn't much more she could want. Besides, there was always that uncomfortable feeling in the pit of her stomach she had to contend with whenever she asked for anything. Like she didn't really deserve it.

'You have to think of something,' Nessa said, frowning.

'Okay.' Belle picked up her pencil.

1. I want the MacGavin family to find their forever home.
2. I want my best friend to find someone who makes her happy.

Belle didn't write Kenzy's name, aware Nessa might read her list again.

> 3. *I want Ms Lachlan to recover from her ankle injury quickly and for her grandson to visit.*

She glanced at Nessa who was still engrossed in her own letter.

> 4. *I want Bob to find a special friend.*

So far the donkey and Jinx hadn't hit it off. Not that they'd had much of a chance – the cat had spent most of his time burrowed under Belle's bed, refusing to come out aside from at mealtimes or for a quick dash to the litter tray. What else did she want? Belle grimaced before writing.

> 5. *I want my da to come home for Christmas.*

He'd not left Kenya for years. When Belle had been younger, just after her mam had died, he'd told her the children he worked with needed him more than she did. He'd been right, of course. Her godmother had given her plenty of attention while she'd been growing up and Belle had adored her. But Annie had been a doctor with a million other important pressures on her time, which meant Belle had often felt in the way.

'There's not much on your list,' Nessa grumbled, leaning over Belle's letter again. 'You need to add something else. My mam says if you can't get to six, you're not trying hard enough.' She hmphed, turning back to her letter.

Belle stared at the blank paper.

6. I want someone to…

Her pencil drifted over the page as she thought about the thing she most wanted. She wrote *put me* but then scribbled it out, shaking her head and putting the pencil down. She didn't need anything. Not even that.

Chapter Three

'What do you mean you let a stranger move in?' a man's voice Belle didn't recognise boomed from the sitting room in Evergreen Castle, and she paused in the hall so she could peer through the doorway. The room had been tided after the lesson hours earlier and Edina sat in her high-back chair with a laptop resting on her knees. A man's face glared out of the computer screen, and even from this angle Belle recognised him from the photo on the mantelpiece. Jack Hamilton-Kirk – so the elusive grandson had finally called?

'Who is she?' he demanded, and Belle felt her hackles rise, uncomfortable with his sharp tone.

'Ach, Jack, settle down, lad, Belle's only staying for a few weeks,' Edina soothed. 'It's nice to have the company and she's—'

'But why?' he interrupted, sounding frustrated. 'You know you're too trusting. The woman could be after money, jewellery, your antiques – who knows.'

Belle swallowed her irritation as she watched Edina's shoulders stiffen. 'The lass knocked me off my bike. I'm fine,' she added when his jaw dropped. 'She's helping until I'm on my feet. Nothing to worry yourself about.'

'You didn't mention she hurt you!' He looked like he was about to explode. There was movement behind him and a voice made an announcement Belle couldn't quite make out.

'It was an accident – and you've been in New York, what could you do?' Edina asked. 'Tell me about your trip.' Her attempt to change the subject was met with stony silence.

'It's work,' he snapped, rubbing a hand across his forehead. He looked tired and Belle fought a wave of misplaced sympathy. 'I'm sorry – I'm not angry with you but...' He let out a long sigh. 'You need to stop wearing the tiaras every day and it would be sensible if you locked your jewellery away.' He grimaced. 'Perhaps we should consider putting the castle in someone else's name? I could organise it. That way your angel of mercy won't be able to take advantage. In light of the accident and this... woman, I wonder if the castle is the right place for you to live now...'

Belle had to force herself not to step forwards. So it was like that? She'd had her suspicions when Edina had been worried about staying in the family home. It was obvious those fears had been planted by someone – and now she knew who...

'I'm fine, lad,' Edina said again, sounding anxious. 'I know you worry, but there's nowhere I'd rather be. I—'

There was another booming announcement and this time Jack turned around. 'I'm sorry – I'm at the airport, I'm flying to Washington and that's my call. I've one more meeting, but I'll be back in London late tomorrow and we'll speak as soon as I land. Make sure you look after yourself and don't give the woman access to anything valuable.' With that final rushed instruction, he hung up.

Belle frowned as Edina shut the laptop, vowing from now on she'd keep a special ear out for the eejit grandson's calls.

Christmas Pud Inn was busy even though it was only Monday evening. Belle sat at a small side table next to the roaring fire, watching as the owners, Moira and Bram McGregor – parents of the twins, Bonnie and Lennie, in her class – efficiently served the crowd, dodging each other like ice hockey players as they made their way up and down the narrow channel behind the counter. Belle had a glass of red wine in front of her and a packet of salt and vinegar crisps. Beside them on her table sat a large pile of red envelopes which included the letters the children had written in the castle earlier today. Belle had already looked them over, but wanted to check everyone's again before she bought stamps and posted them in plenty of time.

Christmas music began to play softly in the background, and she perused the fairy lights which had been strung across the ceiling and the large blue spruce to the right of the pub. It was decorated with silver, gold and red baubles and there was a large fairy gazing at her from the top.

'You still okay to make a batch of cakes for the WI Christmas fete?' Moira shouted across the bar as she pulled a pint, her plump cheeks glowing.

'Aye, no problem,' Belle said, trying to work out exactly when she'd have time to bake. Or how easy it was going to be to navigate the Aga in Edina's huge kitchen. So far she'd cooked their evening meals in a microwave she'd borrowed from Annie's house.

'Sorry I'm late.' Kenzy dropped into the seat opposite and grinned at the Margarita cocktail Belle had bought for her. She drank a quick glug before letting her handbag slide to the floor and shrugged off her pretty black designer coat. 'One of my clients decided she'd like to have a manicure after her facial and I couldn't refuse.' Kenzy was originally from Los Angeles and her accent was strong, despite living in Christmas Village for over five years. She smiled and Belle marvelled again at how beautiful her friend was. With her wavy blonde hair and silver-grey eyes, it was a wonder anyone in the room could focus on anything else.

'Was it dress-down day at the beauty shop again?' Belle asked mildly as she took in Kenzy's blue dress, which accentuated her impressive cleavage. It was silky but demure and stopped just below her knees.

Her friend snorted and shook her head, taking her mobile from her handbag and placing it on the table. Kenzy always kept her phone on standby so she was available to take bookings for the beauty shop at any time. She was a disconcerting combination of sexy siren and sharp businesswoman, but the latter was a side of herself she preferred to hide. 'I have it on good authority Logan Forbes is back from his trip to see his sister in Aberdeen, so I'm in full seduction mode.' A knot marred her forehead. 'Not that throwing myself at the man has worked in the past. But I'm not giving up until he agrees to a date. I get my tenacity from my mom. She wouldn't agree to divorce my father until he gave her the Malibu house.' Kenzy waggled her eyebrows suggestively, but Belle saw the quick flare of pain in her eyes before she took another long sip of her Margarita. 'Logan's wife died four years ago – you'd think he'd be ready for a fling by now.' She frowned.

Belle didn't have a chance to disagree because the man in question walked through the entrance and marched up to the bar. Logan was tall, over six foot, with brown hair and dark blue eyes. He wasn't what you'd call handsome, but his features were rugged and he had deep lines at the corners of his cheeks and mouth, the result of years of working outside. He lived alone and ran a small garden centre a few miles outside the village. He also did gardening and odd jobs for Edina, and was usually responsible for cutting up the logs for her fire. He ordered a beer and turned so he could lean back on the counter. Belle saw his attention rest briefly on Kenzy – he took in her dress, then his cheeks pinked and he sucked in a long breath before turning away.

'Is he looking at me?' Kenzy asked, looking stricken when Belle shook her head. Her friend was confident in almost every aspect of her life, aside from when it came to Logan. Belle knew Kenzy could have any man she wanted. She dated regularly and her relationships were fleeting, but she held herself back, preferring to play the field rather than develop serious feelings for anyone. Which made a traditional man like Logan completely wrong for her. Not that Kenzy would listen if Belle told her that. 'How's Edina getting on?' Kenzy took another sip from her cocktail, her back ramrod-straight.

'Hankering after Tavish Doherty.' Belle's smile dropped. 'She's so lonely, Kenzy. I can't believe she's been living alone in Evergreen Castle for so long without any of us visiting her. She always seemed content to potter around on her own – I'm not sure she even realised how isolated she'd become.'

'No one in the village sees much of her. Tavish delivers her groceries and newspapers – as far as we knew, she was happy keeping herself to herself. We all know her husband was a cantankerous ogre.' Kenzy's full red lips rearranged themselves into a frown. 'You can't go rescuing another stray, Belle, you've got enough on your plate already. It's been five months since you so much as winked at a guy.' She shook her head, wrinkling her nose at Belle's dark trousers and white shirt which, judging by her friend's expression, were completely lacking. 'You said Edina had a grandson?'

'Aye, Jack Hamilton-Kirk,' Belle practically growled – even his pretentious double-barrelled name annoyed her. 'I heard him on Zoom with Edina before I came out.' She shook her head, still riled. 'He's not been to visit her yet and instead of worrying about her ankle, he got angry I was staying in the castle!'

'It's not like you to get irritated so easily,' Kenzy said with a gleam in her eye.

'They've been in touch for five months – it would be so easy for him to come up from London to visit. But instead of organising to see his nana, he starts judging me.' Belle snapped her fingers as irritation pressed against her chest.

'Maybe the man's just worried you've got your eye on the family jewels?' Kenzy laughed.

Belle pulled a disgusted face. 'More like *he* has. He suggested he change whose name the castle is in.' Kenzy gasped. 'And Edina had dressed up for the call, wore her favourite tiara, and Jack told her she should keep her jewellery locked up! Probably so he can get his hands on it.' *Greedy, self-absorbed eejit.*

'Tiara?' Kenzy quirked an eyebrow.

'She's got loads of them.' Belle counted the seven she'd already seen. 'She told me her husband didn't like her wearing expensive jewellery – and since she has limited time left on earth, she wants to make the most of it while she can. She was wearing a tiara when I knocked her off her bike.'

'I love the sound of that.' Kenzy grinned. 'Tell me more about the grandson.'

Belle huffed. 'They only got in touch after his da died six months ago and he has nothing to do with his mam, which is odd.' Her mouth puckered. 'There's a story there, but Edina's yet to share it.'

'What's his mom's name?' Kenzy asked.

'Tara Lachlan.' Belle shrugged. 'I've never heard of her, but I expect she went to school elsewhere, and she lives in Skye now and runs a donkey sanctuary. She phones Edina regularly and from what I've seen she's very attentive. But Edina doesn't want to tell Tara about her ankle because of the sanctuary. Apparently, it'll cause all sorts of problems if she leaves for an overnight stay. I wish I knew more about the family.'

'You'll get it out of Edina.' Kenzy winked. 'You've a way with people, Belle. Do you want another drink?' She glugged down the rest of hers and stood, her attention flickering to Logan who was still standing by the bar.

Belle looked at her half-finished wine and the pile of letters and sighed. 'I've a lot to do this evening, I'd better not.' She watched Kenzy make her way over to the counter, tentatively at first, before she marched up and leaned on it, close to Logan. The man didn't turn his head in her direction, but Belle saw his shoulders stiffen and his left hand squeeze into a tight fist. She turned and picked up the top envelope, sliding the piece of paper out. She smiled to herself when she read a few lines of Lennie's Christmas list.

My mam says I've been good all year. Please can I have a blue
scooter, a Batman kite and Minecraft for my PC. My sister
would like a stefascope.

He'd crossed the misspelled word out and written 'stethoscope'
neatly after it, no doubt after some spelling tips from one of the
parent helpers. Belle checked he'd written the correct school address
on the inside and Santa's address was legible before sealing the
envelope and starting a new pile. She picked up the next letter,
recognising her own handwriting, and shoved it into the pocket of
her coat so she could dispose of it later. She'd only written it because
Nessa had been watching, and planned to destroy it when she got
back to the castle.

'Well, that was a waste of time,' Kenzy huffed, as she placed
another Margarita and a large glass of wine in front of Belle. 'The
man's either blind, dead or a zombie. I could walk into this pub half
naked and I swear he wouldn't look twice. I've no idea what to do to
get him to notice me.' Her lips thinned as she glanced over at Logan
again. 'But I'm not going to stop until he does. I got you another
drink, I thought I could help with the marking. You deserve a break,
Bells. You spend your whole life worrying about other people – you
need to learn to take time for yourself.' She slid an envelope from
the top of the pile and opened it, snorting out a loud giggle as she
read. The sound was natural and unlike Kenzy, who was always so
in control of her emotions. Belle noticed Logan's head jerk around
and he stared at her, his lips curving in response as she chuckled.
'Wow, that's so cute, this one wants a sledge that her puppy can ride
because he always looks so sad when he can't join in. Ahhh.'

Belle nodded and watched Logan deliberately turn to face the bar again. Perhaps he wasn't oblivious to Kenzy after all? 'I love reading what the kids want, it's always so unexpected,' Belle said. It was one of the reasons she enjoyed being a teacher, seeing the children's perspective on the world – all that innocence and desire to do good. In an odd way they reminded her of her parents too, and teaching made her feel one step closer to them. 'If you can make sure the school address is on the top left, please, and they've written this on the envelope.' Belle put one face-up in the centre of the table, before she squeezed Kenzy's forearm. 'Thanks for helping. I need to spend a few hours going through Benji's nativity notes later so this means I might get some time to sleep.' She sipped the wine before sliding the next envelope off the pile and opening the letter inside, immediately recognising Edina's spidery handwriting. She'd told Belle she planned to burn her letter in the fire, but perhaps one of the parent helpers had grabbed it when they'd been tidying up? Belle checked Kenzy was occupied before starting to read.

Dear Santa

I know it's a long time since I wrote. I think for a while I stopped believing in the existence of anything truly good, but over the last few days I've realised there could be some magic in the world after all.

Belle smiled, wondering if that had anything to do with Tavish. The curmudgeon had visited Evergreen Castle twice a day since

Edina had been injured, bringing food and cutting wood for the
fire, making the older woman's face light up.

*I'm getting old, Santa. It happens to us all – perhaps even
you – but I've realised that's okay. We're not put on this earth
to stop time or to live forever, but simply to live our lives in
the best way we can. I'm seventy-seven and I'm starting to feel
it; my bones are either creaking or breaking and I can't do the
things that I once could. I'm a little afraid I may not be able
to stay in Evergreen Castle if things continue as they are. I've
wasted a lot of my life and missed out on so many experiences.
Perhaps I was too afraid, or I'm just from a generation who
accept things, rather than striving to change their lot. But I'm
planning on making up for that in the time I've got left. I just
hope you'll be able to help.*

*Perhaps I don't really believe you exist – I'm a little long in
the tooth and have enough of a hold on my marbles to know
there's no such thing as Santa Claus. But my da used to tell
me if you don't ask for what you need, you're not going to get
it. I suppose he was right – if you don't place an order in a
restaurant, how will the waiter know what you want to eat?
So this is me asking, putting these thoughts out before I burn
this in the fire, in the vain hope that at least one of them will
be delivered.*

*I know that there's a certain order to these letters, so I'm
going to start by telling you I have done a few good things this
year, probably less than most but I plan to make up for that.
I've adopted one of my daughter's donkeys – Bob. He's an ornery*

soul and reminds me of my late husband, Reilly – although Bob is a lot more affectionate and I think the lad just needs to find himself some friends. I've recently been in touch with my grandson who I haven't seen for over thirty years, and I've been encouraging him to visit me in Christmas Village. The lad needs his family, but you can watch out for my letter next year for news on that. As for what I want, some of these are wishes and some are things I should have done years ago. Why are we so afraid to grab what we want with both hands when we have the time?

Belle quickly scanned ahead. This was no ordinary Christmas list. This was a list that could change Edina's life.

I want Jack and his mother, Tara, to reconcile. They need each other and I need to know they'll be looking out for each other when I'm gone.

Belle picked up her wine and sipped, wishing Edina had elaborated. She had no idea why Tara and Jack had fallen out – although listening to him earlier, she had to wonder if at least some of it was his fault. She continued to read Edina's letter as Kenzy worked her way through the rest of the pile of envelopes, stopping now and then to comment, laugh or sip her Margarita.

I want to spend Christmas in Evergreen Castle with my family. A proper Christmas with turkey (and a nut roast for Tara, of course).

Belle frowned as she sipped more wine. She'd love to give Edina everything on her list, but she was unlikely to meet Tara or Jack. Neither of them seemed likely to visit. How could she get them to the castle – let alone encourage them to make up so they'd spend Christmas together?

I want to have a Christmas party, like my parents used to. I'd invite everyone from the village and there would be music, dancing, food and wine. My husband Reilly didn't much like company so the tradition ended with me, and I'd like to start it up again – even if it's just for this year. One final soiree, if you like.

Belle nodded; she could do that. She'd organised parties before. If she enlisted help from the villagers, it wouldn't be too difficult to give Edina this one thing. The next item on the list made her laugh.

I want the old Grinch, Tavish Doherty, to smile or laugh – just once.

'That would be a Christmas miracle in itself,' Belle murmured, as Kenzy picked up the final envelope from the table and began to read it.

I want pink hair. I've never been brave enough to ask for it and Reilly would have had a fit, but I think it would suit me.

That would be easy enough to arrange. Perhaps Edina had a hairdresser they could ask? Or Belle could ask Kenzy for another favour? She eyed her friend, who was sipping her Margarita and stealing longing glances at Logan. She'd mention it tomorrow when Kenzy wasn't so distracted.

I want a tattoo – Tavish has one on his arm which he tries to hide, but I know it's there and I want one too.

Belle grimaced. The only tattoo parlour she knew was located in Morridon…

I want to go to Christmas Cairn. I used to visit every year when I was a child to add a rock to the Lachlan Cairn, but I've not been since Reilly passed. It's a difficult path to navigate alone.

Belle knew of Christmas Cairn. It was a hill not far from Christmas Village with a series of cairns – memorials of stones laid out over the years by the locals. But it would be hard for Edina to get there with a fractured ankle. Belle tapped her chin as she read on, wishing Edina's list included a few easier things.

I want to feel useful. I've no idea how you'd get that in a stocking. But if you can deliver it, I'd be very pleased.

Belle shook her head – she couldn't give that to Edina either. She could barely give it to herself.

Finally, Santa – and I realise I'm being greedy, but I'd honestly be happy with just one of the things on this list. I broke the band on the emerald tiara Reilly bought me when we first got engaged. If you could see your way to fixing that, I'd be able to wear it again.

Regards,
Ms Edina Lachlan

Belle sighed. The last thing on the list would involve finding the tiara and she wasn't going to root around her new friend's house.

'That's me finished,' Kenzy said suddenly, licking the final envelope as Belle shoved Edina's letter into the pocket of her coat. She wouldn't be posting it with the others. Edina was lonely and it was clear no one had looked out for her in a while – so this Christmas Belle intended to deliver at least a few of the things on her list. She just had to figure out which ones.

Chapter Four

Jack Hamilton-Kirk carefully navigated his black Audi TT along the long, wide drive towards Evergreen Castle just as the sun poked its head above the horizon, skidding a little as he went. If he'd stopped to think before hopping in the car on impulse to make the four-hundred-mile trip to Christmas Village from London, he might have hired something more suitable for the wintery weather conditions. He jerked the car to a sudden stop, skidding again on a sliver of ice as a fluffy grey donkey appeared like a devilish apparition from a field to his right and decided to settle itself in front of him, dead centre of the drive. The animal trotted over to sniff the bonnet of the car and Jack rested his forehead on the steering wheel so he could momentarily shut his eyes, wondering if fate was playing a cruel trick on him, or he'd somehow been magically teleported into the movie *Shrek*.

He took a deep breath and looked up again so he could study the castle in the distance. It rose from the snow-covered ground, the almost cream-coloured bricks that formed the turrets and high walls he could still remember from when he'd last visited when he was five. Even after thirty-one years, the place was just as impressive. An ache of emotion caught in his throat and he swallowed. He studied the enchanted building set in the middle of nowhere, flanked by snow-topped mountains to its left and right. He might not be in a movie, but he could be in a fairy tale, complete with a wizened old grandmother who was way too old to be living in the middle of nowhere alone. Jack waited as the donkey let out a loud honk before sniffing one of his headlights as it continued its slow perusal of the car. He could blast the horn, but he didn't want to spook the animal just in case it was startled and hurt itself. He sighed and switched off the engine, deciding to wait it out, wishing he had a flask of black coffee to help clear his head. It hadn't occurred to him to pack one – besides, he probably didn't own a flask anymore. When his ex-girlfriend had moved out of their house seven months earlier, during their particularly bitter break-up, she'd cleared everything from the kitchen and bathroom that wasn't nailed down.

Jack's mind wandered as the donkey continued to work its way past the car, stopping at the front grille so it could press its nose into the ringed logo. Had it only been nine hours since he'd called Edina from his house in London after his long flight home from New York? After learning that a stranger had moved into the castle mere hours after knocking Edina over with a bike, he'd been desperate for more information.

What was a young woman doing, volunteering to move in with someone three times her age? In his experience, no one did anything for nothing. Determined to find out exactly what this woman's intentions were and to protect his grandmother, Jack had packed his car with as many possessions as he could fit into the minuscule boot. Including his computer and all the files and paperwork for the clients he was working on. Edina wasn't expecting him, and he could only hope the WiFi in the castle was good enough for him to be able to log in to work. It worked well enough to run their weekly Zoom calls.

Jack's first video call with Edina had been a shock. His last memory of his grandmother had been of a strong, tall woman with dark hair – but thirty-one years had eroded her. She'd looked old and frail, and he'd realised with an uncomfortable jolt that she may not have that many years left. A fact that had been reinforced by this accident. Which meant it was time for him to get his act together. He'd been putting off this visit for a hundred reasons, but the need to see his grandmother in person had been growing – and this was the push he'd needed.

Jack's mobile began to chirp and he picked up as soon as he read the name Dave Adams.

'What's up?' he asked, putting his mobile on speaker and resting his arms on the steering wheel so he could prop up his chin and watch the donkey's continued investigation. Dave was Jack's best friend from university. He was going through a difficult divorce and regularly used Jack as an agony uncle, although rarely paid attention to his advice.

'Rachel put a padlock on the food cupboard and left me with three empty shelves. I got home from work last night and there was nothing to eat aside from a slice of cheese and a natural yoghurt. She hasn't worked out how to lock the fridge yet, which I'm thankful for. I wouldn't mind, but I bought all the spices and herbs and now I can't use any of them.'

'You need to tell your solicitor about this,' Jack murmured.

'She's not exactly Madhur Jaffrey,' Dave continued, ignoring him. 'Her specialities lie somewhere between boiled eggs, Rice

Krispie cakes and Marmite sandwiches. I love Marmite, but...' He huffed and fell silent. 'What happened to us, Jack? We were happy. *I* thought we were happy.'

'Is anyone ever truly happy?' Jack asked, watching as the light snowflakes began to thicken, landing in icy splashes on the windscreen as they gathered momentum. Would he be stuck here until the car began to resemble an igloo, have to send up a flare and rely on the AA to rescue him?

'You're just jaded, mate. Too many hours dealing with unhappy people.' Dave let out a long pitiful sigh. 'It's why I didn't want you to handle my divorce – that, and I couldn't afford you,' he joked.

'I'd have done it pro bono,' Jack murmured. 'You didn't want me involved because you're too nice – and you know I'm not. You need to tell your solicitor about the cupboard,' he repeated, in the vain hope his friend would listen this time. 'That's not on and you can't let Rachel walk all over you.' At the rate Dave was going, he'd lose everything. Jack had seen it happen a million times. Had been warned a million times by his father.

'I'll think about it,' Dave said, but Jack knew he wouldn't. He was a kind man with a vulnerable heart, a sitting duck in the dog-eat-dog world of relationships. He liked Rachel, but knew you couldn't really trust anyone when it came to money. 'Where are you?'

'Sitting in the car. I'm almost at my grandmother's but there's...' There was no way he could explain the donkey. 'A hold-up.'

'Hang on, you only just got back from New York, aren't you in London?' There was an edge of panic in Dave's voice and Jack used his calmest tone to soothe him.

'Edina's injured her ankle and I decided to visit,' he said.

'She okay?' Dave asked.

'I think so. I'll be here until I know how she's doing' – and until he'd worked out what the woman who'd moved in was up to – 'but I'll still be at the end of the phone. I might take a couple of weeks off...' At least he'd been toying with the idea.

'Holiday – you!' Dave barked out a laugh.

Jack sighed. 'There's a lot going on here I need to sort out. Out-of-control wildlife for one...' As if it had heard, the donkey snapped its head up and sniffed the frigid air, before turning and galloping off down the main drive in the direction of the castle. Perhaps it was time for breakfast? Jack's stomach rumbled. Hopefully there would be some for him too. 'Things have started moving, I'd better go. I'll call when I'm settled. Ring the solicitor!' he added, and didn't miss Dave's grumbled sigh as he hung up.

Jack tried to turn the car over, puffing out a frustrated breath as the engine shuddered, spluttered and died. He tried again, giving up after three attempts. 'Perfect,' he murmured, opening the car door, grabbing his keys so he could stumble out. Stretching his back and rolling his shoulders, he eased himself upright for the first time in seven hours. 'Just perfect,' he moaned, as his impractical leather shoes sank into the snow and ice seeped over the tops. He'd been in too much of a hurry to dress properly for the drive. There were walking boots somewhere in the back of the Audi, along with a thick coat, but it was too cold to look for them now. A gust of wind howled from behind, lifting the bottom of his Armani jacket, picking up the car door and slamming it shut, catching the edge of Jack's thigh hard enough to hurt. 'Dammit!' He shivered, wishing he hadn't given in to the impulse to come without at least chang-

ing. Then he carefully made the slow journey, limping down the
snow-covered drive to Evergreen Castle's front door.

Jack knocked three times on the huge oak door before taking a
step back and stamping ice from his shoes. When he'd been five, he'd
thought the entrance was big enough to fit a tank through – even
now it topped his six-foot frame by another two. There were signs
the building was well cared for which was a relief – his grandmother
had mentioned a gardener in one of their calls. Someone had taken
the time to sweep the worst of the snow from the front steps, and
purple and yellow winter pansies poked from large terracotta pots
to his left and right. Both were set underneath the porch so weren't
buried in a layer of snow. The door swung open and a giant of a
man stood framed in the hallway. He had silver-grey hair, the same
colour beard, and was a few inches taller than Jack. He was difficult
to age – perhaps mid-seventies?

'Aye?' the man said, frowning, taking in Jack's damp suit jacket
and hair before grimacing. 'You lost, lad?' He checked the area
behind him, although the snowfall was so thick he wouldn't be able
to see much. A black Scottie dog came scampering into the hall,
then stood to attention by the man's feet. 'The village is about a
mile from here.' He pointed in the direction Jack had driven. The
man wore big black boots, dark brown corduroy trousers and an
Aran jumper – the clothes looked warm and were an embarrassing
contrast to his own unsuitable outfit.

'This is my grandmother's house,' Jack said, glancing into the
hallway where he could see a table set with a large poinsettia in a
silver pot, multiple family paintings and a trail of fairy lights strung
in between. 'I drove all night from London. Edina told me she'd

injured her ankle. Who are you?' He'd been expecting to find a woman. Had she moved her grandpa and pets in too? And where exactly was his grandmother? Annoyance mixed with concern clutched at his chest and he took a step forwards, only to be blocked from entering by the large man.

'I'm Tavish Doherty, a friend of Ms Lachlan – she's not expecting visitors. She mentioned a grandson, but he's not been here since he was five.' The man narrowed his eyes and spread his legs, looking menacing.

'We've only been in touch for a few months,' Jack said, feeling defensive. 'My visit was supposed to be a surprise. May I come in?' Tavish slid a beefy hand to the edge of the door and for a moment Jack wondered if he intended to shut it in his face. Then he heard footsteps and a woman stepped into the light. She was small and slender with chestnut-brown hair that fell in soft waves past her shoulders. Her face was on the exceptional side of pretty – she had hazel eyes and expressive dark eyebrows that were currently signalling irritation. Thankfully it was all aimed at Tavish.

'Are you all right?' Her voice was gentle, and something about the light Scottish lilt made Jack's blood heat. Then again, he'd always had questionable taste in women, a trait he could trace back to his dad. 'You must be freezing.' The woman signalled into the hallway, practically pushing Tavish out of her way. 'Come in. We've just lit a fire and I was serving breakfast before I leave for work. Did you break down close to here?'

Jack stepped inside, taking a moment to absorb the hard thump in his chest as a memory of his mother hit him. It was the last time he'd seen her. She'd been crying, he remembered, standing next to the bottom of the turnpike stairs arguing with his dad. He cleared his throat, pushing away the unwanted emotions. 'My car's in the drive. I'm here to visit my grandmother, Edina Lachlan. Is she around?'

'Jack Hamilton-Kirk.' The woman enunciated his name as if she wanted to chew each word before spitting them on the floor. Her friendly expression cooled as she drew herself up to her full height, which was at least half a foot shorter than Tavish. 'Aye. She's in here. I expect *she'll* be happy to see you.' With that, she turned and marched away.

Bewildered, Jack followed the woman into a large room he vaguely recollected. It had a long dining table on one side, seating set around a large fire, and had been decorated with an array of Christmas paraphernalia. A tree loomed to the left of the fireplace where his grandmother sat. Her foot was propped on a stool and she had a bowl of porridge resting in her lap. Jack's stomach rumbled as he noticed someone had placed a hot drink onto a small table within easy reach of his grandmother. There was an oak cane leaning against one of the high-back chairs to her right. Edina glanced up as they approached, her face stretching in a wide delighted grin as she spotted him. 'Jack?' She wriggled excitedly, throwing her arms wide as she tried to leap up. Even from where he was standing, Jack could see she had tears in her eyes.

'It's fine, stay there.' He stepped forwards to kiss her cheek – she smelled of lavender perfume which triggered a memory that made his stomach simultaneously swirl with happiness and sink. He dropped into the chair beside her, marvelling that he was actually here.

'I can't believe you're here, lad,' Edina said, echoing his thoughts. She reached out to grab his hand and squeezed it.

Jack squeezed back, embarrassed again that it had taken him so long to visit, especially now he could see how overcome his grandmother was. 'I thought I'd come and see you after you told me what happened.' He looked up at the dark-haired woman, who was glowering at him. 'How's the ankle?' He waggled his frozen feet in his shoes as they began to thaw. He'd change later, once he'd got rid of the audience and rescued his clothes and laptop from the car.

'I don't care about that.' His grandmother beamed. 'It's just so wonderful to see you here in the castle again.' She seemed smaller now Jack wasn't looking at her via a laptop camera. There were deep lines etched across her face and her clothes looked too big for her tiny frame.

'But is the ankle okay?' he asked again, frowning at the enormous blue boot – was that really necessary?

'It's getting a little better every day,' Edina admitted. 'And Tavish and Belle have been taking good care of me, as I mentioned when you called. Oh lad, it's so good to see you. You look even more handsome face to face.' She lifted a hand and held it to his cheek, and he fought the flinch. It had been a while since anyone had touched him and the easy affection was unsettling.

He cleared his throat, taking a moment to look around. Being back here felt strange; a million memories clamoured for attention in his brain and he pushed them away. Instead he concentrated on the surroundings, trying to focus on something practical. There was plenty of artwork still hanging on the walls, a long tapestry to the side of the dining table, and no dusty gaps suggesting anything had been removed. *Yet.* But who knew what the sturdy man and hostile woman were up to? 'I thought I'd stay until you were feeling better.

No need to inconvenience anyone now I'm here.' He glanced back at the woman, hoping his meaning was clear.

'It's been a pleasure helping Edina.' Her tone was smooth but she was shooting unfriendly daggers in his direction. 'But I could leave if you want me to?' Her question was directed at Edina.

'Nae, lass.' The elderly woman frowned at him. 'Belle has loaned her house to a family in need for a few weeks. I've told the lass she can stay until after Christmas. It's been a pleasure having the company. I don't want to bother you when I know your life is so busy.'

Jack let out a long breath, feeling a flicker of guilt as Tavish marched in and picked up the navy coat which was lying on one of the dining room chairs. 'I've chopped more wood for the fire so you've got plenty for this morning. Logan's back from his trip and he told me he'd be here later if you need more. I'll be off.' He frowned at Jack, his expression filled with the same suspicion as Belle's. 'I'll be back this evening to carry you upstairs.' When Jack opened his mouth to say he'd do it, the large man shook his head. 'It's nae trouble. We look after our neighbours in Christmas Village, especially if they're alone.' With that, he turned and marched into the hallway. Seconds later the front door slammed.

Jack frowned. He'd driven up on a mission of mercy on barely any sleep to make sure his grandmother wasn't being taken advantage of – and suddenly he was the bad guy? He wasn't sure how he felt about that. Perhaps because in some small way he agreed. He hadn't been there for Edina; somehow after losing his dad he hadn't wanted to be reminded of his mother too, and he'd avoided visiting the castle. But that had been selfish, and he fully intended to be around from now on.

It was silent for a few moments, but Jack saw Belle check her watch. 'I've got to go too.' He could see she was reluctant to leave. 'The school opens soon.' Her attention ping-ponged between them both. 'It's really no trouble me staying here if you need to get back to London. You can see for yourself your nana's fine.'

'I'm planning to stop for a while. Are there any beds made up?' Jack asked.

'Aye, there's your mam's old room,' Edina said, pointing to the right of the dining table. 'You might not remember. When you were a lad you stayed in there with her. It's got its own bathroom, a desk if you need to work, and a small seating area. The bed's all made up. I always make sure it's ready in case anyone drops by.' How many years had it been since they had? Jack wondered. It was unlikely his mother would have bothered to make the long trip down from Skye when she had her precious donkeys to care for.

'I'm staying upstairs in case your nana needs anything at night. I'll leave you both to catch up.' Belle frowned before turning and marching off. 'I'll be back at midday to bring your lunch from Rowan's Cafe,' she said, turning to speak to Edina as she reached the doorway. Her mouth pursed as she glanced back at him. 'The villagers have all been chipping in, making sure your grandmother's taken care of. Will you be wanting something to eat too?'

'Aye,' Edina interrupted before Jack could refuse. 'We're having soup and cheese toasties today.' Her cheeks pinked with excitement. 'You used to love toasties when you were a wee bairn. Could you ask Rowan to make up two lunches, please, lass? Tell her to add them to my account. I don't expect her to feed us for nowt. I'd like to get your lunch too?'

Jack bristled and Belle's mouth thinned as if she'd read his mind. 'I'm fine, thank you,' she said. She wore pink lipstick – it was a natural rather than in-your-face shade, but it still accentuated the plump curves of her lips and Jack found the way his breath thickened irritating. He turned so he could gaze into the fire, closing his eyes as a wave of tiredness engulfed him. He didn't open them, even when he heard the sound of Belle's footsteps again on the wooden floor.

'For you.' She shoved a mug of hot black coffee into his hands. 'You look like you need it,' she murmured, frowning again as she turned and marched back towards the front door.

Jack stared at the drink. The kind gesture was unexpected, and for a moment he wondered if he'd got Belle all wrong before he shook his head. Everyone wanted something – hadn't his dad taught him that? He'd get to the bottom of what she wanted – and he wasn't leaving Evergreen Castle, or his grandmother's side, until he had.

Chapter Five

Belle was late for school. She half jogged, half ran as she left Evergreen Castle, trying not to trip in the deep drifts as ice splattered her face. She paused for a beat as she passed the ridiculously impractical black sports car that had been abandoned in the middle of the drive. How was Logan supposed to get his truck down here later so he could cut wood and clear more of the snow, allowing Edina to hobble outside to visit Bob? She blew out an irritated breath. Jack Hamilton-Kirk had been everything she'd expected: arrogant, unfriendly and handsome as sin. The photo in the frame on the mantelpiece hadn't done him justice. He had a square jaw, dark ash-blond hair and blue eyes with long dark lashes that he'd probably sold his soul to the devil for. No one looked that good naturally – aside perhaps from Kenzy. Belle had still made him coffee though – all of those annoying helpful and caring genes had kicked in when she'd taken in his pale face and deemed him in desperate need of a shot of caffeine. He hadn't been grateful enough to thank her for it though. Which confirmed everything about him she'd already guessed. Although the small part of her that looked for the best in everyone – the bit Kenzy called her 'Pollyanna persona' – still wanted to be proved wrong.

She reached the end of the drive, a little out of breath, and took a left, tugging her backpack from her shoulders as she continued to run. She'd tucked the pile of red envelopes into the pack's front pocket this morning after sticking on the stamps she'd bought in the post office yesterday during lunch. She pulled them out as she approached the post box, checking Edina's was still in her pocket before she shoved the rest inside the red pillar. There was a lot to do if she was going to give Edina even half of what she'd asked for on the list – and the bit involving Jack and his mother might be difficult. But after meeting him this morning she was even more determined to give Edina the Christmas she deserved. She could definitely help with the pink hair – she'd talk to Kenzy today – and perhaps the Christmas party wouldn't prove impossible…

Isla MacGavin was hovering outside the front of the primary school to the right of the blue front door when Belle arrived, grasping Adam's hand as he watched his friends throw snowballs at each other in the playground. The main school building was small with a triangular arch above the entrance, and a long spire with a bell at the top to the right of the main roof. There were multiple windows filled with mini panes of glass, edged in lead. The classrooms were bright and airy, but sometimes the high ceilings and ancient heating system meant they got cold in the winter, and Belle hoped all the kids had worn at least one extra layer today.

'Miss Albany.' Isla gave Belle a tentative smile as she cornered her on the main doorstep just as Belle was about to open the door. 'I wanted to say thank you again for letting us stay in your home.' The dainty woman pressed a pretty red and green striped box into Belle's hands and indicated that she should open it. Inside were twelve handmade snowman-shaped biscuits. They were exquisite with white and silver icing, button baubles and tiny handmade carrot noses.

'These are amazing!' Belle exclaimed, but Isla shrugged the compliment away.

'I enjoy sewing and baking in my spare time. I wanted to tell you, my husband Clyde's going to see a flat today just a few miles outside the village, but it's not going to be available until after Christmas. I feel bad that we've pushed you out of your house, especially at this time of year.' Isla shoved a hand into the pocket of her coat and tugged on Adam's again as he strained to watch his friends play.

'It's okay if you let him go.' Belle tipped her head towards the playground and Isla released her son. He let out a screech and went hurtling towards his friends. 'Walk, lad, don't run!' Belle shouted after him. She turned back to Isla. 'It's really fine.' But her stomach lurched. If Jack decided to stay with Edina as he'd threatened, it would have been better to move back into Annie's house. A tiny part of her had been hoping the MacGavins would find somewhere quickly, not that she'd ever say so. 'I'm happy staying in Evergreen Castle, and I'm welcome there for as long as I need.'

Isla pushed a strand of curly blonde hair out of her eyes as they filled with tears. 'You're an angel,' she murmured. 'Everybody in the village says so. When the landlord refused last minute to renew our contract I was so worried. I know he had a good reason, because his pregnant daughter needed our place after her husband lost his job.' She swallowed. 'But I had no idea where we were going to go.' She blinked and a tear slid onto her cheek before she swiped at it. 'There's so little available around the area, especially this close to Christmas.'

'It's fine.' Belle felt the familiar flood of warmth pool in her stomach. It was a good feeling, helping people, making a difference. It must be the way her father felt every day. No wonder he'd chosen it over her. She grimaced as the school's bell rang, signalling the start of the day. 'I'm so sorry, I've got to go,' she said, pushing the door open as thirty children charged from the playground towards her.

'Just remember,' Isla said, beaming at her. 'If I can ever do anything for you in return, you know where I am.'

'If I can't be a shepherd, I want to be Joseph.' Doug Wallace frowned as Belle read through the cast list of the nativity play later that morning. She'd only had a cursory glance through Benji's notes when she'd arrived back at Evergreen Castle after her evening in the pub and hadn't had a chance at all yesterday because she'd been baking for the WI Christmas fete after work. Then she'd fallen asleep reading them in her bed wrapped in a dozen blankets, absently stroking Jinx after the silver-grey tabby had emerged from his hiding place. Benji had already listed the main parts and included suggestions as to which children might play them, and she'd decided to test the waters. 'My mam said I have the perfect ears to be a da,' Doug snickered, wriggling one of his earlobes. 'Because I'm really good at switching them off.' Belle chuckled, trying hard not to agree.

'My mam says women can be anything.' Alison Brun turned her brilliant green eyes on Belle. 'Are you sure Joseph was a lad?'

'Fairly certain.' Belle cleared her throat. 'I think you'd make a great king though.' Alison nodded, bowing her head as if Belle had just deposited a crown on it. The children were all sitting at their desks giggling excitedly. 'Does anyone want to be in the chorus?' No one spoke but every head shook. 'That's fine. There are enough speaking parts for you all if you're happy to do them. As you know, the children from the other years normally do the singing.'

Bonnie McGregor put up her hand. 'Can I be Mary?'

Belle tapped a fingertip to her mouth. 'I had a better idea – I thought you'd like to audition for the North Star.' She'd already decided to give the part of Mary to Nessa after she'd confessed to writing it on her Christmas list, but didn't want to upset Bonnie in the process.

The small girl fluffed up her blonde hair. 'Does she speak?'

'Aye.' Belle nodded. She'd add something to Benji's script specially. She couldn't imagine Bonnie getting through an entire performance without being the centre of attention at least once.

'Can I audition to be a sheep?' Adam asked shyly, his large brown eyes serious. 'I like sheep.'

'Aye.' Belle scribbled Adam's name onto her pad. This was going to be easier than she'd expected. Benji had already done a rough draft of the script, including songs, so it would just be a case of adding the odd piece of dialogue, getting the kids to rehearse, and figuring out how on earth she was going to find the nativity costumes to ensure they all fitted. According to Benji, when he'd searched the chest they used for costume storage it had been empty. They were bound to be in a cupboard somewhere – there were always a lot of parent helpers at school performances, so they'd probably been misdirected. She'd have to stay late one evening when she had time, see if she could root them out. The bell rang, signalling it was time for lunch, and Belle hopped up. She had special permission to miss out on playground duty so she could deliver food to Edina.

Belle tugged on her coat and was out of the school and heading for the main high street within a few minutes. She checked her watch. She didn't have a lot of time and needed to hurry if she was going to pick up lunch and get back to school in time for the next lesson. There was a long queue in The Corner Shop as Belle passed and Tavish was serving a customer so she didn't bother to wave; the post office was closed again but Rowan's Cafe looked busy. As Belle stepped inside the steamy shop, she nodded to a couple of the customers as they sat sipping mugs of coffee, accompanied by large slabs of chocolate, carrot, and coffee and walnut cake. The shop was cosy with a large glass counter at the back, showcasing filled sandwiches, various cakes and pastries. Behind the counter Rowan Taylor was busy gathering orders and making coffee, and Belle could hear a clatter from the kitchen, signalling her son Matt was in the back cooking. There were six tables scattered around the room and each had four chairs surrounding it. Someone had painted all the tables and chairs bright green years ago, and Belle knew Rowan and Matt touched them up each summer. Belle did a double-take as she reached the counter and found Kenzy waiting, tapping a foot on the floor as she scrolled listlessly through a dating app on her mobile.

'See anything interesting?' Belle teased, tapping her friend on the shoulder, making her jump.

Kenzy pulled a face. 'I can't summon any interest at the moment.' Her forehead scrunched. 'I need to get Logan out of my system so I can get back to seeing people.' She leaned closer to Belle. 'He comes here on Wednesdays for lunch – I thought I might pick up a salad, see if I can bump into him. I've decided to up my game, be a little more available, see if that encourages him to ask me out.' She waggled her eyebrows. 'I heard Edina's wayward grandson turned up at Evergreen Castle this morning, dressed for a night out on the town?'

'Aye.' Belle grimaced. It always surprised her how quickly news travelled in Christmas Village. 'He's everything I expected. I'm guessing he'll get bored of playing the good grandson in a few days and head back to London.'

'Are you picking up Edina's lunch?' Kenzy asked.

'Aye – and *Jack's*.' Belle said his name slowly, layering it with a dollop of irritation.

Kenzy quirked an eyebrow. 'Is Pollyanna having an off day? I know you weren't that sure about him, but I thought your mantra was "there's good in everyone". Not that I'm complaining. You could do with toughening up – the world's filled with sharks, it's good to have your harpoon sharpened when you meet them.' She laughed, but Belle knew Kenzy believed every word. Years of being stuck in between her warring parents had left her with little time for the idea of true love.

'Let's just say Edina's grandson is going to have to prove himself. I'm really not sure he has her best interests at heart. But perhaps I'm wrong…' Belle shoved her hands into her pockets and her fingers wrapped around two envelopes. She drew them out, frowning when she realised one was the Christmas list she'd written and forgotten to throw out. The other was Edina's. She shoved them both back into her pocket. 'I've got a favour to ask,' she said.

'Anything.' Kenzy turned to Rowan as she approached the counter and ordered a chicken salad and Diet Coke.

'Have you ever dyed anyone's hair pink?' The door at the front of the shop opened and they were hit by a blast of frigid air. Belle saw Kenzy's pupils dilate and guessed Logan had arrived.

Kenzy licked her lips. 'Um.' Logan must have stopped at one of the tables to chat, because her friend's eyes remained positioned at Belle's left ear. 'Sure. Not for a while. The women from Christmas Village tend to favour purple, but I've plenty of dye. You fancy a change?' Her forehead creased. 'I can't imagine you with multicoloured hair, but it's good to see you doing something for yourself for a change.'

'Not for me.' Belle snorted. 'For Edina. I...' She paused, wondering if she should tell Kenzy about the Christmas list. She knew she could trust her, but it didn't seem right. She'd already snooped into something private, hadn't thrown Edina's list away even when she'd known that's what the older woman wanted. It wasn't fair to share her hopes and dreams with anyone else. If she gave Edina just a few of the things she'd asked Santa for, she might chalk the whole thing up to coincidence. If no one else knew about the list, there'd be zero risk of her finding out the truth. 'I thought she might fancy a new hairdo. Edina mentioned the woman who usually comes to the castle to cut and style her hair has gone away for Christmas.' Belle looked at her boots, feeling uncomfortable. 'Her fashion sense is quite eccentric and I wondered if she'd enjoy trying something more dramatic.'

'I can bring a selection of colours.' Kenzy's eyes widened. 'Think she'd fancy a makeover too? I'd enjoy the chance to experiment. I could put some pictures on my Instagram page, see if I can drum up more business.' She looked at Belle critically. 'In return you have to let me get my hands on you. Your hair needs a trim.' She tugged on a strand. 'Yep, the ends are split and you need some make-up tips. You're pretty, Belle, but you never spend any time on yourself.'

Belle opened her mouth to argue but stopped as Kenzy's face brightened. 'Logan,' she purred. 'I'm offering a discount on men's haircuts at the moment. Do you want me to book you an appointment?'

'I'm fine, thanks. My sister gave me a trim while I was visiting her.' Logan's deep voice rumbled next to Belle's left ear and Kenzy's cheeks flushed. Belle had rarely seen her friend off balance. She was the epitome of a man-eater – the girl most likely to chew up and spit out vulnerable hearts. It was just this man seemed immune.

'Here's your order.' Rowan placed a bag with Kenzy's lunch in it on the counter and beamed. 'Aye, it's busy today. Your usual, Logan?' He nodded and Rowan called into the kitchen before turning to Belle. 'I've got the order ready for Ms Lachlan – she called and asked me to add in a sandwich and cake for you. You're looking thin, lass.' She frowned. 'I heard the grandson is a looker. How is the poor woman?' Rowan talked at a million miles an hour and sometimes it was hard to slot in a response. Today she paused, giving Belle a chance to answer.

'She's okay – the ankle will take a few weeks to heal but I'll be staying with her until she's better,' Belle said.

'Aye. I heard the MacGavins are living in your house?' The older woman cocked her head. 'How long will that be for? It would be a shame if they had to move away from Christmas Village.'

'Ach, well, we'll find them somewhere,' Belle murmured, hoping that was true.

'Grand.' Matt brought two bags out of the kitchen and placed them on the counter. 'That's for you...' Rowan pointed to one. When Belle reached into her backpack to pull out her purse, she shook her head. 'On the house. It's about time someone looked after you for a change, lass. Now off with you. If you've got to drop those and get back to school, you've nae much time to waste.' Belle smiled gratefully, before rushing back out of the shop and into the snow.

Chapter Six

'I've wanted to go pink for years! I've no idea how you guessed.' Edina beamed as Kenzy carefully painted gloopy hair dye onto her scalp and Belle bustled around the large kitchen, which was located in the basement of Evergreen Castle. It had taken Belle and Kenzy a tricky fifteen minutes to get Edina down the short flight of concrete stairs, but it had been the best place for Kenzy to work because there was a small bathroom set in the far corner which gave them easy access to a low sink. The kitchen was a long, wide room, with high ceilings that had been painted a bright cream colour. There were large beige and grey flagstone tiles on the floor and two long tables with reclaimed wood on the surfaces, which had been sanded and waxed. Belle had hung a few silver stars she'd found amongst the Christmas decorations onto the walls to brighten up the place. She'd also dangled a sprig of mistletoe from the ceiling in case Edina managed to get Tavish down here. All in all the space felt cosy, but despite the large Aga sitting at the far end of the room pumping out heat, the room was glacial. Belle pulled her woollen cardigan tighter around her middle.

'I'm good at guessing what my clients want.' Kenzy winked at Belle as she put the enormous red casserole dish into the Aga,

containing a hearty chicken stew that she'd thrown together while
Kenzy had been working. She'd finally figured out how to use it, so
Annie's microwave would be redundant from now on.

'Aye, well. Tavish won't know what's hit him.' Edina gave a small
squeak of delight. 'I do so enjoy teasing him. One day I'll get a smile
out of the old curmudgeon.'

Kenzy chuckled. 'A woman after my own heart. We'll do your
make-up next – have a look through what you're using so we can
see what might need refreshing – and I can show you some of the
things you can do to accentuate your eyes.' She bent to look at Edina
properly. 'You've got a magnificent bone structure.'

'Ah, lass, it's been a lot of years since anyone's said anything so
nice. The last compliment I got was from my dentist – and she just
admired that I still had my own teeth.' Edina's face lit with mirth
and Kenzy snorted. The older woman had a wicked sense of humour
and often had Belle belly laughing.

'Where's your make-up?' Kenzy asked, applying another globule
of dye onto her scalp. 'It might be worth Belle getting it now so we
can look while the hair colour is processing? I've almost finished
covering your head.'

'Aye.' Edina nodded. 'I keep it in a drawer in the room my daughter, Tara, uses when she stays. The one Jack's in now.' She pulled a face.
'It's got the best natural light in the castle and a large mirror. I don't
wear make-up often, so I call it the "putting-my-face-on space". Belle,
would you mind getting it, lass? It's just inside the main doorway,
in a small blue bag on the oak shelving to the right of the entrance.'

Belle flushed. She'd not seen Jack since this morning and had
been hoping to avoid him if she could.

Edina must have read her expression. 'Don't worry about Jack, lass. Logan helped him dig his car out of the snow and he went off to visit someone in Tatherfod earlier.' Belle frowned; Tatherfod was a town about a thirty-minute drive from Christmas Village. It didn't have much to recommend it: a restaurant, a large supermarket and a hotel. What would Jack be doing there? 'He came back with a big bag of paperwork an hour ago and then popped into the village because the WiFi dropped out and he had to send some emails,' Edina continued. 'He's not returned – he would have come to find me if he had.' She beamed. 'He's a good lad.'

Belle wiped her hands on her jeans because just the thought of going into the man's room made her palms sweat. 'I won't be long.' She charged up the basement stairs. They led to the end of a large empty ballroom which Edina had shown to Belle when she'd first moved in. The room was empty of furniture and felt even colder than the kitchen. The only source of potential heat was a huge fireplace which clearly hadn't been used in years, because it was sparkling clean. She ran across the polished oak floorboards and opened the door into the main sitting/dining room, listening out for any sounds that would indicate Jack had returned. It was silent; even Jinx didn't scamper out from wherever he was hiding.

A quick knock on the bedroom door confirmed Jack wasn't there, so Belle strode in. It was a beautiful room, with a vaulted ceiling that let slivers of winter sunlight into the large space. There was a door to the left which Belle guessed would lead to the en suite bathroom. She scoured the area, taking in the heavy antique wardrobe, dresser and desk, where a messy pile of what looked like work folders had been laid out. A super king-sized bed with a rumpled dark green duvet

and tangled sheets dominated the back wall. It hadn't been made
– typical. Belle noticed a big black leather holdall had been tossed
onto the bed and was barely balanced against a scrunched-up pillow.
Perhaps Jack had been in a hurry to go out? The zip at the top of the
bag was partly undone and paperwork had slipped onto the floor.
Belle saw something glossy, like a brochure, and took a tentative step
forwards. She glanced around the room and listened again. Hadn't
her da once told her that sometimes it was okay to do the wrong
thing for the right reason? Although he'd probably been referring to
when he and her mam had smuggled four undernourished children
out of an orphanage after discovering they were being mistreated.
Belle doubted he'd approve of this type of snooping. But she didn't
trust Jack and she wanted to know what he was up to.

She quickly pushed the bedroom door closed and took another
step forwards as her heart rate kicked up, shimmying into the top
of her throat, making it difficult to breathe normally. She glanced
over her shoulder. She had to hurry, she'd already been gone too
long; Edina and Kenzy would be wondering what on earth she
was up to, and perhaps Kenzy would come looking for her? Her
stomach made a gurgling sound, indicating she was either hungry
or terrified, and she sprinted the final few steps, kneeling so she
could pick up some papers and the brochure from the top of the
pile of paperwork. Her heart sank. The papers included valuations
for various pieces of jewellery and Belle gasped when she saw how
much some of Edina's rings, necklaces and bracelets were worth.
Did Jack have plans for them? She put the sheets back on the floor
so she could glance through the booklet. It was for a retirement
home – a huge complex of buildings located on the outside edges of

Tatherfod. Belle knew of it. People moved there from far and wide across Scotland because it had an excellent reputation, but Belle knew Edina would hate it there. Hadn't she already confided that she didn't want to leave the castle? Was that what Jack had planned for his nana all along? Was it why he was here?

There was some accompanying literature which detailed costs and included an application form which hadn't been filled in. Belle let out a growl of disgust and closed her eyes. She knew it. With every fibre of her being she'd felt Jack Hamilton-Kirk was up to no good. She swallowed. Should she mention something to Edina? *No.* She flicked through a few pages of the brochure. As she'd heard, the retirement home was beautiful, with landscaped grounds and large self-contained flats. But Belle knew Edina loved her ancestral home, and would hate to move out even if her new home was this luxurious. How much influence did Jack have over her? It didn't matter – Belle had spent a lifetime knowing her da was in the world righting wrongs, fighting for the underdog. It was in her genes and she knew whatever happened she'd protect her new friend. She just didn't know how she was going to do it. She was a teacher, she hadn't been trained for detective work! She jumped up and grabbed the small bag of make-up from the shelf, taking care not to disturb anything. Then she slipped out, closed the bedroom door carefully and made her way back to the basement, determined that whatever happened, she'd be keeping a close eye on Jack from now on.

'Wow!' Edina gasped thirty minutes later, as Kenzy held up a mirror. She'd spent the last quarter of an hour applying eyeliner, mascara and blusher to the elderly woman's face. 'I look twenty years younger, lassie.' Edina giggled, twisting her head this way and that. Even though she still had a plastic bag and pink towel wrapped around her head because the hair colour was still processing, she looked brilliant. 'It's such a tonic having you lasses here.' She beamed as she glanced around the kitchen. 'It's been years since I've had guests. My parents used to entertain all the time, but my Reilly was a right crabbit. He was nice enough to me, but he didn't welcome people. I suppose I got into bad habits after he died, keeping myself to myself because I thought it was what he would have wanted, and I got used to being on my own.' Her face dropped and instantly brightened. 'I need to thank my lucky stars that you knocked me over with your bike, lass, you've changed my life.' Edina stopped Belle to squeeze her arm as she was about to sweep past, intending to check on the stew. Dinner would be ready in half an hour; she just needed to heat some garlic bread.

'Do you think Jack will want to eat with us?' she asked, fighting the frown. If she was going to get to the bottom of what Edina's grandson was up to, she'd have to swallow her irritation and try to befriend him. Adopting one of Kenzy's mantras – 'keep your friends close and your enemies closer'. Perhaps she could rope him into helping her with the Christmas list?

'Aye, I'm sure he should be back,' Edina murmured, looking worried. 'Unless he's got his car stuck in the snow again. I told him to use my old Land Rover, but it wouldn't start.'

There was a loud crash from upstairs and Belle instantly sprang up from where she was kneeling beside the oven, just as the man in question walked down the concrete stairs into the kitchen, clutching

Jinx who was holding on for dear life. The silver-grey tabby's claws were tangled in the thick black jumper Jack had changed into. There were snowflakes in his hair and his cheeks were ruddy from the cold. Kenzy let out a low 'oh, wow' as she watched him descend – his legs, now clad in practical dark trousers, seemed longer and more muscular than Belle remembered.

'Where did this cat come from?' Jack growled, trying to disentangle Jinx's claws from his sweater. As he released first one paw and then the other, the cat reattached them. He tried again with the same result, eventually giving up with a frustrated groan as the cat clung on. 'I thought you owned a donkey?'

'Aye, Bob's mine. Jinx belongs to Belle,' Edina explained, as Kenzy peeled the towel from her head so she could check on the hair colour.

'Figures.' Jack frowned, doing a double-take as he took in his nana properly. 'You look – different.'

Edina snorted. 'Aye, you get your talent for compliments from your granda, all right.'

Jack flushed. 'I mean, you look nice – you always do. But is your hair going to be… pink?' His attention jerked to Kenzy.

'I prefer to call it Shocking Magenta. Pink's so last year.' She grinned. 'I'm Kenzy Campbell, I own The Workshop in the village. If you need a haircut while you're staying…' She waved a hand at the bag of equipment she'd set on the floor.

'I'm Jack. Are you sure you know what you're doing? I'm really not sure pink is the best colour for my grandmother.' He turned to Edina, glancing at Belle, looking a little annoyed. 'Did someone talk you into this?'

'No, I love it, lad!' Edina said firmly. 'Pink hair has been a long-term wish. Your granda didn't like bright colours – I've wanted to do it for years.'

'Okay.' Jack frowned as Jinx began to climb again, attempting to press his nose into Jack's neck. Startled, Jack's eyes shot to Belle. 'Can you take it, please? I found the cat in the middle of the driveway. He looked lost and I thought he was injured so I picked him up. Now I can't put him down.'

Belle frowned; she wouldn't have expected a man like Jack to care about the wellbeing of a stray animal. 'Jinx isn't usually good with strangers.' She approached, trying to ignore the effect his tall, wide body had on her pulse as she drew closer. She reached up to take Jinx from his arms. The cat was purring, rubbing himself against Jack's jumper. It was the happiest he'd been since moving to Evergreen Castle.

'You take after your mam. She's always been good with animals,' Edina murmured, as Kenzy unwound the towel from her head and removed the plastic bag.

'I'm nothing like Tara.' Jack's tone was dark and a little exasperated. 'Is the cat okay?' he asked Belle, as she managed to disentangle Jinx from the jumper and put him on the floor. Instead of shooting off like usual, Jinx wound himself in and out of Jack's legs, purring loudly.

'He's fine, he's taken to you...' She paused. 'Perhaps he has a head injury?' Belle knelt to stroke Jinx's soft fur and check him over. The cat was usually such a good judge of character. By rights the man should have lost an eye by now.

'Thanks,' Jack muttered, but his mouth twitched as he sniffed the air. 'Is that garlic bread?' He looked at the space beside the Aga where two thick sausage-shaped rolls had been wrapped in foil. Belle had to put them in the oven in a minute.

'Aye, and the lass made a chicken stew to go with it,' Edina said. 'We'll eat in the dining room if you don't mind helping me get there, lad?'

'I need to wash the colour out of your hair first,' Kenzy said. 'If you help me get your nana to the bathroom, I can finish up in there. I've got my dryer so we can complete the makeover.' She winked at Edina. 'I'm sure Jack can help Belle get everything ready here.'

'That's not necessary,' Belle snapped.

'It's no trouble.' Jack frowned, then picked Edina up as if she weighed nothing and followed Kenzy into the bathroom. He folded his arms when he walked back out and glanced around the kitchen. 'What needs doing?'

Belle shrugged. 'Laying the table – the food will be ready in twenty minutes. I'll need you to help me serve, but we can use the dumbwaiter.' She pointed to the corner where an arch of cream-coloured tiles framed what looked like a wooden cupboard with open shelving. On closer inspection Belle had discovered a rope and pulley system inside.

'Ahh, okay.' Jack sauntered over to it and ran a hand across one of the shelves. 'I remember this.' He cleared his throat, a low guttural sound which hit Belle clear in the solar plexus. It was an unhappy noise, one she wasn't expecting. 'Where will I find the cutlery?'

Belle pursed her lips, trying to dismiss the wave of sympathy she'd been feeling, and pointed to a long wooden cabinet to the side of him. 'Everything's in there.'

'Right. I'm going to wash my hands and change first.' He glanced down at his jumper which was covered in cat hair. 'I'll be back in a sec.' Then he marched up the stairs with Jinx scampering closely at his heels, leaving Belle wondering what he'd looked so sad about.

'I adore it,' Edina declared, flapping her hands around her new hairdo as she sat at the end of the dining table wearing a diamond tiara. The colour was almost neon and Belle blinked, trying to get used to the vibrant vision, resolving to tick 'pink hair' off Edina's Christmas list. It felt good – and as she watched her new friend giggle, enjoying being the centre of attention, something inside her expanded, filling up the empty void. In that moment, she knew she had to continue with the list. If Jack encouraged Edina to move out of Evergreen Castle, this could be her last chance to get some of the things she'd asked Santa for.

Someone knocked on the front door and Belle started to get up, but Jack beat her to it, striding to the hallway, waving at her to sit. A few minutes later he led Logan into the dining room, with Jinx dogging his heels. The gardener was wearing his outdoor coat, and as he pulled off his woollen cap a flurry of snowflakes fluttered to the floor. He squinted, his eyes crinkling at the corners in surprise as he spotted Kenzy sitting at the table next to Belle.

'Ach, I'm sorry I interrupted.' He squeezed his hat between his fingertips. 'I wanted to tell you I managed to get the Land Rover started.' He turned to Jack, looking serious. 'I'd advise you to use it for the time being and to leave the Fisher-Price car here – at least until it stops blizzarding.'

'Thank you,' Jack said mildly, absorbing the jibe about his car with a quiet chuckle.

'You should join us, Logan.' Edina waved a hand at the table. Jack had laid it earlier with placemats, cutlery, and pretty wine glasses which he'd filled with Merlot. There were spare bowls next to the large casserole dish which Belle had set in the centre. 'There's a space opposite Kenzy, and extra cutlery and a placemat in the dumbwaiter. I always keep some there, ready for when Tara visits.' Edina beamed.

'I'm fine,' Logan ground out, glancing at the exit.

'You'll be finer after you've eaten. Go on with you, you've done me enough kindnesses over the years; the least you can do is let me feed you. Especially when I'm not the one cooking – I wouldn't subject you to that.' Edina shuddered. 'Lay the lad a place, someone, pour him some wine – it's from the cellar.'

Kenzy got to her feet so she could grab the cutlery and a glass, before laying Logan a place opposite her. She wasn't dressed up this evening, which may have explained the deep flush marring her cheeks. Belle knew her friend felt vulnerable if she was seen in anything other than her full vamp outfit. She used her sexuality as armour and relied on it. Today she wore jeans and a baggy red sweater. She'd put her hair up into a knot and curls swung around her cheeks as she moved. Her face was devoid of make-up, aside from a light swipe of lip gloss. Belle thought she looked prettier than she ever had.

'That okay?' Kenzy pressed her lips together when Logan continued to watch her without moving. Then he nodded and tugged off his coat, pulling up a chair. Belle could feel the tension coming off him as she spooned the casserole into his bowl and offered him the garlic bread.

He took a slice and gazed at Kenzy. 'You've been working?' He cleared his throat and forked up some casserole.

'Nope.' Kenzy shook herself and gave a more confident grin. 'I'm doing a favour for a friend. Do you like it?' She pointed to Edina's hair. She was still preening, gazing at herself in one of the shiny spoons Jack had laid out earlier.

'Aye… it's definitely… bright,' Logan said, as a smile played at the corner of his mouth. Logan didn't smile much. It was interesting Kenzy had managed to elicit one.

'Just say the word and you too can have pink hair,' Kenzy teased, seeming to relax as Logan continued eating, pausing to let out a gruff bark of laughter in response to her offer. Jack chuckled too, then Kenzy set her sights on him and pursed her lips. 'You could pull off green – if you want to make an impact this Christmas, I'm on the main high street.'

'I'll remember that,' Jack said, letting out a deep belly laugh that made Belle's stomach flutter in response because the sound was so warm and light.

Perhaps there was something about the normality of breaking bread – like it was a sign they could all let their barriers drop, even if it was just for half an hour? Even Belle felt more relaxed, despite the memory of what she'd found in Jack's bedroom earlier hovering at the corner of her mind. Maybe there was a reasonable explanation? The Pollyanna part of her brain was at work again. But whatever happened, Belle knew she was going to get to the bottom of that, and why Jack Hamilton-Kirk was really here.

Chapter Seven

An hour later, Jack stood by the large butler sink in the basement kitchen and scrubbed another of his grandmother's antique plates. 'No dishwasher,' he grumbled. 'No central heating. No mod cons at all. I've no idea why anyone would choose to live here.' Especially a frail old woman in her late seventies who normally lived alone. How long would it be before Edina had another accident, lost her footing on the stairs, or froze when the weather raged as it sometimes did for days in the Highlands?

Out of the corner of his eye, Jack saw Belle frown at him as she dried a couple of the silver forks he'd just washed up, before placing them carefully into the wide drawer he'd got them from earlier. Before today Jack might have been tempted to count them – perhaps he still would once everyone was tucked up in bed? It was important he ignored the hard tugs of attraction he'd been feeling towards Belle this evening, and was mindful of the lessons his dad had taught. *Trust no one* – the words should have graced his epitaph.

He heard a deep laugh from upstairs and guessed it was his grandmother, teasing Tavish who'd arrived with his dog ten minutes before to carry her up to bed – despite Jack insisting again he could do it. The old man's jaw had dropped when he'd seen the ridiculous hair, and after Tavish had checked Edina's ankle she'd asked him to join her for a nightcap to toast the new locks. She was so trusting, Jack thought, shaking his head, so willing to accept anyone into her world for the price of a chicken stew, new hairdo or a little conversation. How would she feel if one of them used the friendship as a way to cheat her out of her money? Jack turned just as Belle pulled her thick coat tighter around her middle and secured a couple of the large buttons at the front. She'd grabbed it from her bedroom just before they'd headed into the kitchen to wash up. 'Cold?' he asked as she moved to the Aga to hover her hands over the top, rubbing them together and shuddering.

'Freezing,' she murmured through gritted teeth. 'I can't seem to warm up.'

'These old basements are almost impossible to heat,' he said, glancing at an old fireplace at the edge of the kitchen which now featured wooden shelving. He suspected the chimney had been bricked up by his grandad years before, no doubt in an attempt to make it warmer – but Jack guessed removing the fire, one of the only possible sources of heat aside from the Aga, would have had the opposite effect. 'It would be difficult and expensive to add central heating. I looked into it a few weeks ago.' He placed another plate on the drainer and watched Belle out of the corner of his eye as she scowled, before shoving her hands into the pockets of her coat. She jerked in surprise, then pulled out two square red envelopes. She stared at them, twisting them in her hands, and Jack turned to the sink to pick up another plate, washing it slowly.

What was in those envelopes?

He heard Belle's feet on the flagstone floor and had to force himself not to turn and track her movements. Instead he was drawn to the clear glass splashback to his right, set into the wall above the wooden counter. He could just make out her silhouette in the reflection, and watched as she popped open the lid on the large silver recycling bin set in the far corner of the kitchen, before turning to see if he was watching. Jack rolled his shoulders as he washed another plate, and the nonchalant movement must have reassured her, because she ripped one of the envelopes in half and tossed it into the bin. Then she let the lid drop and came to join him.

'I want to ask for your help with something,' Belle said after a moment of silence. She picked up one of the plates from the drainer and began to dry it as Jack's heart sank. Was she going to ask for money?

'With what?' he asked, keeping his voice steady.

Belle put the plate away and whipped the remaining red envelope from her pocket. 'With this,' she murmured, opening it so she could draw the letter out and unfold it.

Jack dried his hands and took it from her. He recognised Edina's handwriting immediately, the long curly strokes and defined tilt of the letter 'e'. She'd written to him a lot when he'd been younger – he'd only discovered how often when he'd been clearing out his dad's house after he'd passed a few months earlier. He'd found a pile of unopened letters and cards and read them. His father had raised him alone since he was five after his mother chose money over a son. Until that moment he hadn't known about his grandmother – so the fact that she existed and wanted a relationship with him was a surprise. He'd been angry his dad had kept the letters from him, but he wasn't surprised. Reading them had been the catalyst for him getting in touch. Jack was essentially alone in the world, and for the first time in a long time he felt adrift. He didn't belong anywhere or to anyone now, and it bothered him. Perhaps it was just grief?

'This is my grandmother's Christmas list.' He scanned down the sheet of paper and his attention caught on one of the things Edina had asked for.

'Pink hair…' His eyes jerked up to meet Belle's. 'Now I understand.' He wasn't sure if he wanted to thank her, or if it just made him more suspicious. Why would someone do that for a stranger?

Belle shrugged, looking embarrassed. 'It was one of the easiest things to cross off. Edina doesn't know I kept the letter, and it was easy to convince her that Kenzy choosing pink was a coincidence.' The red flames that crept up her cheeks were endearing and Jack had to fight his reaction to them. 'Your grandmother wrote the list in a lesson with my primary two class. The letter was supposed to burn in the fire, but…' She shrugged. 'Once I found it with the others, I thought it might be nice to give her a few of the things… as a thank you.' She waved a hand. 'She let me move in here and because of that, I've been able to help another family.'

'You want my help?' Was this just some cleverly staged manipulation – and if so what did Belle want? If Jack said he'd help, he could keep an eye on her at least. Work out exactly what her motives were for staying in Evergreen Castle. Everyone wanted something; his dad had instilled that lesson and he saw it every day in his job. If you waited long enough, you'd find out what that something was.

Jack started to read the letter properly and stopped at number one. *I want Jack and his mother, Tara, to reconcile.* His whole body stiffened. 'No.' He wished now Belle had tossed the whole thing into the fire. 'That's not going to happen. Tara let me go for the price of a better life.' His tone was hard. 'She never looked back, never contacted me. There'll be no reconciliation with my mother, not even for Edina.'

'I'm so sorry,' Belle said softly, sounding genuinely upset. She reached out and squeezed his arm, and Jack took a step back. The unexpected contact, her sincere look of compassion, had an odd effect on his insides. 'I had no idea... Edina never mentioned it.'

'That rules number two out as well,' he said, feeling a wave of emotion he couldn't define. 'There'll be no big family Christmas – at least, not with Tara. But...' Jack paused; it wasn't like he had anyone to spend the festive season with. 'I could be here. I'm not sure what my long-term plans are yet. As long as I don't need to travel to London to attend court, I'll be living and working in Evergreen Castle until my nana is back on her feet.' His forehead squeezed – and, of course, until he'd worked out exactly where she'd be safest. Staying here alone, or moving somewhere more suitable.

He read on, stopping when he got to his grandmother's wish for a Christmas party. He had a recollection of a celebration in the castle – of huge lavishly decorated fir trees; dancing in the main ballroom; all kinds of tantalising food. Had he danced with Tara? Had she even been there? He searched his mind for more memories. He vaguely remembered Father Christmas had put in an appearance and brought him a black truck which he'd kept under his pillow. Perhaps for a while he'd hoped it would somehow bring his mother back. He could still remember the crushing pain of losing her, the visceral ache in his gut when he'd seen his friends with their mothers, and he'd clung to the hope that she'd return for months. But when he'd realised it would never happen, that she didn't care, he'd chucked the truck in the bin. It might have been over thirty years since he'd attended that party; had Edina held any since? Had his mother attended? He pushed the thought away. 'Look, I'm not sure this is a good idea.' He shook his head. 'I think you should leave it alone. My grandmother isn't related to you. I'm not sure why you want to do this.'

Belle put her hands on her hips and frowned. 'Edina's becoming a friend. Why wouldn't I?'

Jack stared at her. 'You've only just met.' His voice was incredulous and he watched emotions play across her face. Surprise, irritation and then anger. Was he getting in the way of her careful plans, or did Belle really want to do this for his grandmother? He wasn't sure.

'We've only just met too,' she said softly. 'And I think I have your measure. But I still don't understand why you wouldn't do a few simple things to make your nana happy.' Her expression seared him, made him feel guilty. 'I'm going to give her some of the things on this list with or without you.'

Jack looked at the letter again. It would be better if he stayed involved. 'The Christmas party might be possible.' He frowned. 'Not sure how we'd arrange it without my grandmother knowing though. I'm assuming you want all this to be a surprise?'

Belle nodded. 'I could organise most of it, or get help,' she murmured. 'If we had it on Christmas Eve, Edina wouldn't need to know about it until just before. I've already sorted a lot of downstairs – got a tree, put up decorations; we may need to find a few more, and I'd love to put lights up around the turrets and castle walls. Perhaps a few in the grounds. It'll just be a case of organising the music, food and inviting everyone. I've no idea how we'll get Tavish to smile.' She laughed, a high sweet sound he'd not heard before. 'I swear if that curmudgeon ever tried to grin, his face would crack. Perhaps if we found the right inspiration, gave him a strong enough whisky…'

Jack leaned on the counter and read on, fighting a smile. 'Where's Christmas Cairn?' He had a vague recollection of the name.

Belle pulled a face. 'A few miles up the valley. It's a rocky climb and at the moment there's a lot of snow on and around it. I've no idea how to get Edina there. Especially with that ankle. I've been racking my brains to think of a solution…' She looked truly upset.

'You can leave that one with me,' he said finally. 'Do you know anything about this broken tiara?'

Belle pulled a face. 'She's not mentioned it and I don't know where Edina keeps her jewellery. She's worn a few tiaras but they looked fine…'

'You can leave that with me too,' Jack said. He wasn't going to encourage Belle to search through Edina's stuff. She'd given him a pile of valuations when he'd arrived so he could look into insuring her jewellery – so he knew she owned a small fortune in trinkets. 'If you can think about how we can make her feel useful.' He let out a long puff. 'I thought Christmas lists were supposed to be about perfume, iPads and Smart TVs.'

'When you're in your seventies I'm guessing those things don't matter,' Belle said, searching his face. 'For some they never did,' she added lightly.

'Not in my world,' Jack said, turning so he could empty the water from the washing-up bowl. A door slammed upstairs and he guessed

Tavish was leaving. 'I've got some work to be getting on with,' he said gruffly. He had to look over documents for a divorce settlement before the morning. 'Do you want to discuss this again tomorrow? Perhaps we can agree more of the details for the party.' He waved the letter and she shrugged. 'We could meet in the pub I saw on the high street. It might be better if we had these conversations out of the house? There's nothing wrong with Edina's hearing.'

'I'll be working late at school tomorrow,' Belle said, looking unhappy.

'I could meet you there.' Jack shrugged. It might be nice to see her on her home turf, to get a better lay of the land. Like, did she have a boyfriend?

She shook her head. 'I'm organising the nativity play and we've lost the costumes somewhere in the school. There are a lot of places to search – I could be hours.'

'Then I'll help,' Jack said, wondering why he'd offered. It wasn't in his nature to push himself into other people's lives – not outside his work anyway. But if he was going to understand this woman, figure out what she wanted from Edina, he'd have to spend time with her. If he was going to do that, he might as well be nice.

'Oh, okay. Thank you.' Belle looked surprised. 'Um, I'd better get to bed, it'll be an early start for me. I'll leave you the letter. We can discuss everything tomorrow. Don't stay up too late working.' She turned and walked up the stairs and Jack tried not to watch, tried not to notice the curve of her cheek or the way the trail of Christmas lights on the walls picked out the highlights in her hair. She drew him in, confused him. Had Tara done the same to his dad?

He waited until the sound of Belle's footsteps quietened and disappeared, guessing she was probably in the sitting room by now. Then he went to the recycling bin and picked out the torn red envelope. There was a flutter of feet on the stairs and he jerked around guiltily. The silver-grey tabby was sitting on its haunches on the concrete step, staring at him. Those green eyes, a brilliant contrast to all its silver fur. He let out a slow exhale. 'Fine, you stay quiet about this.' He waved the two pieces of envelope in the air. 'I'll feed you. Quid pro quo.' The cat blinked and he rooted through one of the cupboards where he'd noticed cat food earlier, grabbing a small saucepan when he couldn't find a bowl. He poured the food into it and watched as the cat proceeded to devour the lot.

Jack pulled the pieces of letter out of the two halves of red envelope and pushed them together so he could read. The first five things on the list weren't even for Belle. Jack frowned. No one was this nice. What was her angle? Belle had written *I want someone to…* next to number six, and scribbled out the following words. He couldn't decipher them through the squiggles of black biro. Had she been too embarrassed to reveal her final wish? Or would it have revealed her true intentions?

He frowned and shoved the pieces of envelope and letter in the pocket of his trousers. If he spent more time with Belle, he'd figure out what she really wanted.

Jack switched off the lights in the kitchen and walked upstairs, almost jumping out of his skin when the cat darted through his legs and trotted ahead of him in the direction of the sitting room. The fire was still burning in the grate, throwing off a toasty heat, but it was getting low so he added another couple of logs before getting his laptop from the bedroom. He could do a few hours' work, add in some research into Belle Albany from Christmas Village. There was something about the woman… something he didn't trust. He just had to fight those irritating tugs of attraction until he got to the bottom of exactly why she was in Evergreen Castle.

Chapter Eight

The small shed at the back of the school was full of spiders – okay, they might be frozen spiders, but still, Belle tentatively opened the door and shone a torch into the tiny space. It was jam-packed with shelves and the PTA used it for storing fundraising supplies. Belle stepped inside the darkness and fought a shiver, shining the light from her torch over multiple pots of glue, glitter, paint, and large pieces of card the team used to create signage for school events. She spent a few minutes scoping each shelf, like a forensic expert in a detective series on Netflix. 'Nothing, nada.' She sighed after she'd checked them all, and poked around the deepest, darkest corners of the small area, shaking her head before inspecting the ceiling to see if someone had magically installed a secret loft. 'Where are these eejit nativity costumes? I've checked every logical location.' Now she only had the illogical places to search. She began to back out just as her mobile buzzed in her pocket. Was it Jack? They hadn't agreed an exact time to meet, but she'd expected to see him when the children had filed out of school after their last class. When he hadn't turned up, she'd had to fight a wave of disappointment.

As soon as she saw it was her da calling, Belle picked up, backing further out of the shed and using one hand to relock the padlock as the other held the phone to her ear.

'Belle?' Hunter Albany asked, as if he'd expected someone else to answer.

'Da. How's it going?' Belle trudged along the narrow pathway which led past the side of the school playground to the back of the main building, only just avoiding slipping on the snow which was coming down in droves, layering over the grit and salt which had been scattered by the caretaker earlier. The lights were on inside the school, but she knew almost everyone had left. Robina was somewhere in her office – she'd agreed to stay later so Belle could root out the missing costumes. But she hadn't offered to help.

'Busy – there's always so much to do here. The kids are good though, we've been vaccinating this week. You wouldn't believe how brave some of them are.' Belle was used to her da regaling her with stories of the young children in the orphanage, but he stopped suddenly and there was an awkward pause. 'How are you?' he asked.

'Fine, all good,' Belle said, tiptoeing the last few metres to the back of the school. It wasn't worth going into specifics; her da was ill-equipped to deal with anything beyond a basic conversation, sans emotion of any kind. Besides, she *was* fine. She eased the door open and stepped into the school hall, stamping her feet on the mat and swiping snowflakes off her coat, absorbing the blast of warmth as it enveloped her.

'I was calling about Christmas.' Her da sounded guilty.

'Ah.' Belle's stomach sank, because she knew what was coming. Tears pricked the corners of her eyes, which was ridiculous. In the twenty-two years since her da had sent her to live in Christmas Village with Annie, he'd only made it back for the festive season a handful of times, often leaving early because of an emergency. Sick children, food shortages, or volunteers who needed to see their family more – family who didn't have a woman like Annie taking care of them.

Belle took her coat off so she could hang it over a chair, then walked up to admire the large Christmas tree she'd helped set up over lunch because she knew it would make her feel better. It was decorated with an eclectic array of ornaments; some of the younger classes had drawn and coloured pictures in their lessons and added ribbons to the artwork to make it easy to hang; there were also dozens of multicoloured baubles Belle had picked up from an all-year-round Christmas shop in Lockton last year. White fairy lights flickered off and on at intervals.

'I'm sorry, Belle, but I'm not going to make it,' he confirmed. 'There's too much to do here, too many children who need me. A couple of the other volunteers have kids at home who are younger than you. I said I'd stay so they could go home for a visit.' Weird how her da had rarely used that excuse to see her. 'I feel bad now Annie's gone, but I didn't think you'd mind…'

'It's fine.' Belle cleared her throat, pushing the hurt down, knowing she was being selfish. 'I understand. I'm not sure what to do about your present.'

'Ach, lass, don't worry about that.' He paused. 'Did you get the parcel I sent over? It should have been posted last week?' Belle's da regularly sent small packages over with people who were flying home to the UK, asking them to post them on. They contained a variety of things, from handmade wood carvings and beads to pretty woven baskets and even sculptures. Annie's house was filled with them. Belle appreciated the gifts, but wished just once her da would realise she'd rather see him.

'Not yet,' she murmured. 'I'd like to send you something for Christmas, Da.'

He sighed. 'You could wire some money if you really wanted – there's a million things we could do with here.'

'Okay.' Belle thought of the pile of items she'd already accumulated in case he visited this year. She'd mentioned he might come to Edina, who'd told her he'd be welcome to stay in the castle. After losing Annie to cancer in January, she'd hoped he'd find the time... She sighed. She'd already wrapped his presents. Practical gifts she knew he'd appreciate – soap, a state-of-the-art shaver, a few clothes, and a new iPhone because he'd given the last one to someone who needed it more. If Annie were here, she'd encourage Belle to tell him about them. Her godmother had always been good with advice. They hadn't been hugely close, due to the demands of Annie's job, but Belle had known she had somewhere to turn. 'That's fine, I'll wire you what I would have spent,' Belle promised. Posting items was pointless; they often went missing. She'd donate what she'd bought to charity, or give them to the PTA for raffle prizes.

'I'm sorry, lass, I've got to go, someone's just arrived.' Her da sounded weary but in an odd way, Belle knew he enjoyed it. Enjoyed that feeling of being needed. She wished he'd appreciate just once that she needed him too.

She rolled her shoulders, annoyed with herself. She was thirty, for goodness' sake. She had everything she wanted here; the children, school, Jinx, Kenzy, and all the people in Christmas Village. There was no need to feel this… emptiness. But the feeling was still punctuated by a stab of irritation. 'It's fine – let's speak later in the week. Take care, Da.'

'Bye,' he said and hung up, leaving her staring at the mobile. 'Just once…' she said softly. 'Just once, would it kill you to put me first?' She winced, knowing the wish was unfair. She didn't need him… not really.

'Everything okay?' The deep chocolatey voice startled Belle and she jerked her chin up to find Jack standing in the doorway. She could tell from his face he'd been listening, but clearly had no idea what to make of the call. 'Sorry I'm a little later than I intended.' He looked around the school hall and Belle did the same. It was a large room, with a high ceiling and a pretty dark wood parquet floor. There were ladders lining one of the walls which each of the classes used for PE lessons, and on the opposite side of the room sat a small stage made from large black plywood blocks. The stage had a piano on it, and behind that a set of gold velvet curtains had been drawn. Those hid a small space the teachers used to store musical instruments and PE equipment. 'I was on the phone to a client, got caught up. Did you find the nativity costumes?' Jack asked.

'Nope.' Belle pulled a face. 'There are a couple more places I can look.' She put the mobile into the pocket of her trousers, feeling something warm in her belly when Jack followed the movement. He wore jeans and a dark grey sweater that made the blue of his eyes pop – for an insane moment Belle wished she could grab the poster paints from the PTA shed and recreate that exact shade. The spell was broken when he shrugged off his coat and wrapped it over his arm. Was he planning to help? She let out a long huff and marched over to the curtains so she could pull them open. It took just a quick glance once she'd got to her knees to confirm there were no costumes hidden at the back.

'No luck?' Jack asked, appearing behind her.

Belle shook her head. 'I've got two weeks to put on a nativity play and we use the same costumes every year.' She grimaced. 'The children will audition tomorrow and the first thing they're going to want to do after I tell them who got which part is dress up. I've no idea if the costumes will fit, and for all I know a moth could have got to them.'

'Is there anywhere else you can look?' He glanced around the hall.

Belle rose to her feet and brushed dust from her trousers. 'There's a staff cupboard with a small loft. It's the only other place I can think of.' She shuddered at the idea of climbing up into the small space. 'After I look, can we discuss your nana's Christmas list? I've not had much time to think about it today.' She rubbed a fingertip against her temple. She had a headache starting.

'Sure,' Jack said, as she grabbed her coat and marched out of the hall into the children's dining area. Jack's footsteps on the parquet floor told her he was following.

'Belle?' Robina appeared at the door which led into the main entrance to the school where a small library, reception area and her office were located. Her eyes flickered to Jack and she straightened, swiping a hand over her crisp black suit and offering him a stunning smile Belle rarely saw. 'We have a visitor?'

'This is Jack Hamilton-Kirk, Ms Lachlan's grandson.' Belle swept a hand to introduce him. 'Jack, this is Robina Sinclair, our headmistress. Jack's helping me look for the nativity costumes.'

'Aye, good to meet you.' Robina's cheeks flushed as Jack shook her hand. Then she shifted her attention reluctantly to Belle, taking a few moments to let go of his hand. 'I need to leave, lass, the snow's getting heavier and I've got a fair drive. Can I leave you to liaise with the caretaker about locking up? The cleaners finished twenty minutes ago, so it'll just be you in the school now.' Belle nodded. 'Can you come in early tomorrow? I want to have a meeting about the new literacy curriculum and some of the things I need you to look at. Don't stay too late, lass – and don't cycle.' She wagged a finger at Belle. 'You know what happened last time.' She winked at Jack. 'Thank goodness your nana was all right.'

'Sure.' Belle nodded and Robina flashed another brilliant smile, before wishing them good night.

After Robina had left, Belle led Jack through the dining hall, where she'd set up another Christmas tree and helped some of the children hang garlands across the walls in the break this afternoon. There was a door on the right of the room, opposite the kids' cloakroom, and she switched on the lights as she led Jack inside. The room was small but cosy, with a brown leather sofa across the back wall one of the parents had donated, and a large table with chairs set around it. Belle and the other teachers came in during breaks when it wasn't their turn for playground duty – to mark homework, create lesson plans, or simply because they were craving adult company and a reviving hot drink. Belle switched the kettle on and searched the cupboard, taking out a tin with some cookies she'd baked this morning, happy there were a couple left. The staff were supposed to take turns bringing in snacks, but most were too busy so her biscuits didn't last long. 'Make yourself at home.' She pointed to the table. 'I'll make you a drink and you can put your feet up while I check the final place.' Jack placed his coat carefully on the sofa and dropped his laptop next to it, as Belle searched in her handbag for paracetamol and knocked a couple back.

'Wouldn't it be quicker if I helped?' Jack asked, watching as she put the pill bottle back in her bag.

His offer surprised Belle. 'It might be dusty.' She looked meaningfully at his clothes.

'I'll risk it.' He put his hands in the pockets of his dark trousers and gave her a lopsided smile, making her stomach twist because it was so genuine and unexpected. 'Your clothes are smarter than mine.'

'Oh…well…okay,' she said, leading him back out of the staffroom, through the dining hall, into a dark corridor which had the primary one classroom to the right. Straight ahead was a storeroom the teachers used for supplies. The PTA didn't normally have access, but there was a tiny loft space in the roof, which was the final place Belle could look. Perhaps someone had managed to get in last year? She crossed her fingers as she unlocked the door and stepped inside, suddenly aware of how small the space was when Jack followed. It was immediately obvious from a quick glance around the tidy shelves that the bag of costumes wasn't there. She glanced at the ceiling and then eased out the small white stepladder wedged to the right of the shelves, bumping into Jack as she tried to open it. Her heartbeat kicked up a notch. The last time she'd been this close to a man was when her ex-boyfriend, Ted Jones, had told her of his plans to move to Australia. Plans that hadn't involved her. She set the ladder up, propping a foot onto the bottom rung before letting out a long, calming exhale.

'Okay?' Jack asked.

'Um… yes.' Belle took another step up as he reached around to hold the ladder, encircling her with his arms.

'You're shaking?' He put a hand on her shoulder.

Belle pulled a face, pleased he couldn't see her expression. 'I'm not keen on small spaces,' she admitted. In truth she was terrified; just the thought of climbing any higher and sliding into that tiny loft had her whole body quaking.

'Let me do this. Come on, get down.' He stepped back, giving her room to move, and she sighed when her feet touched the ground before patting a hand on her chest.

'I know it's ridiculous,' she murmured. 'I've always hated them, right back to…' She trailed off and looked up to the ceiling. 'You've no idea what you're looking for.'

'A bag?' He quirked an eyebrow. 'Can I have the torch?'

Belle handed it over before moving so he could pass. She held on to the ladder, staring straight ahead rather than looking up at his legs and bum. She heard the loft door squeak open, then gave in as the top half of Jack's body disappeared. He must have switched on the torch because the area above his shoulders was suddenly illuminated and Belle went onto her tiptoes, craning her neck. 'There's not much here,' Jack shouted. She heard shuffling as he moved further inside. 'There's a bag filled with… beanbags.' He sounded disappointed. 'I'm guessing this is PE equipment?'

'Aye.' Belle nodded. 'No costumes then?' What was she going to do?

'Hang on. There's something else.' Jack moved again, snaking further into the small space until all Belle could see were his feet.

She winced, hoping his clothes would survive. She heard more shuffling, a creak, then glitter fell like snowflakes from the ceiling. Belle swiped the tiny flecks from her face as Jack slid back, pulling out a black bag once his feet were back on the ladder and handing it to her. Belle put the sack on the floor, then held the ladder as Jack eased the lid to the loft back in place. When he was down she winced at his clothes. He was caked in glitter and dust.

'You're covered.' Belle brushed a hand across his jumper, pulling away when she felt the hard muscles of his chest. 'Sorry.'

'It's fine.' Jack brushed at the particles, frowning at the places where he'd rubbed the glitter in. 'It's just dirt, no harm done.'

Belle pointed to the bag. 'You think these might be costumes?'

'I glanced in the top and saw something promising.' Jack closed the stepladder and put it to the side of the shelving unit. He swung the bag under his arm and edged past Belle, leading her out of the cupboard. As soon as they were in the corridor, Belle felt herself relax. There was something about Jack in close proximity that had made her uncomfortable. Perhaps Kenzy's man-mad hormones had somehow rubbed off?

As soon as they were back in the staffroom, she flicked on the kettle as he opened the black bag and began to empty it onto the table. First out was a billowing red velvet cloak with white fur lining the edges, then a woolly beard, a huge red sack and a furry red and white hat. 'This is definitely a Santa costume. There are elf ears too.' He placed four large plastic ear-shapes onto the table.

'Can you see an angel? Maybe a shepherd costume? I'd definitely expect a star if those are from the nativity,' Belle said.

'Not yet.' Jack put a long set of bandages onto the table. 'Think this is a mummy costume?' His eyebrows rose to the edge of his hairline, drawing attention to his glossy hair, which was layered in dust. 'Am I hallucinating or do I need caffeine?'

'Sorry.' Belle jerked herself from the fantasy where she'd been brushing her fingers through his hair and cleared her throat. 'Do you want coffee?'

'Please.' Jack nodded.

She made hot drinks as Jack continued to empty the bag, then put the two remaining cookies on a plate and brought everything to the table. 'Is this a donkey? This is exactly what I need for the nativity!' Belle picked up the furry pieces of material; each had two legs with black feet. She put the pieces to one side as Jack took a head with a cape-style body from the bag.

'I think that's supposed to be a reindeer.' The head was oval-shaped and it had odd-coloured eyes, a bright red nose and antlers. 'If you cut these off – he indicated to the two pointy twigs – 'it might pass for a donkey. You've got all the main elements.' He grabbed an antler and pulled. 'These have been attached really well.'

'I'll take it home and see what I can do.' Belle swallowed. Annie would have known how to fix the costume; she missed her godmother at times like this. There was no one else to ask.

Jack squinted at Belle before reaching out to run a fingertip across her cheek. 'You're covered in glitter.'

'Hazard of the job.' Belle swiped a hand across her face and sparkles fell on the table and floor. 'When I was little I used to think it was fairy dust.' She frowned at the carpet; Robina wouldn't be happy when she saw the mess tomorrow. 'I wish it was – that way I'd be able to conjure up the nativity outfits.'

'There are a few more costumes in this bag.' Jack picked out a dark cloak. 'I'm guessing this is Darth Vader without the ominous mask?' He put it to one side, then grabbed a red cape and a chequered dress. 'Little Red Riding Hood? Ah, and a wolf.' The papier-mâché face was very distinctive. He quickly pulled out the rest of the clothes. 'No star, shepherds, kings or angels though. I'm sorry.' He shook his head, looking genuinely disappointed. 'These aren't your nativity costumes.'

Belle let out a long sigh. 'There's nowhere else to look. I'm going to have to ask the MacGavins if I can get my godmother's sewing machine from my house and make them myself. It's too late to ask the parents to help and the PTA are flat out on the fair they've planned for January. I'll take these back to the castle so I can work out if there's anything here I can reuse. Maybe Edina will have some ideas…'

Jack looked away and picked up his coffee and biscuit. 'Speaking of my grandmother, shall we look at this Christmas list?' He helped her stuff the costumes back into the bag before carefully pulling the envelope from the pocket of his coat, along with a notebook and fountain pen.

Belle got a pad and pencil from her handbag and pulled up a chair opposite. 'About your mam,' she started. 'I've been thinking… Edina said you were five when you last saw her, that's a really long time…'

'Not long enough.' Jack cleared this throat, but he must have sensed her watching him because he lifted his head until their eyes met. His were filled with emotion, none of it good. 'I get that you want to help my grandmother and I appreciate it.' There was an edge to his voice and Belle sensed he wasn't telling the truth. 'I'll help with the party and some of the other things she wants.' He frowned. 'I'm really not sure about the tattoo… but I'm not meeting Tara.' He folded his arms and leaned forwards. 'I want my grandmother to be happy. She's all the family I've got. My dad died earlier this year.'

'I'm so sorry.' Belle leaned forwards. 'I lost my godmother in January.' She swallowed. 'It's hard losing people. Was it… did you know it was coming?'

'No. It came from nowhere.' Jack's voice was toneless.

'What happened?' Belle asked. She could tell he didn't want to talk about it but wanted him to open up, wanted to get to know him. So she'd understand his motives, what made him tick.

'He was in the courtroom of all places,' he said.

'So he was a lawyer?'

Jack nodded. 'Same as me. He was only in his mid-fifties and he'd led a healthy life. Blood clot in the brain.' He splayed his fingers. 'Catastrophic – instant. It was a shock for all of us.' He looked away.

'Annie… well.' Belle's eyes filled as she was transported back to the start of the year. 'It was cancer. We knew, but… it always happens more quickly than you expect. I was lucky we got that last Christmas.' She frowned. When her godmother died, she'd felt like she'd lost another link to her parents. Felt even more alone.

'I'm sorry too,' Jack murmured. Belle could tell he'd had to drag the words out and wondered if he'd always struggled to share his emotions, or whether it was just with her. 'So this party?'

'Aye.' Belle picked up her pencil. The abrupt change of subject marked the end of their conversation. But he'd shared something with her, a tiny piece of his life, and she felt a little better knowing he had a human side, that he could care – perhaps even hurt. Maybe there was a heart in there somewhere? 'So… I can speak to Rowan in the cafe about catering,' she said, feeling more enthusiastic suddenly. 'I could make some invitations myself – I was thinking Edina might want to invite everyone in the village? She's started to reconnect with a few people; this would be a good opportunity to expand her social circle and introduce her to the rest.'

'Sure,' Jack said, but his mouth tightened. The difference was almost imperceptible but Belle noticed immediately. Was it because if Edina re-joined the community, it would be harder for Jack to encourage her to move?

She frowned, wanting to kick herself. She'd started to let him under her skin, started to look for a kinder and gentler side that probably didn't exist. She'd have to watch herself, keep her Pollyanna persona under control before she got the true measure of the man and figured out what he had planned – and exactly how far he was prepared to go to get it.

Chapter Nine

The snow was thick as Jack steered Edina's Land Rover into Evergreen Castle's drive. Belle glanced at the back seat where her bike had been perched next to the bag of costumes, after Jack had insisted on driving her home after their meeting. He hadn't spoken after she'd settled in the car beside him, choosing instead to switch on the radio which was belting out a series of Christmas songs, and Belle glanced out of the window. She squinted as they headed down the drive towards the castle, seeing something move in the darkness out of the corner of her eye. She pressed her nose to the glass, attempting to see through the dense curtain of snowflakes. The moon was high tonight and threw enough light over the fields to draw out shadows and shapes. As they drew closer, she could just make out Bob standing beside a tree. She watched the donkey lift its head and zero in on the car. The creature seemed to sniff the air before setting off at speed across the field, its stubby legs thundering on the ground, throwing chunks of ice in the air like a racehorse at the Grand National.

Belle bashed a finger onto the electric button which opened the window as she saw the animal approach the drive. 'Stop!' she shrieked as Bob trotted to a halt in front of them, and Jack slammed on the brakes. 'No, I didn't mean you!' she screamed at the donkey.

'What—' Jack shouted, as the car jerked and then skidded. He hadn't been driving that fast but the layers of fresh snow meant the wheels couldn't find a proper purchase. Edina hadn't driven for so long no one had bothered to put snow chains on the tyres. Bob stood blinking in surprise as they approached, his feet planted firmly on the ground like a gladiator about to take on a chariot.

'Noooooo!' Belle shouted again as the car slowly bumped into him – the hollow thud echoed around the small space, making her want to throw up.

'— the hell?' Jack finished.

'Oh God.' Belle shoved the door open and stumbled out. 'Is he hurt?' She almost fell as she half ran, half staggered through a drift so she could reach the animal, her heart thundering so hard she could hear nothing but the fast pump of blood. Bob was lying on his side in front of the car, and she knelt and stroked the rough fur on his head, willing him to open his eyes. She searched his body and the snow for signs that he was bleeding. 'There's no blood – is that good?'

'I don't know.' Jack was with her in seconds. 'How does he look?' He dropped down beside her in the snow and put a hand on the donkey's chest, looking upset. 'He's still breathing.' The words came out in a whoosh. 'What's he doing out here? I thought donkeys didn't like cold weather? Not that I know anything about them…'

'No idea.' Belle shook her head, still stroking Bob's fur, watching for a flicker of life. 'Edina told me he gets lonely and sometimes goes out looking for company.' She watched as the donkey slowly opened one blue eye and blinked, sniffing the air before his attention jerked to Jack, and the animal seemed to grin. 'He's moving,' she murmured as he wriggled his body this way and that, before gracefully getting to his feet.

Belle stood too and Jack followed, reaching out to ruffle Bob's head. His handsome face was a picture of guilt and relief. 'He's okay.' He shook his head, suddenly looking annoyed. 'Shouldn't he be locked in a barn so he can't just wander wherever he wants? It's dangerous.'

Shards of snow splattered Belle's face as the wind picked up and she swiped at her eyes, moving closer so she could hear. 'Aye,' she shouted, watching as the donkey nuzzled Jack's armpit before dropping its head so he could sniff the knees of his jeans. Instead of stepping back or shooing him away, Jack continued to stroke the donkey as his expression softened. He looked different, more vulnerable, and Belle felt something inside her warm. 'He's got a barn of his own, by the garage where Edina keeps the car,' she explained. 'She told me Bob doesn't much care for being alone. He keeps escaping – even after Logan fixed the lock… I can walk him back now, check he's not limping. See if I can lock him in. This weather's not going to get better before morning.' She patted the animal's behind, ignoring the cold wind as it tore at her. She was just thankful she'd changed into her snow boots before leaving school, but wished her coat was thicker.

'Better if we both go – just in case he decides to make a break for it.' Jack frowned, looking towards the castle. 'I'll get my laptop and leave the car here.' He patted the hood of the Land Rover. 'I'm getting used to abandoning vehicles on this drive. If Tavish is looking for another reason to hate me, this should do it.' He winced. Did the older man's derision bother him after all? 'Is it okay if we leave the bike and costumes in the car until morning?'

'Aye,' Belle said. She was supposed to be making cupcakes tonight for a fundraiser at the school anyway, so she'd have no time to do anything about the costumes. She waited while Jack collected everything he needed, stroking Bob's head as he followed Jack with his eyes.

'That animal's got a crush on you – just like Jinx,' she said, as they started to trudge through the snow with the donkey glued to Jack's side. 'Are you related to Doctor Dolittle?'

Jack laughed as if the idea were absurd. 'Nope. I didn't even have a pet when I was growing up. Dad wasn't keen on animals… A reaction I think to Tara. Perhaps I smell of those cookies you made…' He sniffed the sleeve of his coat.

'Animals can sense things about humans, sometimes things they don't even know about themselves,' Belle said quietly. 'I always think they're a bit like children.'

'You think they need company, like we do?' he asked quietly, as they got to the bottom of the drive which would lead them around the perimeter of the main castle, towards the back where the garage and Bob's barn were located. Lights flickered on, triggered by their movement, illuminating the path and surroundings. The donkey seemed content to follow them; he nudged his nose against Jack's leg every now and then as if to remind them he was there. Belle found it endearing and a little surprising. What was it about this man that attracted Bob and Jinx to him? It wasn't biscuits… Was there a whole other layer he hid, a softer, gentler side?

'I think we all need someone who cares about us.' Her voice was husky, and Belle was pleased the racket from the wind would mask the emotion she could hear. She had lots of people in her life, but losing Annie and Ted this year had left a gap she was struggling to fill. 'Do you have anyone special?' Her cheeks warmed and she tugged the hood of her coat so it covered the side of her face.

When Jack didn't answer, Belle wondered if he would. 'Not really.' His voice was matter-of-fact. 'I had a girlfriend, but she... left me.'

'I'm sorry,' Belle said. 'My boyfriend did the same – he emigrated to Australia in July. You can't get much further away than that.'

'You didn't want to go with him?' Jack asked. 'Isn't it twenty-five degrees in Sydney now? Dammit,' he said, as in an act of irony a gust of wind blew snow into his face.

'He didn't ask,' Belle said quietly. 'It was his dream.'

She heard Jack let out a sympathetic grunt and was pleased he didn't ask more. It wasn't like Ted had been her big love story, but being left behind had hurt, opening wounds she'd worked hard to heal. They passed a small shed filled with a large pile of tree trunks where Logan chopped wood for Edina. There were two more sheds, followed by a small kitchen garden which was sheltered by the wooden buildings. Belle knew Edina grew vegetables and fruit here in the summer, and Logan helped out when he wasn't mowing the grounds or doing odd jobs.

The door to the garage on the right of the allotment was open and lights were on. There was one empty space where the Land Rover should have been, and beside that Jack's Audi had been parked next to a Rolls-Royce Silver Ghost. Belle stopped to gaze at it. The garage had been closed each time she'd walked this way before, so the car was a shock. 'Isn't that…?' She pointed as Jack pulled the door shut.

'Sorry, but we need to get out of this snow,' he said, trudging to the small barn beside the garage. 'I'm guessing this is where Bob's supposed to be living?'

Belle nodded and followed as Jack pulled the barn door open and flicked on a small bulb, before guiding the donkey inside. It was warmer out of the wind and the ground had been layered with fresh hay. Belle had helped Logan refresh the stall a few days before and knew he tried to do it every other day. Bob trotted to a trough which had been secured at the far wall, dunked his head and began to chew loudly.

'What?' Jack came to a sudden stop as he noticed the colourful pencil drawings pinned to the walls of the barn. Belle folded her arms as he walked up to one, taking time to study it. 'It's a donkey?'

'Aye,' Belle said. 'I asked my class to draw Bob some pictures.' She shrugged when he turned to look at her, his face incredulous. 'Edina mentioned he was lonely and I thought he might appreciate a little colour in here.' She shrugged. 'The children enjoyed drawing him some friends. Perhaps I'll get one of them to sketch you.' She grinned.

Jack barked out a laugh as he moved to check out another picture. It was a joyful and surprising sound from him. 'This one is… what, the castle?'

She nodded and pointed to one where a woman sat on a throne, wearing a tiara. She had her foot on a stool with a cushion tucked under it. 'That's Edina. When the children came to the castle to write their Christmas lists, they heard about Bob going on a walkabout and wanted to do something for him. We turned it into an art lesson.'

'I don't understand you,' Jack murmured. 'The donkey would have no clue why you all did this... He's not going to say thanks.' He glanced back at the pictures as Bob came to nuzzle his hand. Then he turned to Belle and stared, absently stroking the donkey's mane. He looked so off balance, she felt almost sorry for him.

'Why does that matter? Besides, it's the wee lads and lassies, not me – I told you, children and animals see the world in a completely different way.' She nodded at Bob who was still vying for Jack's attention, nudging at his leg. 'Why don't you come to school with me tomorrow, meet my class, see what I mean?' The words were out before Belle could stop them. She couldn't tell if it was a desire to see a repeat of Jack's smile, or because she'd promised herself she'd keep an eye on him. He was charming her again though, she could feel it.

'Why?' He looked suspicious.

She shrugged. 'I think you might enjoy it. Maybe bring Edina?' Perhaps if Jack saw his nana with the kids, saw how happy they made her, he might even reconsider his plans for the retirement home. 'You could help me with the auditions.' She clapped her hands, warming to the idea. 'The children would love an audience – and I know Edina would enjoy it. I need to go into school early tomorrow, but...' She stared through the barn door where the snow was still coming down in thick droves. 'Perhaps if Logan helps you dig out the car again, you could drive her in for eleven o'clock?'

'I... well.' Jack frowned, clearly torn. 'I suppose I could bring her.' He checked his watch. 'I might have to take a video meeting then, but…' He pulled a face, his chiselled jaw tightening as he thought about it. 'Okay…'

'Also,' Belle said, going for broke now he'd agreed to come to the school. 'I've got an idea about those tattoos, so you can leave that part of the Christmas list with me.'

'I'm really not sure—'

'Trust me,' Belle said.

Jack winced as his mobile began to ring, and he pulled it out of his pocket and checked the screen. 'Let's talk about that later. I'm sorry, I've got to take this… I can lock up?'

He answered the mobile, patting Bob on the head, turning away without waiting for an answer. Belle watched as he took a turn around the barn, running a hand through his hair as he talked. He looked tired and she felt a wave of compassion before forcing it away. If she was going to help Edina stay in the castle, she'd have to stay focused – and that meant fighting all the unexpected feelings she was beginning to have for Jack.

Chapter Ten

'Rachel's moved all my clothes into the spare room.' Dave sounded stressed as Jack paced, turning so he could watch Belle walk towards the castle, pulling her coat tight around her waist as wind and snow lashed at her. She stumbled suddenly then righted herself, and Jack fought an unexpected desire to rush out and take her arm – to prop her up and guide her safely to the back door. Instead he turned so he couldn't watch, and stroked Bob's head as the donkey bumped his arm.

'I didn't think you were sharing a room anymore?' Jack asked, trying to engage his brain in the conversation.

'We weren't – but she hadn't moved my clothes!' Dave exclaimed. 'She's started sorting our books into piles. We used to read each other's… I've no idea which of them belong to me. I don't want to know…'

'What did your solicitor say?' Jack asked, wondering if he should just get the woman's number and call her himself.

'She said we should talk,' Dave said eventually. 'She told me she'd be happy to mediate any conversation. All I want to know is why? Rachel asked if she could take the car. Who cares about the damn car, she's ending our marriage and I've no idea what I did wrong!'

Jack blew out a breath and went to rest his head against the side of the barn wall, close to a particularly colourful drawing of the sun – talk about irony. He closed his eyes. 'Do we ever truly know anyone?' he asked quietly, feeling the weight of his friend's pain.

'You never knew Rosalind,' Dave said grumpily. 'You forgot her surname when we met, do you remember?' His laugh was hollow. 'She said, "It's Foster, Jack, you'd think you'd recall it by now, we've been dating for almost two months."' Dave's imitation of his ex-girlfriend's husky voice was accurate and Jack found himself chuckling. 'You probably should have seen the writing on the wall then.' Dave paused. 'I'm really not sure why I'm asking *you* for relationship advice. I've never met anyone who's managed to cock up quite so many... the worst thing is, your girlfriends were all perfectly lovely.'

'Rosalind stole all my china and cutlery,' Jack grumbled. 'The woman has a mean streak a mile wide.'

'You hurt her,' Dave countered. 'Rachel told me all about it, they used to talk. She spoke to a lot of your exes – did you know that?'

Jack pulled a face, horrified. 'Not until now.'

'Apparently you have a very suspicious nature, and find it difficult to trust.' His friend was obviously warming to the conversation now it was no longer about his impending divorce. '*And* you avoid intimacy.'

Jack let out a long breath and turned so he could pace the small space again. 'Is that right?' His tone was tight. He wasn't angry at Dave, but he hated being analysed. He knew what he was and what he needed, his father had taught him that – a lot of navel gazing wasn't going to change it.

'Sorry.' Dave must have realised how he was feeling because he went quiet. 'I think it's easier to focus on other people's faults, that way you don't have to consider your own. I think Rachel is seeing someone at work. I'm scared I wasn't enough.'

'It would be better if you tried to stop thinking about the why and focus on what it is you want out of your assets.' Jack straightened his neck, more comfortable with the conversation now. 'How are you planning to split the house? Do you want to buy her out? Which pieces of furniture are yours? Think about the future, protect what you have. You can't trust Rachel now – you're on opposite sides. Book a singles holiday, download a dating app – look forwards, not back.' Jack knew he'd said the wrong thing when Dave didn't respond. When he did his voice was toneless.

'I know I tease you about your girlfriends, mate, but… I think sometimes you spend so much of your life concentrating on endings, the unpicking of marriages, you've forgotten what being happy looks like. All your solutions are about splitting things up, putting people in separate boxes. But humans aren't like that. We *need* people… enduring relationships and happy endings, we need those too. I'm not going to walk away from a marriage I've been in for almost ten years without a fight.' He sighed. 'I'm not going to give up on Rachel.'

'Okay…' Jack sighed, knowing he was ill-equipped for this conversation. 'I'm sorry.' His voice was soft. 'I… honestly, I don't know what to say. How to help.'

'That makes two of us. Believe it or not, just talking to you helps. Even if it reminds me of all the things I don't want…' Dave laughed; it was an unhappy sound but Jack was still pleased to hear it. To know his friend was still capable of finding humour in the situation. 'I'll talk to my solicitor again. Maybe I'll make dinner for Rachel tonight, see if she'll talk to me. She's been living on boiled eggs. I can do a lot better than that... Except, dammit, she's locked away all of my spices and herbs. Takeaway,' he chirped. 'I'll get an Indian takeaway. That's her favourite. I'll call you with an update. I hope your grandmother's feeling better,' he added, his voice lighter. 'How is she, and how does she feel about moving into the retirement home?'

Jack thought of Edina's Christmas list and desire for a resolution with Tara, of her pink hair and the tattoo Belle had mentioned – and that he still hadn't broached the subject of her leaving Evergreen Castle. 'I've no idea,' he said, feeling a sliver of uncertainty for the first time in years.

'So which of you lads and lasses is going to be first?' Edina clapped her hands as she perused the ten children who made up Belle's primary two class. Jack had helped her into the classroom, propping her up with his shoulder while Belle had pulled out a chair and got a stool ready for her leg. The room was charming, and Jack took a moment to look around at the walls where Belle had hung glittery stars, coloured streamers and pictures of Father Christmas, a reindeer herd and various other characters, alongside carefully handwritten stories. The children were all sitting on the carpet at the front of the room by the door. Jack didn't have a lot of experience with kids, but were they always this small? The chairs and tables had all been pushed back to make room at the front. A couple of tables had been placed in the centre of the classroom facing them – and Edina was seated behind one. Jack hung out at the back, keeping an eye on his phone.

'Me, I'll go first!' A young boy with freckles and red hair shot an arm in the air, almost shaking with excitement.

'Angus.' Belle nodded as she pulled out one of the seats, looking serious. She looked pretty today. Her chestnut-brown hair was tied back and she'd worn barely any make-up but her hazel eyes still seemed to take up her entire face. Jack had only seen her briefly this morning when he'd offered to walk her to the car to get her bike. She'd been carrying a tin, and had pulled out a chocolate cookie and handed it to him as a thank you for his help. He hadn't known whether to be suspicious or to ask for another. The woman confused him, he couldn't figure her out – which, for a man who prided himself on his ability to read people, was disconcerting. 'Is there a part you're interested in playing?' Belle asked, scribbling something onto a pad.

'I wanna be a king.' The boy grinned, displaying a set of pearly white teeth with a large gap in the centre. He pointed to Edina's ruby tiara. 'I like your crown.' Jack had tried to convince his grandmother not to wear it earlier – he knew exactly how valuable it was – but Edina had insisted. Belle had watched the exchange and a deep groove had marred her forehead, making him back off. Since when had he cared about her opinion? 'Will I get to have one like that?'

Belle nodded. 'Something similar,' she said, and Jack hoped she wasn't going to ask Edina to lend her one of hers. 'The king has a speaking part. If you'd like to walk to the stage… I marked the area with tinsel, just step over it.' She pointed to the wide space next to the children which had been outlined with a garland of silver sparkles. 'If you can use your loudest voice and offer Baby Jesus your gift – what is it?'

'It's *maaaaaaa*,' Angus tried, flushing, the colour joining the dots between his freckles as the children began to shriek with laughter. '*Meeeeeerr*,' he tried again.

'Ach, you sound like my da's sheep!' a boy with curly brown hair snorted from behind his hand.

'That's enough, Magnus Thomson, we don't laugh at our friends,' Belle said firmly. She had a way with the kids – gentle but firm. Jack watched as Magnus nodded and apologised, looking contrite. 'It's *myrrh*, Angus. But that was an excellent audition. Very loud and clear. We can work on the pronunciation in rehearsals.' She clapped and Edina whooped, then the children joined in as Angus exited the stage. 'So we need a shepherd – does anyone want to try for that part?'

'I want to be a sheep!' Adam put his hand in the air.

'We'll be auditioning for those in a minute,' Belle soothed, as Magnus shot to his feet and wiped his hands on his black trousers.

'I'll be a shepherd.' The young boy marched to the stage without waiting for an invitation and regarded Belle and Edina seriously, before puffing out his small chest. Even Jack could see the child meant business when he punched an arm in the air and yelled, 'Sheeps, come here!' Adam grinned before making his way slowly to the stage on all fours while the rest of the children roared with laughter, falling into each other as they watched.

'Ach, that would do it,' Edina said, sounding impressed. 'You've a talent, laddie.' She pointed to Magnus. 'I could use you at my castle when my donkey goes walkabout. Before I leave, I'll take your mam's number so I know how to contact you,' she joked. 'And you.' She gazed at Adam. 'There'll be a place for you too at Evergreen Castle if you ever want to come and visit Bob. I've a feeling he'd enjoy the company of a sheep.'

The boy giggled and his cheeks went even redder. Edina leaned in to whisper something to Belle. She was in her element, buzzing with excitement, obviously enjoying being in company. His grandmother was lonely, Jack could see it now, and he fought a wave of guilt. What would happen when Belle moved back into her own house and he headed back to London? The retirement home was obviously the best solution, he just hoped Edina would agree.

'Anyone else want to audition for one of the shepherds – we can have two?' Belle asked, but the children fell silent and looked at their hands. She nodded then glanced at her pad, which was sitting on the table. 'I'm looking for an angel, someone with a really clear voice.' A couple of the girls murmured to each other but didn't volunteer. Then a small child with dark brown hair shot to her feet.

'Mam says I'm like an angel,' she said, fluttering her long eyelashes prettily at Edina and Belle. She did look like one – was that normal for kids too? Jack didn't spend a lot of time in their company – any, to be exact. Even when he'd been younger, after his parents had split he'd socialised with his father's friends, joining them at their dinners and days out like a mini mascot because his dad had been loath to let him out of his sight. Which meant he'd matured quickly, but had been out of sync with his own generation.

'Okay, Lara.' Jack could only see the back of Belle's head as she gave the kids 100 per cent of her focus, holding the attention of the room in a way that was almost surreal. Even in the courtroom, Jack had rarely commanded this much respect. The little girl carefully made her way to the centre of the glittery stage. 'So I need a loud voice, but you don't want to scare the Baby Jesus, so—'

'Baby Cheeses, don't be afwaid!' Lara boomed, lifting her small arms in the air and gracefully performing what Jack assumed was a pirouette.

'Ach, it's almost like there's an angel right here in this room with us!' Edina said, wiggling excitedly in her chair, almost tipping it backwards. Jack stepped forwards to save her, but Belle had already stretched out a hand and pushed her chair back onto its feet. His mobile buzzed, and he switched it off and put it in his pocket without checking the screen. He could catch up with work later. It was fascinating watching Belle managing the lesson and it was giving him an insight into the real woman underneath that helpful exterior. Perhaps she'd eventually expose her true nature. No one was this kind or so thoroughly good. 'Ten!' Edina declared, leaning over to whisper loudly to Belle. 'I think the lass has got the part? Ach, I feel like Simon Cowell.'

Belle chuckled and nodded. 'Nessa, do you want to try out for Mary?' A little girl with long blonde hair nodded slowly and stood, staring at the top table. 'Come and get the baby first.' Belle reached under her table and pulled out a doll wrapped in a white muslin cloth, which she handed over. Nessa made her way back to the stage and stood in the centre, cuddling the toy.

'Well, you've got the hold right, lass.' Edina nodded and held up both hands, spreading her fingers. 'That's another ten out of ten from me.'

Belle checked the pad in front of her. 'You're doing brilliantly, Nessa. Lennie, can you come onto the stage too, please? I thought you could try out for Joseph.' A little boy with light blue eyes and blond curls who looked remarkably like the little girl sitting next to him shot to his feet. 'Alison, how do you feel about being the innkeeper?' Another girl stood; this one had green eyes and a long angular face. She was taller than the other children, so when she joined Nessa and Lennie she towered over them both. 'Lennie, you ask Alison if there's room in her inn and Alison—'

'I have to say no, but that I have room in the barn with my donkey.' The little girl's voice was crisp and clear.

'Wonderful stage presence, lass,' Edina gushed, throwing her arms up and making the chair wobble again.

'I agree, that was perfect,' Belle said. 'Nessa, if you can put the baby down for a moment, please.' The little girl dropped the doll on its head. 'Aye, just there's fine. Now if you can say something about being tired. Then Lennie and Alison, do your lines. You know what to say – don't worry about getting this perfect.'

The children performed their mini scene without a hitch and Belle started to clap at the end, the rest of the class joining in as Edina whooped. Jack found himself clapping along, wondering what weird tangent his life was taking. This time last week he'd been in New York, negotiating on behalf of his client in a very bitter divorce. His life felt so negative in comparison to this. When Belle had finished allocating parts to each of her class and all the children had taken a turn on stage, one of the small boys put up his hand.

'Aye, Angus?' Belle said.

'When can we try on our costumes, Miss Albany?' The rest of the class began to wriggle and mutter in agreement.

'Um. *Shhhhhh.*' Belle placed a finger on her lips and leaned forwards. 'I've got some very exciting news for you all,' she said as the children quieted. 'This year we are going to be getting brand-new costumes.'

There was a gasp from the children as they turned to face each other.

'Even the star?' The little girl called Bonnie frowned and her lower lip wobbled. 'I like the star costume we use every year.'

'And I like Mary's costume,' Nessa piped up.

Belle blew out a long breath. 'I'm sorry, lasses, but we can't use the old costumes because they've been lost. All of the costumes have been lost.' One of the girls started to sniffle and Jack stepped back into a table, almost tripping over it. Wouldn't it have been easier for Belle to make up a story about them being at the dry cleaner's or something? 'Shhh. It's okay!' Belle put a finger over her lips again and the room fell silent. 'The good news is there'll be new ones made especially for you.'

'Aye,' Edina joined in, sounding excited. 'It's just like being in a movie. All those actors and actresses get costumes made just for them.'

The boy with inky black hair who'd been given the part of a sheep put his hand up. 'Yes, Adam?' Belle's voice held a hint of uncertainty.

'I'll get my own costume, a new one?' he asked and she nodded.

'Who's going to make them?' Bonnie's forehead knotted.

Jack could almost hear Belle swallow. 'Me.' Her voice cracked and a few of the children began to chatter loudly amongst themselves.

'Can you sew?' Adam asked, his small features so serious that Jack wanted to smile. It was like looking at himself thirty years ago.

'Well, not...' Belle started, and he wondered if the woman knew how to lie. Or understood when it might be a good idea.

'I can,' Edina said firmly. 'And I've got my own sewing room at the castle, so if Miss Albany needs any help, I'll be able to make whatever you need.'

'There you are, children,' Belle said, visibly relaxing. 'We've an expert working with us now, so you've no need to worry about the costumes. I can take all your measurements before the end of the lesson and we'll get started on your outfits this evening.'

'And I've crowns galore for the kings, and even the angels and star!' Edina patted a hand to her tiara. Jack winced and shook his head just as his grandmother turned her head and gave him a huge wink.

As the children filed out of the class for lunch twenty minutes later, with Belle steering them towards the cloakroom so they could put on their coats and hats, Jack helped Edina to her feet.

'Ach, that was fun, lad,' she said, grinning as he helped her half hop, half walk towards the exit until she was steady on her cane. She looked so buoyant and full of life, so different from the woman he had been talking to on his laptop. Was it all because of Belle? 'I forgot how much I enjoyed being around children.' His grandmother's face clouded. 'I was so sad when we lost you. I want you to know, I hated not having you in my life.' She patted Jack's cheek and looked up into his eyes. He felt something dip in his chest. Was it the memory of losing her, or a timely reminder of the connection he'd been missing? The kind Dave had accused him of avoiding.

'I'm sorry,' Jack said quietly, meaning it. 'My father – well, you know how he was…'

Edina's smile dimmed. 'Aye,' she murmured, her voice changing. 'I do know, lad.'

'He didn't tell me about your letters. I know he had his reasons,' he said, feeling defensive when Edina's eyes glittered. 'If he had… I would have got in touch sooner. I honestly didn't think you wanted to see me. I was so young when we left.'

'Of course we wanted to see you.' His grandmother sounded angry. 'Your mam did too…' she added gently. 'There's a lot you don't know, lad… Remember, there are two sides to a story and you've only been told one.'

'I know everything I need to.' Jack shook his head, shutting down the conversation, as Belle walked back into the classroom holding her coat.

'I'm on playground duty.' She grinned at Edina before looking up at Jack. There was something in her eyes, something different. She looked less defensive than she had when he'd first arrived in Christmas Village; something had changed yesterday and he wasn't sure if he liked it. He had no idea what to do with the sweet openness of her expression, the way her eyes seemed to be saying he could tell her anything, ask for anything and she'd give it. Perhaps it would be better for both of them if she didn't let her guard down? It would certainly feel less dangerous for him. 'I want to thank you both for being here today – it made such a difference to the children to have an audience.' Belle dragged her eyes from his.

'Ach.' Edina clapped her hands, almost toppling over when she stopped leaning on the cane. Jack caught her under the arm and held on. 'The pleasure was all ours. I loved every minute.'

'I was wondering,' Belle said quietly, 'if you meant it about helping with the costumes?' She scraped a hand over her forehead, looking weary. 'I don't want you to feel like you have to… It'll be a lot of work and your leg…' She pointed to the cast.

'Ach, lass, I'd love to!' Edina said, grinning. 'I haven't had so much fun in years and I love using my sewing machine – my poor wee ankle won't get in the way of that.'

Belle's shoulders sagged. 'Would you mind if we talked more about it at the weekend?' She chewed the edge of her lip. 'Decide what we need to do. Perhaps I could invite Kenzy over to the castle tomorrow? She's got a creative eye and I thought I'd ask if she could help. I need assistance with creating the set too…'

'Jack can help with that,' Edina said without looking at him. 'He used to be a whizz with Lego when he was a wee boy.'

'I…' Jack let out a long sigh. 'Sure,' he murmured, surprised he didn't hate the idea.

'Logan will probably pitch in if I ask.' Edina nodded again. 'He's a good lad. Perhaps Tavish would even join us?' Her cheeks flushed.

'I'll make cakes and biscuits and we can have a meeting. I can think of at least one other person who might be able to help,' Belle said, and Jack wondered if they did tattoos. She reached out and squeezed Edina's arm. 'Thank you, you've no idea how much I need your help with these costumes.'

'Ach, thank *you*, dear. I asked Santa to make me feel useful – I've felt aimless since Reilly passed. That Christmas list might have burned up in my fire, but you delivered something Santa could not.' She mimed blowing a kiss and then took hold of Belle's arm. Jack watched as the two women walked slowly out of the room, wondering exactly what was happening to all his carefully laid plans…

Chapter Eleven

Rowan added another log to the fire as Belle finished putting the cakes and biscuits she'd made out onto the long dining room table. Isla had brought up two teapots and placed them next to the steaming coffee pot Belle had already set out – now she glanced around the large room. 'I can't believe how big the place is,' Isla gasped, taking in the multiple chairs Belle had reorganised earlier for the guests.

'Aye, it hasn't changed a bit since I last came to a party the family hosted when I was a wee lass,' Rowan said rapidly, glancing around. 'You should see the ballroom.' She gestured to the far corner, spreading her arms wide.

'I've heard about those parties,' Isla murmured, her voice lowering. 'I'm so happy to be here.' She turned back to Belle. 'It was good of you to invite me to help with the nativity costumes. Adam is so excited about being a sheep and I want to contribute in any way I can.'

'The lad was brilliant! A natural,' Edina declared, speaking earnestly to the two women Belle had persuaded to help.

'Ach, you're helping me,' Belle said. 'The biscuits you made were delicious. You're an incredible baker, Isla, as is Rowan. I'm hoping you're both as talented with a needle and thread.'

Isla shrugged. 'I'm not bad,' she murmured, threading a dainty hand through a blonde lock. 'I made this.' She pointed to the swirly patterned skirt she was wearing. It had ruffles and a series of complicated pleats.

'Wow,' Belle said, admiring it.

'I wanted to talk to you.' Isla put a gentle hand on Belle's arm and steered her into the corner of the room, lowering her voice. 'The flat Clyde went to see didn't work out. The person who saw it earlier decided to move in. We're searching for a place but there's still nothing close to Christmas Village.' She glanced around the dining room. 'I asked my mam and we can stay with her whenever we want, but she lives past Aberdeen. I hope it's okay but I'd rather not go until after the nativity – Adam's so looking forward to playing his part…'

'Where will Adam go to school?' Belle asked, thinking of the small boy with dark hair and soulful eyes. He was a quiet child and it had taken him a long time to make friends. She hated the idea of him moving away and having to start again.

Isla shrugged. 'There are schools where Mam lives…'

Belle winced. 'I hope moving away won't be necessary. I'll help you look for places as soon as I have time… I'm sure we'll think of something.' She hadn't had a spare moment, what with the nativity, Edina's Christmas list and the added distraction of Jack.

'Ach, lass, if it doesn't work out, we'll be happy enough with my mam – and we can keep looking back here until something comes up,' Isla promised.

'Are we ready?' Edina boomed from the chair Tavish had placed next to the fire. Her leg rested on the appliqué cushion and she wore a sapphire tiara, looking every inch the lady of the castle.

The doorbell rang and Rowan trotted into the hallway to answer it.

'Sorry I'm late.' Kenzy came rushing into the main room, wearing knee-high boots and a dress that should probably have been illegal, it was so tight. Belle knew her friend had decided to dress up because Logan was coming to the meeting later to offer his help with creating props for the set. 'One of my suppliers visited the salon yesterday afternoon and he brought me these temporary tattoos. They're really popular, apparently – I was wondering if I should offer them in the shop? I thought we could try applying some of these samples tonight. I'd welcome your opinion.' Belle had hatched the plan with Kenzy the day before after telling her friend how much Edina wanted a tattoo. This meant the elderly woman would have one in time for Christmas, without dragging her into Morridon to get something permanent done. Kenzy shoved a hand in her bag and pulled out a pile of white strips, then placed them on the coffee table Belle had got Jack to drag in front of the fire.

'Ach!' Edina's eyes widened in delight and she gazed into the roaring flames. 'It's almost like Santa reached in and pulled my Christmas list out of that grate before it burned and disappeared.' She shook her head and Belle felt her conscience twitch. She wasn't used to lying. This might be for a good cause, but how long should she keep it up?

Jack was currently with Logan and Tavish, working on installing a better lock on Bob's barn. The donkey had gone walkabout again this morning, and Jack was concerned he was going to get lost or hurt. Belle hadn't expected the man to get so caught up in the welfare of the animal; it showed a softer side to him, proving she'd misjudged him when they'd first met. He'd not mentioned the retirement home to Edina either, so perhaps now he'd seen how happy his grandmother was, he'd changed his mind? Or maybe she'd got it wrong and he'd never been after her money at all?

'Ach! These look so realistic, lass,' Edina sang, looking delighted. 'I've wanted to get a tattoo since my Reilly died and I watched a programme about them on TV. Can we try them now, do we need needles? I've not brought my sewing equipment down from upstairs, but Belle knows where I keep it all.'

'No needles required,' Kenzy said cheerfully. 'Just choose your tattoo and all I need is warm soapy water and a sponge. They're not permanent, just a bit of fun.'

Edina grinned and rolled up the sleeves of her jumper, exposing the pale wrinkly skin on her forearms. 'I'll get a few done, see if I can get a rise out of Jack.' She chortled. 'Tavish has one just here on his arm.' She pointed to the spot just above the inside of her wrist. 'I've had a glimpse, but he keeps pulling down his sleeve so I can't make out what it says. Perhaps if I show him mine, he'll show me his?' She waggled her eyebrows, beaming.

'Why don't we chat about the costumes while everyone chooses their favourite design?' Belle suggested, walking to the dining room table. 'Anyone for cake? There's chocolate, carrot or mince pies, and I've made coffee and tea.'

'Aye – and I've a wee dram to go in it to warm you.' Edina laughed as she pulled a small bottle of single malt from where she'd tucked it down the side of her upright chair.

Belle took it as Edina leaned forwards and picked up the pile of tattoos, carefully sifting through them. Belle poured out drinks for all the women, adding a small splash of whisky to the mugs, missing out her own. She had a new literacy report to finish reading and comment on later and needed a clear head. She'd been working on it all day and was almost at the end.

'This one says "Best Before 2021" – ach, I've a few more years left in me than that!' Edina laughed, continuing to search through the temporary tattoos, handing some of the bundle to Isla as Jinx wandered into the large room. The cat blinked and searched the assembled faces before he sneaked under Edina's chair so he was closer to the fire. '"Here Today, Gone Tomorrow", not if I can help it,' Edina continued. '"I'm Not Going Anywhere" – yep, I prefer that one.' She continued to leaf through the mound.

Isla sipped her tea and picked up a couple of the tattoos. 'I'm not sure if it's a good idea. What if Adam sees it?' she said, snorting out a laugh as she read. '"Warning: May Contain Bones".'

'Kenzy could put it on your shoulder with one of those red hearts, make your husband chuckle, and you could hide it from the wee lad until it washes off,' Edina suggested as she laid a small pile next to her. 'I'm going to have three.' Her eyes sparkled and she wriggled in her seat, leaning forwards to grab her coffee which Belle had added an extra shot of whisky to. '"The Book Was Better"; "So Much To Do, So Little Time" and "Choose Wrong".' Each of the tattoos was accompanied by a corresponding picture, from a skull and crossbones to a smiley face. 'Oh, I've spent far too much of my life doing the right thing… It's such a delight to realise it's okay to be wicked every now and again…' Her face lit as she roared with laughter.

'I've known that for years,' Kenzy said mildly, picking up a tattoo that had fallen on the floor. '"90 per cent naughty, 10 per cent nice."' She giggled. 'Sounds about right.' She placed it onto the seat of her chair. 'I'll just pop to the kitchen for a bowl of water and sponge and then I'll put these on. By the time the men return, they'll all be done.' She set off towards the ballroom which led to the kitchen so fast Belle was worried she'd slip in her high heels.

Rowan let out a snort of laughter as she lifted a tattoo from the small mountain. '"Be Nice or Starve" – aye, I'll have that one.' She stabbed a finger on the back of her hand. 'Right here. That'll stop any eejits complaining in my cafe when they have to wait.'

'What about you, Belle?' Edina asked, and they all turned to look at her.

'Oh.' Belle frowned; having a tattoo hadn't been part of the plan. This was supposed to be for Edina.

'You need to choose something…' Isla said. 'We're all having one.'

'Well…' Belle pawed through the pile, sipping some coffee and almost spluttering. She hadn't added whisky when she'd been pouring the drinks, but someone obviously had. She sipped a little more. 'There's nothing here…'

'Let me look,' Kenzy said, returning with the bowl and sponge. 'I'll choose for you, otherwise you'll go for something that's all wrong.' When Belle started to protest, she shook her head. 'I'll put it somewhere discreet.' She leered suggestively. 'That way only the people you want to see it will. This is it!' She waved a tattoo in the air. '"Shut up and Kiss Me" with some pretty pink lips. Simple and it says it all. It's been way too long since you've smooched anyone. I'll put it on your shoulder, same as Isla, so the kids won't see it at school.'

Belle decided not to argue. She could scrub the tattoo off in the shower later. Besides, it had been a long time since anyone – aside from Jinx – had been in her bedroom or seen her undress. Even Ted hadn't stayed over much towards the end of their relationship because she'd always been so busy helping at events, school or bake sales. He'd accused her of avoiding intimacy – had he been right?

'I'll do yours first, before you change your mind.' Kenzy propped herself on the edge of the coffee table and pushed the wide collar of Belle's jumper down so she could access her shoulder.

'Hey.' Belle blushed but Kenzy swiped away her hand.

'So, these costumes!' Edina declared, taking a large sip of her coffee. 'Do we know what we need? Have you any material, patterns?'

'Oh… no.' Belle leaned to the side so she could see past Kenzy. She had so much to sort, and she'd barely had time to focus on anything this evening because she'd been reading Robina's report. 'I've got no material or patterns. I need costumes for Mary, Joseph, an angel, three kings, two shepherds, two sheep, a donkey, and a star.' She winced. 'The children in the other classes who make up the chorus will be decorating their own halos and crowns in Art.'

'Those costumes won't be a problem, lass,' Edina said. 'Aside from the donkey – that will depend on if we can repurpose the reindeer.'

'Finished.' Kenzy eased Belle's jumper back on her shoulder. 'Don't touch it yet.' She picked up the bowl and sponge and sat in front of Edina, before picking up the three tattoos.

'What about the stage?' Isla asked. 'I worked in a theatre in Edinburgh years back, so I know a few things about keeping things simple. But you'll need props, a backdrop. Wasn't there a painting of the desert and the outline of a barn last year?'

Belle pulled a face. 'It's all missing. I've searched everywhere. I'm guessing someone mistook it for rubbish and threw everything out.'

After doing a bit of detective work, she'd discovered the caretaker had been sick last Christmas and a friend of Robina's grandson had come to help… Belle had missed the whole thing because Annie had been sick.

'That's fine, lass, we can make what we need together,' Edina said. 'I invited Logan tonight because he's good with his hands.'

Kenzy made a low humming sound.

'I've plenty of material in my sewing room. Once we decide who does what, you can take a look through and decide what you want to use. If Tavish or Jack can carry my sewing machine downstairs, I can whip up as many costumes as you'd like,' Edina offered.

Kenzy finished applying her tattoos and Edina admired her forearms, before putting her sweater back on and tugging it down to cover her arms.

'I'm good at painting,' Kenzy said. 'So if you've got sets to decorate, I'm happy to help. Now, whose tattoo should I do next!' She grinned as both Isla and Rowan's hands shot up.

'I'll help you tidy everything,' Kenzy said, as Belle went to let Isla and Rowan out of the castle, waiting until they were both safely in their cars and heading down the driveway before returning to the sitting room. It was almost ten o'clock and she wanted to read through the literacy report once more so she had time to digest it before making notes tomorrow. She stretched as she got back. Tavish was sitting on the seat opposite Edina and his dog Iver was curled at his feet. He gazed at the Christmas tree and sipped a glass of whisky, enjoying his daily nightcap before he carried her upstairs.

Jack had told Tavish he could get his grandmother to her bedroom, but the shopkeeper had insisted he wanted to keep an eye on her ankle. Belle suspected it was an excuse, because the older man's eyes lit whenever he saw Edina.

Kenzy was balancing most of the cups and plates from the dining table in her arms, and Logan loped over to take some into his large hands. He'd been quiet this evening, but Belle had seen him staring at Kenzy when he thought she wasn't looking.

'I think you managed to organise everyone. I'll find some music for when the kids get on the stage, check it's okay to use.' Jack walked over to join Belle as she went to the table to pick up the empty tea and coffee pots. He grabbed the small bottle of whisky and held it up to the light. 'It's empty.'

Belle pulled a face. Rowan and Isla had barely drunk any because they were driving. But she could feel the alcohol swimming around her head, making her limbs feel loose. Kenzy must have sneaked more into her mug when she hadn't been looking. 'The nativity will be a lot of work.' Belle changed the subject, watching as Jack picked up the remaining plates and headed towards the ballroom which led to the kitchen. 'But it'll be worth it. Will you be around to see the play?' she asked, wondering if it was bad that she hoped he'd say yes.

'I'm planning to stay until just after Christmas. I'm a partner in the law firm so it's my call, and working from here is going okay while I don't have to be in court.' Jack opened the door into the ballroom and waited for Belle to walk through first. She was quiet as they made their way across the empty room to the stairs which would lead to the basement kitchen. When they were halfway down the steps, Belle heard voices and put an elbow out to stop Jack from going any further, jerking it away as it connected with the hard muscle of his chest.

She listened as Kenzy cleared her throat. 'I wondered if you'd like to come to my house for dinner tomorrow?' she asked, in the sexy purr that felled men faster than a seasoned lumberjack. Jack raised an eyebrow and Belle shook her head. Her friend had been trying to get Logan alone for months – now she had, she didn't want to interrupt.

'I…' His voice sounded even more gravelly than usual and Belle wondered if he was embarrassed at being asked out. Not all men could handle Kenzy at her most forthright –fewer could resist her though. 'If I do, you'll have to do something for me, lass…'

'Well…?' Kenzy hummed.

'I'm not propositioning you.' He cleared his throat. 'You're a beautiful woman. You know that well enough. No one in this village, or probably the entirety of Scotland, is out of your reach. One look and most men are toast.' He shrugged. 'I've noticed…'

'You have?' Kenzy sounded surprised. 'Well then, why—'

'I've been waiting,' he said seriously. 'Waiting, because I thought you had things you needed to get out of your system.'

'Okay…' Kenzy trailed off.

Belle moved again, and Jack followed. She peered around the corner, feeling the warmth of his chest hovering close to her back as he looked too. She could just make out the shadowy silhouette of her friend. She was standing next to the counter in the middle of the kitchen, opposite Logan. He stood with his legs wide and his hands planted in his pockets, as if he wasn't sure what to do with them. Dangling above them, Belle could just make out the sprig of mistletoe – did they know it was there?

'So... what do you want?' Kenzy asked, wrapping her arms around herself. 'I don't understand.' Her tone was less confident now.

'I'm looking for something real, lass. I don't want to just date you, or bed you. I'm not looking for shallow and short-term. I was married for twelve years before my wife passed. I'm not built like that.'

'And I am?' Kenzy tossed her head, sounding hurt.

'Nae, lass,' Logan said quietly, studying her intently. 'I dinnae think you are. But I'm not sure you're ready to acknowledge that.' He took a step forwards then and Belle saw her friend jerk as if he'd touched her. Thought she might stumble backwards on those sky-high heels she was probably regretting. She held her breath, transfixed by the transformation in her confident kick-ass mate as she seemed to deflate, shedding the armour Belle had always suspected she used to keep herself safe. Instead she looked... vulnerable. Logan carefully caught a strand of her blonde hair between his fingertips and began to stroke as his voice deepened. 'It's easy to flirt. It's easy to make men want you when you look like you do. And it's easy not to care. The hard work starts when you're ready to make a commitment to someone. When you're ready to risk feeling something.'

Kenzy swallowed, leaning forwards as if he were reeling her in. 'I don't know what you mean,' she murmured, but even Belle could tell she was lying.

'Well, when you do' – Logan dropped the shiny strand of hair and took a step backwards – 'you let me know. I'll be waiting. I've been waiting for a while now.' He put his hands back in his pockets and rocked on his heels. 'I'm a patient man, I can wait until you're ready.'

'I am ready. I just asked *you* out – jerk.' Kenzy looked annoyed but Logan just shook his head and gave her a crooked smile.

'Nae, lass, you're not ready for me,' he said, turning and walking away. 'Yet.'

Belle let out a squeak and lurched around as she realised exactly where Logan was headed. She widened her eyes, thrusting her chin upwards, signalling to Jack that they had to retreat. She tried to edge past him, as she heard Logan's feet on the bottom of the stairs and ran, still holding the pots, hoping he'd follow. She let out a sigh of relief as she heard Jack behind her and took an instant left when they got to the ballroom, using her little finger to prise open the door of a narrow cupboard where she knew Edina kept the cleaning supplies. She dived in, almost knocking over a mop. 'Quick!' she squeaked to Jack and he followed, easing the door until it was only open a crack. Belle could see Logan as he sauntered across the ballroom. 'Ach, that was close,' she whispered, clutching the pots to her chest which was now heaving. She glanced into the empty room again, as Kenzy marched out of the kitchen in the direction of the dining room.

'What happened?' Jack's forehead knotted. It was dim in the cupboard but she could still make out his face.

'A lad just said no to Kenzy Campbell,' Belle hissed. 'I think the sky's about to fall in.' She looked up at the ceiling as Jack chuckled.

'I think it's still intact. Perhaps they should both chalk that up to a lucky escape,' he said quietly. 'In my experience, chemistry like that is a route to a whole load of misery – and a very expensive divorce.' He sounded serious.

'That's…' Belle felt her stomach turn over, but she wasn't sure if it was due to sympathy or all the whisky she'd drunk. 'Sad,' she finished, suddenly feeling sorry for him.

Jack shrugged as his blue eyes scanned her face. She felt her body warm through to her bones; even her knees wobbled. *Woah.* There was no room to move, no air, and suddenly she was very aware of the enclosed space and how near they were. Perhaps Jack realised it too, because he straightened and moved away. 'Hazard of the job,' he said, his lips twisting into that lopsided smile she was beginning to recognise. Then he lifted the plates he was still holding. 'Think it's safe to go down to the kitchen now?'

'I guess.' Belle nodded, but even as she followed Jack out of the cupboard, through the ballroom and back down the short flight of stairs, she wondered if it was.

Chapter Twelve

Belle woke with a dry mouth. Jinx was beside her, curled up on a pillow on the double bed, and the cat opened one eye when she turned over, then yawned before closing it again. She dragged an arm out from under the duvet and shivered, glancing at her bedside table and frowning when she realised it was 3 a.m. Worse, she'd forgotten to bring water up from the kitchen – there should have been a glass beside the clock. She ran her parched tongue across her teeth, tasting whisky and toothpaste, knowing she needed a drink. If she didn't hydrate, she'd still have a headache tomorrow – and teaching a class of six-year-olds with a banging head was a terrible idea.

Sighing, Belle pushed the bedding back and winced. 'Freezing!' she squeaked, and leapt out before she changed her mind, pulling on her slippers and the thin dressing gown Annie had given her last Christmas. It was as impractical as the matching pink silk slip she wore underneath, but since losing her godmother, it was her go-to outfit for bed. There was something comforting about knowing Annie had chosen it. She wrapped her arms around herself as she padded out of the large bedroom, past the end of the solid oak four-poster bed, then the enormous matching wardrobe which loomed beside the door, taking care to step lightly on the floorboards because she knew her bedroom was directly above Jack's.

She listened for movement as she crept into the dark hallway, then trotted down the turnpike stairs, pausing at the entrance to the dining room before slowly padding across it. Someone had left the Christmas lights on and the tree sparkled, lighting up the entrance to Jack's bedroom. The door was shut and he was probably asleep. *He* hadn't drunk a load of alcohol before bed. She'd murder Kenzy later – after she'd got her to talk about her conversation with Logan. Her friend had left Evergreen Castle before she and Jack had finished tidying up the kitchen and hadn't responded to any of Belle's texts.

Belle opened the door to the ballroom and winced when the hinges squeaked. She waited to see if anyone stirred, then slowly made her way across the large room, skipping quickly down the steps into the basement kitchen. There were multiple small windows at the top of the walls on two sides edging the ceiling, and enough light from the moon shone through them to help Belle to see. She grabbed a glass from a cupboard and ran the tap, filling it and glugging down two large mouthfuls as she stared into the white butler sink.

'You okay?' The deep voice made Belle jump and she screamed as she spun round, splashing water all over Jack who was standing just behind her. He swiped a hand across his face as liquid dripped from his cheek onto his navy long-sleeved pyjama top. It was open at the collar and Belle watched a tear of water slide into the dip at the base of his throat, unable to drag her attention from the smooth skin.

'Ach, I'm so sorry. You startled me.' Shaking herself, she grabbed a chequered red and white tea-towel from the counter and tried to wipe the water away, but Jack took it and used it to slowly dab his face.

'That'll save me taking a shower in the morning,' he said dryly. 'I didn't mean to frighten you. I heard a noise and…' He stopped suddenly as his eyes fixed on something under Belle's right ear and his mouth stretched into a wide grin.

She tried to look and realised the silk dressing gown had slipped, exposing the pale skin across her collarbone and the spot on the top of her shoulder where Kenzy had put the eejit tattoo.

'"Shut Up and Kiss Me"?' Jack read, looking amused. 'Is that an order?' He glanced up at the ceiling and Belle realised she was standing exactly where Kenzy had been hours earlier, directly under the mistletoe. She swallowed and tugged the silky material back in place, hiding the ridiculous words.

'Of course not. The tattoos were for Edina,' she said, embarrassed. 'For the Christmas list. Kenzy insisted we all had one. It's only temporary and no one was supposed to see it.' Heat pooled in her stomach, gravitating lower, and she tried to ignore it, to ignore the warmth flickering across her skin. She wasn't even sure she trusted this man – how did he affect her this much?

'I like it.' He smiled slowly. 'Think she's got any left?'

'Um… I…' Belle felt the flush creep up her neck and flood her cheeks.

'I'm joking,' he said, studying her. His eyes were so dark she could barely see the blue; it lined the edges of his pupils like a narrow frame.

'Of course.' She nodded a few times and tried to laugh but the sound came out all wrong. She cleared her throat. 'It's a stupid tattoo.'

'Why?' His lips curved.

'Who tells someone to shut up before kissing them? It's so contradictory. Besides, doesn't kissing fall under the same category as chemistry?' she babbled.

Jack quirked an eyebrow, looking confused, and she took a small step back, a little overwhelmed by the affect he was having on her.

'You know. A path to misery and an expensive divorce?' If Belle thought using Jack's words would make him laugh, she was wrong. Her hand gripped the glass tightly as he frowned and tipped his head.

'I'm not a monk,' he said softly. 'I happen to enjoy kissing – and I don't necessarily connect the meeting of lips to the insanity of a marriage contract. They aren't mutually exclusive.'

'Oh…' Belle nodded as her stomach lurched. Where the hell was this conversation headed and why had she started it? 'I—' She lifted her glass, unable to form words. 'Need…'

'Do you like kissing?' Jack asked quietly, taking a step forwards.

'Yes,' Belle squeaked, wondering if her response was triggered by the alcohol she'd drunk this evening or something far more dangerous. Because if she thought that was going to make Jack do anything but step closer, she was wrong.

He stepped closer.

'I mean… doesn't everyone?' she gabbled, wishing she hadn't when he gave her a wolfish grin. Had she thought he was cold when she met him? Because all she could see in his eyes was heat – and all she could hear was blood rushing through her body, whooshing in her veins. She found herself leaning forwards, much like Kenzy had done when Logan had been playing with her hair. It was almost involuntary, as though he was some kind of man magnet. 'I…'

She swallowed, losing her thread when he reached out and caught a strand of her hair, and stroked it between his fingers, mimicking what they'd seen earlier.

'Soft…' he murmured. 'I wondered.'

'I use shampoo,' Belle said, wishing she could just stop talking. Jack chuckled.

'And conditioner,' she added. *Dear God.* 'Could you please just tell me to shut up?'

'Shut up,' he whispered, leaning forwards and brushing his mouth over hers. His touch was gentle but it had the desired effect. His lips were soft and he smelled really good – like expensive aftershave and fabric conditioner. A fragrance she would never have expected to have such a powerful effect on her pulse. He deepened the kiss and Belle sighed, putting a tentative hand on the muscles across his chest as they slowly explored each other's mouths. If someone had told her a few days ago that she'd be kissing Jack Hamilton-Kirk, she'd have laughed. Even now she wasn't sure if this was actually happening or if she was still in bed upstairs, half asleep.

But it wasn't a dream. She knew that because when he stroked a hand across her collarbone and under the silk of her dressing gown, then pushed it off her shoulder, she felt the cold settle on her skin. Felt goosebumps rise and spread across her body in a slow wave. She lifted her arms and wrapped them around Jack's neck and he let his hands drift down until they were clutching her waist, then gently kneading her bottom. She heard a low groan but couldn't tell if it had come from her or him. Jack gently eased her backwards until she was stopped by the kitchen counter. She was glad she had something to help hold her up because gravity had ceased to work. He pressed his body into hers and she felt a sharp punch of heat as the chemistry surging between them notched up. He must have felt it too, because suddenly he was pulling up the bottom of her nightdress and his warm hands were exploring the sensitive skin on her waist and back. *Oh boy.* Heat pooled in her centre and Belle wondered where this was going to end. She didn't fancy dropping onto the hard flagstone floor, but wasn't sure she was capable of stopping. And Jack didn't seem inclined to either. Perhaps he was caught up in the same madness as her? He moved his head and began to nibble at the delicate skin close to her ear, dipping down to kiss her neck before feathering his lips across her collarbone. This was insane – just a few days ago Belle had hated Jack. Now she couldn't seem to stop herself from running her arms down his chest and lifting the material of his shirt so she could trace her fingers across the warm hard skin on his stomach. She let her fingertips rise to his chest, nudging him back a little so she could investigate all those hot, hard muscles properly, exploring every solid inch as if she were mapping and committing it to memory.

Then there was a crash. It wasn't loud, which suggested it was a floor or two up from them, but since the castle was so quiet and the only noise Belle could hear was the rapid rise and fall of their breath, she heard it. Jack did too because he jerked back and stared at her. His chest heaved in and out, a reminder of the sharp rush of chemistry and heat that had been at work until this moment. 'Did you hear it too?' Belle asked. Her voice was husky and the pitch lower than normal. She swallowed as Jack blew out a breath, as if he needed a moment to gather himself.

'Yes.' His voice was gruff as he stepped back and tugged her silky nightgown back in place, pulling his shirt down over his beautiful, toned chest. Belle let out a small cry of complaint just as there was another crash from above. This one was louder.

'Dammit,' Jack said. 'That can only be Edina.' He turned and half ran across the kitchen and up the stairs, checking behind him to see if Belle was following. She charged after him, taking deep, ragged breaths as she tried to calm the rampant chemistry still surging through her blood, wondering exactly what had got into her.

It took just a minute for them to run up the turnpike stairs to the hallway, and they heard another crash as they reached it. Jack was at Edina's bedroom door in seconds, wrenching it open without knocking. 'Are you okay?' He sounded worried, and any lingering doubts Belle had had about his affection for his nana were gone in that instant.

'Ach, I'm an eejit.' Edina groaned from underneath what looked like a heavy drawer that had come from the big set of antique oak cabinets looming over her. She wore a thick navy nightgown which covered almost her entire body, aside from the parts they could see poking out from underneath the piece of furniture resting on her lower half. The boot protecting her ankle still looked intact. There was no blood and none of her limbs appeared to be at an unnatural angle. Belle blew out a sigh of relief as she dropped to her knees.

'Are you hurt?' she asked. 'Can we move the drawer?'

'Aye, lass,' Edina said, and Jack carefully lifted it and put it back where it had come from. Belle helped her into a seated position on the floor, checking her for injuries, experiencing a moment of déjà vu. Jack's grandmother looked a little dazed but was fine otherwise.

'I was trying to get to my tiaras for the nativity. I promised the wee lads and lassies they could borrow some. But I had to shove the cabinet trying to get it open and the bampot light fell.' She pointed to a pretty Tiffany-style lamp which was in jagged pieces a few metres away. Next to it Belle saw a picture frame lying face down on the oak floorboards. 'Then when I tried again, I gave it a good shove before pulling it and the drawer came out too quickly and knocked me flat – all my jewellery fell out.' She winced as she regarded the assortment of stunning rings, necklaces, bracelets, earrings and tiaras scattered around her. Belle even spotted some pieces glinting under the four-poster bed.

'Was it important you found them all now – at three thirty in the morning?' Jack asked, incredulous.

'Ach, lad, when you get to my age you don't sleep that well.' Edina shrugged. 'I thought if I was careful I'd be able to look through everything and choose the right pieces so Belle could take them to school tomorrow.' She reached out and picked up two fragments of silver-coloured band – one half had a huge emerald set in the top and the other was just a rounded curve. She twisted the pieces between her fingers, pointing to the place where it had obviously snapped before holding them together until they formed a complete semi-circle. 'I used to wear this tiara all the time. Your granda bought it right after we met.' She frowned. 'I fell, and it bounced on the floor and snapped. He didn't want me to wear any of my jewellery after that and I never did get it fixed.' She sighed.

At least they knew which of Edina's tiaras needed mending now and where to find the pieces. When Belle shifted her eyes to meet Jack's to see if he'd realised, he was staring at his grandmother with a worried expression. 'Shall we get you into bed?' Belle asked quietly. Now she wasn't running or kissing Jack, she was getting cold.

'Aye,' Edina murmured, groaning when Belle tried to guide her to her feet. Jack came to help, and together they got her into bed and under the duvet and blankets. 'Can you pass me the photo, please, lass?' Edina asked Belle, pointing to the frame on the floor. 'I'd forgotten I'd put it in that drawer.' Belle handed her the picture, twisting it round at the same time. It was Jack's mam; Belle recognised her from the photo on the mantelpiece. She was standing in a field filled with lush grass and four grey donkeys were gathered around her. You could see mountains in the distance and the sky was clear and blue. The woman was smiling, but despite that, she had a sadness around her eyes. 'I still haven't told Tara about my ankle. I wish she were here...' The words held an ache, and when Belle looked at Edina she was frowning. She sat on the edge of the bed and put a hand on her arm. 'That's your mam, lad,' Edina said softly, lifting the picture and looking at Jack. 'You look so much like her...'

He let out a long breath. 'I told you, I'm not talking about that.' He sounded so different from the man Belle had been kissing earlier. All that heat had burned away, leaving something cold in its place.

Belle watched Edina's shoulders droop. 'So stubborn,' she said sadly. 'If you'd just meet her, listen... you'd understand.'

'It's not important.' Jack shook his head. 'What is...' He faltered. 'What *does* matter is that it's becoming increasingly clear this isn't the right place for you to live.'

Edina paled and glanced up from the photo. 'What do you mean, lad?'

'I was beginning to come around to the idea of you staying.' He swallowed, looking genuinely upset. 'But what would have happened if you'd been alone tonight? Who would have come? This is a big house, that turnpike stairway is...' He shuddered. 'Terrifying. Every time I walk down them I imagine you falling. The kitchen is in the basement via another ludicrous staircase, there's no proper heating—'

'I'm fine, lad.' Edina's voice was firm but Belle could hear a hint of uncertainty in it. A smattering of fear. 'This is my home, where I've lived my whole life.'

Jack looked at her, his eyes dark but his expression clear. 'Sometimes we have to make difficult choices. Change isn't always easy...' He trailed off as Belle turned to him too, narrowing her eyes.

'Your nana is fine living in Evergreen Castle,' she said, feeling her heart rate pick up, only this time for a different reason. She could read the writing on the wall, could feel her blood beginning to boil. 'There's plenty of us in Christmas Village who'll be happy to take her under our wing. A lot who already have.' There was a fire burning inside her, a fire she recognised. It lit whenever she knew someone was in trouble. Whenever they needed her help. Those flames of indignation filled her, made her feel needed.

His lips pursed. 'You're spread too thin already. Anyone can see that.'

'What does that mean?' Belle snapped.

'School, the play, making cakes and biscuits, literacy reports, nativity costumes, families in need of accommodation.' He ticked everything off his fingers, daring her to argue. 'Besides,' he said, more gently now. 'She's *my* grandmother.' He turned back to Edina.

'I went to see the Tatherfod Retirement Home the other day.' Edina let out a shocked squeak. 'It was luxurious, safe and very warm.' Jack stepped forwards. 'Just come and look with me – no one is saying you have to do anything you don't want to, but we can have a day out.' His lips curved but he didn't look like he was smiling. 'If you hate it, we'll think of something else.'

Belle could feel her insides hardening. She was seething. He was a snake – a chameleon. She'd been kissing him earlier. He'd taken her in completely, and she'd been suckered in by those dark brooding eyes, that sexy body, the way he'd treated Bob and Jinx. She shook her head. She could see he cared for his nana, but was it really in her best interests to move?

'Laddie…' Edina let out a long breath.

'I've got a brochure,' Jack said quickly, his attention darting to Belle and back to Edina when she glared at him. 'Let me get it now. You can take a look, and I can make an appointment for us to visit together so you can see for yourself.'

'Ach,' Edina said, as he turned on his heels and disappeared out of the room. Belle sat on the edge of the bed, staring at the jewellery on the floor, feeling numb. She got up and began to gather the pieces, putting them into the large drawer. Carefully putting the two sections of tiara to one side so she could find them later, she gathered the pieces of lamp, still seething. She wasn't going to let Jack get away with this, and she was going to make sure her friend got everything on her Christmas list. The whole thing felt so much more important now she knew Jack wanted Edina to move. 'I wish Tara were here,' Edina repeated, sighing and picking up the photo from the bed so she could stare at it. 'If she was, I think everything would be okay. Do you think I need to go into a retirement home, lass?' Belle looked at her, at the lines around her face, at how tired she seemed. Sure she was frail, but what seventy-seven-year-old wouldn't be after being run over by a bike and then attacked by a drawer in the middle of the night? She was strong too, full of life – and over the last week, Edina had seemed so happy.

'Nae.' Belle shook her head, thinking about her mam and da, what they'd do in this situation. *Anything and everything they could.* 'I don't.' She heard the hammer of Jack's feet on the floor, then turned back to Edina. 'Do you have Tara's number?' she whispered.

'Of course, lassie.' She nodded. 'I haven't lost my marbles, despite what the lad might think.'

'Give it to me later,' Belle whispered as Jack headed back through the door.

Belle didn't know what she was going to do about Jack Hamilton-Kirk. But she did know she wasn't going to let him move Edina out of her home – or get his hands on Evergreen Castle without a fight.

Chapter Thirteen

Jack steered the Land Rover out of Evergreen Castle's drive, ignoring the squeeze of sympathy in his chest for his grandmother who was sitting in the passenger seat, staring out of the window. He was doing the right thing, he had to remember that. Edina was his only real family now and he had to protect her. 'Are you warm enough?' he asked, reaching over to ratchet the heating up, but she nodded without looking at him. 'We're only visiting and it'll be quick,' he said quietly. 'I'm not going to make you move into the retirement home if you don't want to.' He sighed when she didn't respond and took a left out of the drive. He'd had a quiet few days in Evergreen Castle, feeling slightly more popular than an axe murderer, but less welcome than someone with a really contagious cold. Belle had barely spoken to him, choosing instead to narrow her eyes every time she saw him in the castle. He wouldn't mind, but they were pretty eyes and every time he looked at them, he was reminded of that moment in the kitchen when he'd leaned down for that kiss. Of the heat that had ignited between them. A heat he'd heard about but had never experienced for himself. He let out the breath he'd been holding. 'I'm not my father,' he said, fully aware of the man's reputation for getting his own way, no matter what.

'Aye,' Edina said finally. 'Well, if you were, I'd already be living wherever he decided. Separated from my family, alone and afraid.' She knotted her hands in her lap as they passed a pretty spruce tree decorated with red baubles and laden with snow, which marked the start of the main high street.

Jack let her words sit for a moment. 'What?' he asked finally, shocked. His dad had had his faults, but that reaction was a little extreme…

Edina sighed. 'You don't want to talk about your mam.'

Jack gripped the steering wheel tighter and decided he might circle back to what she'd said later. Preferably after a glass of whisky. Any conversation about Tara would be a mistake at the moment, especially when his grandmother wasn't happy with the idea of visiting the Tatherfod Retirement Home. He wasn't looking to upset her, he simply wanted to keep her safe. To make sure that when he was in London he didn't have to worry about her falling down a set of turnpike stairs, getting stuck under a heavy drawer or run over by a wayward bike. Worse – of having some stranger insinuate themselves into her life in an effort to fleece her out of everything she owned. His mind drifted to Belle and he shook his head. No matter how many times his head told him not to trust her, his heart kept screaming something else. He didn't understand her, had no compass to guide him; nothing aside from his feelings, and he knew he couldn't rely on those. Just look at how much he'd adored his mother.

As they reached the part of the high street where the small parade of shops began, he saw Kenzy heading out of the beauty salon, waving. Edina wound the window down as Jack slowed the car to a stop. 'How's the ankle after your accident?' Kenzy asked, smiling as she approached.

'Much better now, thanks,' Edina said, her lips curving for the first time since she'd got into the Land Rover. 'The drawer didn't do any harm and this cast should be off in another few weeks. Mind you, not sure how I'm going to get Tavish to visit so often once it is.' She frowned, perhaps considering her potential move away from the village.

'I'm sure you'll think of something.' Kenzy grinned. 'Belle told me you had a day out planned?' The warmth in her grey eyes dropped a few degrees as she glanced at Jack, and he realised the whole village probably knew where they were headed. Something knotted in his chest; embarrassment, guilt or doubt? He didn't know, wasn't ready to examine it. 'I wanted to ask if the tattoos were still there.' Kenzy smiled again when Edina nodded and pulled her sleeves up to reveal the three that had been applied on her forearms. His grandmother had been ruthlessly teasing Tavish, trying to encourage him to show his, but so far the man hadn't relented. 'Just say if you want any more,' Kenzy sang. 'I'll see you tonight, at the nativity meeting. I'm ready to help with the costumes and I'll bring my most creative head! Before you leave, Rowan asked me to tell you she wants to see you.' She pointed to the cafe a little further up the high street, which had been adorned with an array of red, green and gold Christmas garlands. Jack had stopped there once to have a coffee and to use the WiFi. The food had been tasty and the company warm, but he guessed he wouldn't be so welcome now.

'Aye, okay.' Edina smiled. Kenzy tipped her head at his grandmother before heading back to the salon without sparing another look for him. 'Can you pull up when we get closer, please, lad?'

Jack nodded and drove another few metres along the road, before stopping outside the cafe. Rowan must have been looking out of the window for them, because the door swung open and she came trotting out, wearing a thick black coat and carrying a large hessian bag. 'Edina, I packed you sandwiches, Christmas cake and a flask of my best coffee.' She spoke rapidly, ignoring Jack. 'I wasn't sure if you'd have a chance to stop in Tatherfod – I know there's a restaurant but I've no idea what the food's like. Belle said you didn't eat much breakfast, lass?' She scowled at Jack. 'I expected you'd have no appetite. Never mind, I packed enough for two in case there was anyone you wanted to share it with.' Her tone suggested that including enough for him to eat too had been against her better judgement. 'I'll see you at the castle later.' She squeezed Edina's arm, handing over the bag before picking her way back through the snow towards the busy cafe.

His grandmother put the package on the floor between her feet without saying a word and Jack took a deep breath. He started the car, only to immediately switch off the engine again when he saw Tavish walk out of The Corner Shop at the end of the high street and wave. The older man tramped through the snow with his dog Iver at his heels, making a beeline for the car as Edina leaned out of the window. 'You come to show me your tattoo?' she teased, and Tavish flushed.

'Nae, woman.' He tugged the sleeves of his sweater down, fully covering his forearms. 'Someone just came into the shop blathering about a donkey.' He pointed up the road in the direction they were about to drive in. 'It's a few miles on apparently, close to the entrance of the riding school.' Jack had passed the riding school on his way into the village on that first morning so knew it wasn't far. 'Could it be Bob?' Tavish rasped.

Edina pulled a face. 'I dinnae know. Belle went to feed him for me this morning; the lass didn't mention he wasn't in the barn. But she might have let him out, or the wee thing escaped. Perhaps he's gone for another wander? I've not been to visit for a few days because of the snow.' She sounded worried. 'I hope the lad's all right.'

'I called Belle's mobile,' Tavish said. 'But the lass must have been teaching because she didn't answer.' His forehead creased. 'I can shut the shop and mosey up, see if I can find the donkey if you want? I know you're busy,' he growled.

Jack cleared his throat. 'We can stop in and check if it's Bob. It's on our way.'

Tavish's green eyes glinted dangerously as he turned to Jack and frowned. 'I wouldn't want you to get distracted,' he snarled. 'There's plenty of us here who are happy to help out.'

Jack put his hands on the steering wheel and shook his head. 'You think I don't know what you're all doing?' he asked, looking back down the high street at the shops, wondering if the villagers were staring at them even now. 'This is obviously some kind of theatrical attempt to show me my grandmother will be taken care of when I'm not around.'

Tavish's lips thinned and he leaned in through the open car window so he could look Jack in the eye. He was menacing and a little scary, not that Jack was going to admit it to his face. 'Or what if it's true, lad? What if this is less about fiction and more about the way things really are? What if we are all here to look after your nana? Sometimes the truth can be exactly what you see…'

Jack swallowed a wave of emotion. 'Not in my experience,' he said quietly.

'Then I feel sorry for you, lad. Seems to me you're searching for a whole lot of things that aren't there.' Tavish sighed and stepped back when Jack didn't respond. He cleared his throat when Edina didn't say anything either. 'I'll see you later, lass.' Tavish put a hand to his forehead in a gesture reminiscent of a gentleman tipping his cap.

'We'll go and check on Bob,' Jack said gruffly, starting the car as Edina waved goodbye to the old man and wound the window up. 'It won't take long.'

The road was quiet and no one else from the village tried to stop them, as Jack navigated his way out of the high street to the road that would ultimately take them in the direction of Tatherfod. There were about a million sparkly lights hung along the fences that lined the highway and a large Christmas tree someone had erected and decorated. It was pretty and so unlike anything he'd seen in London. To the right and left of the road were fields, flanked by a range of mountains with multiple peaks piled with snow. They were dotted with fir trees that lined the tips and steep sides, providing colour and texture to the picture, which could have graced the front of a festive card. The sky was a muted blue with strips of cloud that signalled more snow was on the way. Jack just hoped they could make it to Tatherfod and back without getting caught in any. At least the Land Rover had snow chains, thanks to a visit from a friend of Logan's, so there was little chance of them getting stuck.

Edina cleared her throat. 'I need to talk to you, lad.' She shifted in her seat, turning to look at him. Jack could sense whatever she was about to say mattered and slowed the car, but didn't take his eyes off the road.

'Okay,' he murmured.

'I'll come and see your retirement home.' Even from the corner of his eye, Jack could see the pinch of sadness around his grandmother's eyes and fought a wave of guilt. He was doing the right thing… wasn't he? His dad would have thought so.

'I sense a but…?' He cleared his throat.

'Ach.' She shrugged. 'I just think I'm better off where I am.'

'Alone,' Jack said, watching the road. There had been a big dump of snow last night and it had piled up, creating wide twinkling banks on either side of them. He couldn't imagine how Bob could have made it this far without walking in the middle of the highway, straight in the path of any traffic. He winced, hoping the donkey was okay.

'I'm not alone, lad, not anymore. Not since Belle came into my life and I started to reconnect with the village.' Edina sighed. 'I've realised it's easy to get used to,' she said softly. 'Shutting yourself away from people. Sometimes because you decide it's easier or not as painful. Perhaps because there's less risk of getting hurt…' She let that sit between them and Jack suddenly realised she was talking about him.

He shook his head. 'I'm fi—'

'Your mam's done the same – ever since she lost you. Hiding herself away with her donkeys.' Edina swallowed and waited but Jack wasn't going to ask about her. It was easier when he pretended she didn't exist. 'Your granda wasn't keen on people. He always said your mam and I were enough for him, that he didn't want or need anyone else in his life…' She sighed. 'I thought I didn't either.'

'And now you do?' Jack asked gruffly.

She let out a raspy exhale. 'Now I'm enjoying having company. Realising what I've been missing. Belle made me realise what it is to be part of a community. She's a good lass. Her heart is in the right place.' She cleared her throat. 'I thank my lucky stars for the day she ran me over with her wee bike. Because I've realised I'm not alone. Not if I don't want to be.' She reached out and touched his arm. Her skin looked paper thin but there was a strength to her grip. A strength that surprised him. 'And neither are you.'

'We have each other. You've always had me,' Jack said. 'At least, since…'

'Aye.' She nodded. 'And I'm grateful for it. Not grateful your da died, of course. But I'm happy you're in my life now and I appreciate you want to take care of me. But you have to know, I'm okay. I can take care of myself, and when I can't, I've plenty of friends here now to help.' She pointed to the bag between her feet. 'I think that's what Tavish was trying to say earlier – in his own ornery way.'

Jack sighed. 'Meaning… you don't want to move?' He could feel a headache forming behind his eyes. The same one he often felt when his father had been pushing him to do something against his better judgement. He fought the urge to rub his temples.

'Ach, lad.' His grandmother linked her fingers and looked out of the car. 'I just wanted to tell you how I felt.'

'I get it,' Jack muttered, wondering again what he was doing. Following the same path as his dad…? Trying to put a round peg in a square hole, thinking it would fit as long as he tried for long enough, or found exactly the correct weight and size of hammer. He'd never thought he was like his dad, but perhaps they were more similar than he'd thought? He stared at the road as he drove, noticing a turning on the left with a signpost that read, CHRISTMAS CAIRN, 1.5 MILES. Was that the place Edina had written about on her Christmas list; hadn't she wanted to go? There had been something about laying stones – and he'd promised Belle he'd make sure his grandmother got to tick it off her list. But he'd done nothing to make it happen. Instead he was taking her somewhere she didn't even want to go. He winced.

'It's the next turning, lad!' Edina said suddenly, pointing to a left turn a few metres along the road. 'The riding stables.' Jack indicated and drove in, almost skidding as he took the corner too fast. It was a longish driveway lined with trees peppered with snow, but he could see a large grey stone house, a set of stables in the distance, and a few horses in a field further out. About two thirds down the drive, a fluffy grey donkey was standing in the snow sniffing the air.

'What is it about this animal?' Jack complained as they drew closer, and Bob's large eyes brightened as he recognised them. He pulled the car to a stop, ensuring there was enough room for others to get by. 'Give me a minute.' He hopped out and paced up to the donkey. Bob let out a loud honk of delight and trotted over to nuzzle Jack's coat. 'What are you doing here?' he asked, stroking the rough fuzz of fur on the animal's head, glancing back the way they'd come, feeling ridiculously happy that he was okay. 'How are we supposed to get you home?'

Edina must have heard, because she wound the window down. 'There's a tow bar on the back of this car and we might be able to borrow a horse box from the owner. I've known Duncan Knox for years. We went to school together. I used to ride with him right up those mountains when I was a wee lass.' She pointed into the distance with a wistful expression. 'Perhaps Duncan could put Bob in his paddock today and we can pick him up on the way back from your…' Edina paused. 'Retirement home.'

Jack frowned. 'Let's go and ask.' He walked back to the car and climbed in. The donkey stared at them and blinked. 'I'll drive you down and walk back to get Bob.' He checked his watch. 'We can't stay long.' He'd made an appointment for a tour and they were already going to be late.

'Aye, lad.' His grandmother sounded resigned.

He started the car, gripping the steering wheel, and Bob's ears pricked up but he stayed put. Jack eased out of the space so he didn't startle the animal and slowly made his way down the drive, hoping the donkey wouldn't use them leaving as an excuse to escape.

'He's coming too.' Edina clapped her hands and turned in her seat so she could watch Bob follow the car. 'Ach, lad, you're a regular Pied Piper, just like Tara.' Jack shook his head, glancing in the wing mirror as the donkey trailed behind them. When they reached the wide clearing at the end of the drive, he got out of the car as a portly grey-haired man emerged from the house to greet them. As soon as he saw Edina, his face lit and he went to open her door.

'I've not seen you for years, lassie, how many is it…?' His green eyes flickered as he tried to calculate the exact number, but Edina held up a hand.

'Ach, best if you don't, unless you plan to knock a few decades off. I prefer my history vague and peppered with inaccuracy.' She grinned as Bob jogged over to sniff Jack's jacket pocket. 'Duncan, this is my grandbaby. Jack, this is my good friend Duncan from way back.'

'Best horsewoman I ever met, your nana.' Duncan strolled over to greet Jack. He didn't bat an eyelid at the donkey, but he did reach out and rub his head. 'This fellow is looking for snacks.' He grinned as Bob gave up on the pocket and dipped lower, checking Jack's trouser pockets, then his boots. 'If you carry some chopped carrot, apples or swede, he'll likely do anything you ask.' Bob honked. 'Didn't I hear you used to ride this guy?' Duncan turned to Edina, who had twisted in the car seat so she could see them better.

'Aye.' His grandmother nodded, her mouth pinching. 'When I first got him. Bob enjoys going out for jaunts. I rode his mam a few times too when I visited Tara.' She looked to the left. 'Christmas Cairn is a few miles in that direction – I'd often ride one of our donkeys there when we visited.' She frowned as something shimmered in her blue eyes.

Duncan looked sympathetic. 'I could saddle him up – you could take a quick ride before you leave? I've not been for a few years, but there's a short cut behind the stables. It'll only take half an hour from here.' He patted Bob's back. 'He's obviously a strong wee lad and you still look as light as a feather.' He looked at the thick blue boot on Edina's ankle and frowned. 'You injured? I hadn't heard.'

'Just a wee fracture. It's almost healed. Besides, that wouldn't stop me, not if someone helped me climb on.' Edina winked, then her attention shifted to Jack and she frowned. 'But we have to go.' Her voice flattened. 'The lad's got a place he wants me to see…'

Jack put his hands in his pockets and stared at his grandmother, then at Bob. He remembered the way Belle had glared at him. The shock in her eyes when he'd talked about the retirement home. Why did what she thought matter? 'Is it really safe?' He turned to

Duncan as something thudded in his chest. Uncertainty? Or the uncomfortable realisation that he'd been wrong?

'If we saddle him up, and you walk beside them both. Your nana's a good enough rider to hold on.' Duncan smiled as Bob nudged Jack's hand. 'I'll give you some snacks to take. The wee lad will be fine.' He glanced up at the long fluffy clouds. 'There's snow coming, but it won't fall until later. You'd probably be safer going on a walk with that donkey than you would going for a long drive.' His green eyes met Jack's and he wondered if Duncan knew about the retirement home too. Had word about their visit travelled this far?

'Ach, lad, I'd love to go,' Edina said, sounding excited. 'I've not been to Christmas Cairn for years, not since your granda passed.' She looked across the fields, her expression filled with longing.

'Sure, okay,' Jack said reluctantly. 'But my grandmother needs to be secured properly, I need to know she won't fall.'

'Aye, lad.' Duncan's lips curved and his expression suddenly warmed. 'I can promise your nana will be fine.'

'Then saddle Bob, please.' Jack sighed. 'I'll walk beside him, take them up.' He squinted into the distance, wondering what Belle would say when she found out what they'd done. Imagining her grin of approval before he blocked it out.

'Really?' Edina's jaw dropped. 'We're not going to Tatherfod?'

'Nope.' Jack shook his head, wondering if he was losing his mind – and was rewarded with a beaming smile.

Jack slowly walked beside Bob as the donkey made its way up the small rocky incline behind the riding stables that Duncan had directed them towards. It was layered with a smattering of sparkling snow, but it wasn't too slippery because it was clear no one had been this way for a while. 'You okay?' he asked Edina, looking up into her face. Her eyes were shining and she hadn't stopped grinning since Duncan had saddled Bob and helped her to climb on.

'Aye, lad,' she said, shaking her head as each of the donkey's steps rocked her from side to side. 'I can't believe I'm here, I thought I'd never come again.' She cleared her throat as she took in the stunning views. They were on a narrow pathway which edged the side of a large hill with a gentle incline. The track was uneven and Jack had to keep checking ahead to make sure Bob didn't accidently stumble on any unexpected rocks. In the distance, he could just make out the outlines of the mountains that flanked either side of Christmas Village. Their peaks were covered in snow and framed by a vibrant blue sky. 'It's not far now,' Edina said, sounding excited. She was holding on to Bob's saddle and her legs were positioned on either side. Jack was walking close to the donkey, with a small drop to his right. His grandmother's other leg, with the injured ankle, was positioned on the left, away from him so he didn't accidently knock it when he walked. 'We could go faster,' she said, wiggling a little on the saddle and nudging the donkey with her knees.

Jack shook his head. 'We'll take it slow. I'd never forgive myself if Bob tripped, or you fell off.' It had been a long time since he'd let himself care about anyone and the thump of pure emotion was unsettling.

Edina chuckled. 'What would Belle say if she could see us now? Think she'll talk to you again when we get back?'

Perhaps for the first time in a few days Belle wouldn't narrow her eyes. Maybe she'd even understand that his heart was in the right place. Jack grimaced, annoyed her opinion mattered. Was he going soft? His dad would have blamed it on her pretty face and told him to watch himself...

'Ach, I see the cairns, lad!' His grandmother bounced in the saddle, stretching her neck so she could see further, and Jack gripped the donkey's reins tighter. Bob had been happy enough on their walk, content to stay beside him. Duncan had given Jack a handful of snacks for the journey. But he wasn't ready to trust the animal entirely, fully aware the right incentive – an Audi perhaps – might have Bob charging in the wrong direction. 'I'll want to get off when we get closer. I don't care about my leg,' Edina said, her voice growing quieter as they turned the rest of the corner to find around forty cairns – piles of smooth oval grey rocks layered into stunning towers, some half buried in snow. The view was impressive and Jack found himself faltering as a memory swept through his mind. Of a woman with long dark hair, laughing as he held out a smooth pebble he'd found. She'd admired it and swept him onto her shoulders so he could place the stone on one of the cairns.

He remembered the sound of her laugh, the light musical tinkle, and felt something move inside his chest. Pain followed – that familiar visceral ache – and he shoved the memory away as Edina directed them to the left. The tower of stones was positioned at the far corner of the other cairns, set away from them. 'My granda started it.' Edina pointed and Bob began to walk towards it. 'I used to come here every year to put a new stone on the pile. It's good to have you here again, lad. Thank you for bringing me.' Her voice was hoarse.

Jack could feel an answering response in his throat and fought to dismiss it. There were so many feelings welling up inside. Feelings he had to ignore so he wasn't blinded by them. 'It's okay.'

His grandmother pressed a hand on his shoulder and squeezed. 'I appreciate you listening, not trying to force me to visit the retirement home – or to move there.'

Jack shook his head without looking at her. 'I told you, I wouldn't do that. I might have to visit you more often though…' He gave her a thin smile. 'And I'll definitely be staying for Christmas this year.'

'Aye, then I'll consider that yet another gift delivered from my Christmas list,' she murmured, making Jack's chest warm.

Jack drove slowly through Christmas Village a few hours later, pulling Duncan's large horse box on the back of the Land Rover. The old man had welcomed them into his house when they'd returned after the slow and bumpy ride, and his wife had fed them huge slabs of Christmas cake and hot tea while Duncan had hooked the box onto the back of the car. Jack had promised to return it tomorrow and Bob had happily trotted inside, probably exhausted after his adventures. It was snowing heavily, and no one wandered out of their shops to stop them to chat as they navigated down the high street.

Jack almost wished someone would; he'd get a kick out of seeing their faces when they discovered Edina hadn't been to visit the retirement home after all. Jack turned slowly into the castle drive, feeling something flare in his chest, imagining Belle's smile when she learned that instead of going to Tatherfod they'd ticked something new off Edina's Christmas list.

Someone – probably Logan – had cleared the worst of the snow from the entrance, and Jack drove quickly towards the back of the castle, suddenly in a hurry to arrive, pulling up outside the garage where a dark grey Toyota HiLux had already been parked.

'Are you expecting visitors?' Jack asked, turning to Edina and noticing her face had paled. 'What's wrong?' He reached out to touch her arm.

'Ach, lad…' His grandmother shook her head, squinting at the castle. 'I'm so sorry. Belle was worried about you taking me to the retirement home today. I gave her the number, it's all my fault.' She swallowed. 'Please don't be annoyed with the lass…'

'Whose number?' he asked. Frowning, Jack shut off the engine and climbed out of the car at the exact moment the back door of the castle swung open – and something in his chest froze.

Because framed in the doorway, standing beside Belle, was his mother.

Chapter Fourteen

Belle could feel the weight of Jack's fury across her back as she stood in the centre of the sitting room, watching him pace the large space without looking at anyone. Tara sat in one of the high-back chairs, her face pale, and Edina sat opposite looking grim, her foot resting on top of the cushion and stool. A large fire blazed in the grate, but even the heat blasting from it didn't have the power to warm the icy atmosphere.

'If you came to see me, you might as well leave,' Jack said, his voice stiff as he stood looking at the jaunty baubles dangling from the branches of the Christmas tree, his hands clasped rigidly at his sides. 'I'm not interested in why you came, I don't want you here.' His voice was gruff.

'Lad, my daughter is welcome to stay in my castle for as long as she likes,' Edina said, sounding distressed. 'I like having you together, I've dreamed of this moment for…' She stopped for a moment and it was obvious she was gathering herself. Tara's eyes widened, and even from where she was standing Belle could see they'd filled.

'This is my fault.' Belle swallowed, feeling awful. 'I rang your mam…' She grimaced. In truth she'd done it out of anger. A need to protect Edina from the wicked grandson who was out to steal her castle. A fantasy she'd created in her mind, it seemed – because they hadn't visited the retirement home at all. Instead, Jack had taken Edina to Christmas Cairn, fulfilling one of the things on her Christmas list. Now she felt wretched.

'This has nothing to do with you.' Jack's voice was tight and Belle felt something squeeze in her chest as he turned to look at her, his eyes flaming blue.

'The lass isn't to blame,' Tara said, standing slowly so she could face her son before wrapping her arms around herself as if she'd lost her nerve. Belle had only spent a few hours in her company and hadn't got to know her well yet. She had the same dark hair as Jack, only hers would have reached her shoulders if it wasn't in a ponytail. Her blue eyes matched his too, but the similarities ended there. She was thin and delicate rather than tall and broad-shouldered. Belle had a sudden urge to protect her from Jack's wrath – she waited to see if she'd have to step in. 'I've been wanting to visit Mam for a while, perhaps to come for Christmas.' She frowned at Edina's blue boot. 'I had no idea she was injured.' She gave her mother a wistful smile. 'Then when Belle called and told me she was hurt and that you were here…' Tara swallowed and Belle could see the emotions streak across her face. 'I've wanted to get in touch for a long time. I've just been…' She shrugged. 'Scared. It's always hard to be here, every time I visit, but especially now you're here too.' She looked around the large room. 'There are so many memories…' Her face filled with pain. Belle could feel it in her chest, wanted to reach out and help. 'I can't believe how much you've changed.' Her voice dropped to a whisper as she took Jack in. 'How much you've grown, how beautiful you are.'

'This isn't going to happen.' Jack's voice was like ice. 'Whatever you're hoping for. The grand reconciliation, forgiveness. It's Christmas – I know that's what you're expecting. That's the fairy tale, isn't it?' His eyes shot to Belle and narrowed. 'You left me without a backward glance when I was five. Let my father take me to London, and I haven't heard from you since. As far as I'm concerned, I have no mother. There's no place for you in my life.' Belle saw Tara take the hit as if it were a physical blow, saw her step back and nod. 'You think you can have no contact for over thirty years and then just turn up because my father's no longer here to stop you. I've got no money to give you, if that's why you came. I believe my father gave you plenty, didn't he?' There was something vulnerable in Tara's face as she absorbed the impact of his words. She turned to look towards the door. Was she really going to walk away?

'Don't leave!' Belle found her voice and it sounded angry. 'Edina wants you here, she needs you – and what about your son? You haven't seen Jack for years – isn't he worth fighting for?' She didn't know where the words had come from. Years of feeling like she'd been abandoned by her father were swirling up inside her, like a volcano bubbling and waking after an eternity of lying dormant. She felt furious and protective. This was the opposite of what she'd wanted. Somehow the man she'd thought was the enemy had become a victim. 'You left him when he was a bairn – aren't you even going to tell him why?'

'I…' Tara opened her mouth and closed it, her eyes shining with unshed tears. Why didn't she speak?

Jack stared at her, watched her swallow, then he slowly twisted his head until his eyes met Belle's. She felt the punch in her solar plexus, could see the vulnerability shining inside the blue. As if someone had reached into his chest and pulled his heart out, laid it bare for everyone to see – and she was responsible.

'I didn't expect this...' she whispered, knowing the words were inadequate. Knowing she'd made a huge mistake. For the first time in her life, Belle realised doing the right thing for the right reason might not always bring the happiness you'd expect.

Jack nodded once before turning on his heel, marching to his bedroom at the edge of the sitting room and quietly shutting the door.

Belle knocked on Jack's door ten minutes later. She held a bottle of single malt and two glasses. Kenzy, Rowan and Isla were due at the castle to make nativity costumes in an hour and a half, but she couldn't settle until she'd spoken to Jack. She squeezed her fingers tightly around the glasses and bottle as she waited for him to respond. When he didn't, she tried the door and walked in.

Jack was sitting at his desk in the corner, working on his computer. He didn't look up when she entered, but she could tell by the way his shoulders tightened that he'd guessed why she'd come. She put the glasses on his bedside table and poured them both a drink, before putting one next to him. 'Annie always told me that when I did something wrong, I should apologise.' She sipped some of the liquid, felt it slide down her throat, but could barely taste it. Her insides felt scratchy and her whole body felt wrong – as if the bones had somehow rearranged themselves, making her stiff and uncomfortable. 'I'm sorry.'

Jack didn't speak, so she moved the bottle next to the paperwork on the desk and turned to walk away. She'd try again later, think of some other way to make him listen. 'Wait,' he murmured, turning to look at her. His eyes were just as blue, but the hints of vulnerability from earlier were gone. He drank the contents of the glass in one and indicated the small leather sofa on his left, spinning his chair so he could face her when she sat. He leaned forwards so his elbows rested on his thighs and she could see the fine hairs on his golden arms, the toned muscles under his skin. He hadn't shaved this morning and there was a rough scrub of stubble across his chin. It made him look less finished than usual, more human – less like the polished lawyer he was. Belle swallowed what she recognised as lust. He twisted around and poured himself another whisky from the bottle, then turned back, cradling the glass between his hands. 'You're sorry…?' he said, his voice toneless.

She nodded. 'I…' She sighed. 'I'd like to say I invited your mam because I wanted to give you a happy ending, a grand reunion.' She nibbled her bottom lip. 'But that would be a lie.' He didn't respond but she saw something flash across his face; she had no idea if it was good.

'Would it?' he asked, leaning further forwards.

Belle fought a desire to fold her arms. She wanted to be open, to show him the truth. His eyes skimmed across her body and she knew he was trying to read her. Was that a lawyer thing, or was it just Jack? And why was her skin now burning from the inside out? 'I was angry when you took Edina to visit the retirement home. I thought…' She dropped her eyes to the floor before lifting them again to meet his. 'If I invited your mam, she'd distract you.' She pulled a face, disgusted with herself. 'I thought she'd side with me, help your nana stay in the castle. It's where she ought to be.' She swallowed again.

'That's your professional opinion, is it?' he asked, his expression unreadable.

'I...' She puffed. 'It feels right, and there's plenty who live in Christmas Village who'll help to take care of her if she needs it. I know I will.' He gave her a blank stare and she blew out a frustrated breath. 'You arrived out of nowhere, you've barely visited or seen your nana before. I thought...' She stretched her neck, knowing she had to tell him, to expose all of the ugly truth. She couldn't live with herself otherwise. 'I assumed you wanted the castle. I believed you were trying to get her out of the way.'

'Ahhh...' Jack watched her face and something about his expression softened. 'I can understand why you might have believed that.' He shrugged. 'I expect I'd have assumed the same. But the castle will be passed to Tara – she's next in line, the beneficiary.' He watched as she absorbed the words, accepted everything she'd believed about him had been wrong. 'Since we've been estranged. I wouldn't expect – or want – any of it.'

'Oh,' Belle murmured, feeling even worse.

Something darted across his face. 'You thought I was after Edina's property, yet you kissed me anyway?' Jack raised an eyebrow.

'Ach... well, maybe not' – she winced – 'at that *exact* moment.' When he'd kissed her she'd barely been thinking at all.

She was expecting anger, or at the very least indignation. Instead a slow smile crept across Jack's face, startling her. 'I always used to believe you could never truly know someone – but you're an open book. You really can't lie, can you?' He shook his head. 'I'll bet you're terrible at poker.'

'Well… I… Yes,' she admitted. There was a rustling from underneath Jack's bed and seconds later Jinx wriggled out. The cat's ears pricked and he regarded them both regally, before sauntering over to Jack and rubbing against his legs. Jack leaned down to scratch the cat's head absently as he watched her. Belle wondered if he realised how comfortable he'd become around animals, how much they were drawn to him – if what Edina had said was right, he was exactly like his mam.

'I'm not going to say I'm happy you invited Tara here. I will say, I appreciate you did it for the right reasons – or at least reasons you believed were right – and that you didn't lie about it.' His forehead mashed. 'It's… refreshing. You like to help people – to put others first – and I don't meet many people like that in my line of work.'

'That's sad,' Belle said, meaning it.

Jack shook his head. 'I've never met anyone who puts other people's feelings before their own, even strangers. Until you, I thought they only existed in fairy tales. You have the perfect name for it, I suppose…'

'Belle.' She nodded. 'My mam used to love Disney movies. She saw *Beauty and the Beast* just before I was born and named me after the heroine. We used to joke about it.'

'Figures.' He laughed. 'You need to know I don't believe or deal in happy endings. I'm going to do everything in my power to stay out of Tara's way if she decides to stay on at Evergreen Castle. That means while we'll do as much as we can to give my grandmother what she wants on her Christmas list, it's not going to include an emotional reunion with my mother.' His eyes bored into hers. 'I'm going to ask you to respect that, regardless of how you feel about it. Is that okay?'

She swallowed. 'You're not going to give Tara a chance to explain?'

'I've no interest in what she has to say.' He sipped the rest of the whisky and Belle toyed with the desire to argue. To tell Jack he was wrong. That everyone deserved redemption. She sipped her drink, letting it burn her throat as she nodded her agreement, unable to say the words aloud. Not helping went against everything she believed in, but she owed Jack now and she wasn't going to try and help or interfere again…

Chapter Fifteen

'It doesn't scream "donkey".' Kenzy frowned at the two pieces of beige costume that Belle had laid out on the dining room table, before fiddling with the inside of its papier-mâché skull, trying to see if she could detach the reindeer's antlers without destroying the head. 'He's the wrong colour for one – and those eyes…' She shuddered, looking at the pinkish pupils someone had painted on. 'All the make-up in the world couldn't disguise those. The animal could have a hangover. Are you sure this costume isn't meant for Halloween?' She took a delicate sip from the large mug of hot coffee Belle had laid out earlier, adding a dash of Edina's single malt.

'I don't think so,' Belle said.

'Which of the wee ones is playing the part?' Rowan asked, looking up from the yellow material she was sewing gold sequins on. It would form the basis of the large pointy star that Isla was building from thick cardboard boxes, which she'd positioned on the square coffee table in front of the fire.

'No one,' Belle sighed, frowning at the strange eyes – could they be repainted, and how were they going to get rid of those antlers? 'I'm trying to persuade some of the children from primary one to do it, but they all want to be in the chorus. I think they like wearing the halos and crowns.'

'Have you thought about using Bob?' Edina looked up from her sewing machine, where she was stitching three pieces of stripy cloth that would ultimately become one of the shepherds' costumes. She'd already finished the first and it hung over one of the high-back chairs. The woman was a whizz with a thread and had finished the angel outfit too. Even her broken ankle hadn't got in the way of her using the machine. Belle could only imagine Lara's face when she took the angel costume into school tomorrow so she could try it on. The children had been working on their lines over the last few days and the whole thing was beginning to come together. Robina had started to murmur about a programme, but Belle hadn't had a chance to think about it yet. She'd tried to refuse when the headmistress had asked her to organise it, but in truth it had been easier to say yes.

'I'm not sure how Ms Sinclair would feel about having a real donkey in the school.' Belle pulled a face. 'Besides, I'm not sure how we'd persuade Bob.'

'Tara could do it. She's got a power when it comes to donkeys,' Edina said quietly, glancing towards Jack. He was seated at the opposite end of the table, reading through the nativity script after Belle had asked him to check it. He'd only agreed to stay because Tara had gone to bed soon after they'd eaten, having barely touched any of her food. 'Tara and I are going shopping tomorrow while you're working. But I was thinking of taking Bob out for a ride on Saturday. Tara's going to join me – Jack, perhaps you'd like to come too?' Edina suggested, using her most wily voice.

'Sorry – I've got plans with Belle on Saturday.' Jack turned to look at her.

'Is that right, lass?' Edina asked, frowning.

'Um…' Belle stumbled.

'We're going to measure the stage at school for the nativity scenery. As it's the weekend we won't have to worry about the kids getting in the way.' Jack gave Belle a piercing look. 'I said I'd help.'

'Aye.' Belle let out a long breath as someone knocked on the front door and Rowan hopped up to answer it. Logan followed her into the dining room a couple of minutes later. His hair was wet from the snow, but he'd removed his coat and held a small wooden structure. As soon as he entered the room, his eyes sought out Kenzy and Belle saw the flare of heat when he spotted her.

Her friend continued trying to unglue the antlers from the reindeer head, but she could tell from the shudder across her shoulders that Kenzy knew Logan had arrived.

'Ach, lad, what's that?' Edina asked, peering out from behind the sewing machine.

'It's a crib for the nativity,' he said, holding it up. 'It needs to be painted. I've sanded it so it won't take long. But it'll need small fingers, it's fiddly work.' He placed it on the dining table beside Kenzy before shoving his hands in his pockets and rocking back on his heels. 'I thought you might like to do it, lass?' he asked quietly, as Belle took a seat on the other side of the table and Isla and Rowan began to talk amongst themselves. 'Since you're good at…'

'Painting nails?' Kenzy asked, turning to blink at him. She looked pretty today – then again, Kenzy always looked gorgeous.

Her make-up had been applied extra carefully and Belle wondered if it had been because she suspected Logan would be here.

'Aye, well…' He shrugged his large shoulders but didn't back away. He had an intensity to his expression now, as if his conversation with Kenzy in the kitchen had triggered something. 'Did you think on what we talked about the other day? I was hoping you'd give it some serious thought.' His eyes caught Belle's before she picked up her sewing and gave it her full attention, pretending not to listen. Kenzy hadn't confided in her about what had happened in the kitchen, but Belle knew it had affected her. Usually her romantic conquests were a major feature of their conversations, and the fact that Kenzy hadn't mentioned it meant this was different.

'Have you changed your mind about coming for dinner?' Kenzy shot back, looking at Logan, her back ramrod-straight. 'Because I kept next Tuesday free. I'm afraid I'm either working late at the salon or out for the rest of the week. My date's cooking me seafood this Saturday.' She raised an eyebrow and it was obvious she was trying to rile him.

Logan gave her a slow smile. 'Still not ready, lass…?' Kenzy's cheeks flushed.

'Do you want a drink, Logan?' Belle asked, keen to smooth over the situation before things got heated. 'We've got Christmas cake.' At the end of the table, Edina's face lit, confirming she'd been listening too. 'I'll bring enough for everyone.'

'Aye, thanks.' Logan nodded, glancing towards the front hallway. 'It's cold outside. I'd appreciate a drink before I leave.'

'I'll help,' Kenzy snapped, marching after Belle as she made her way towards the kitchen.

The basement was freezing and Belle worked quickly, putting the royal blue kettle on the Aga to boil and slicing the Christmas cake Rowan had brought with her. 'Can you believe the jerk!' Kenzy complained, pacing the flagstone tiles in her sky-high heels. She was wearing dark trousers today in homage to the weather, but her soft pink top was silky and clung to her curves. 'I'm just looking for a date – one.' She stuck her index finger in the air. 'He's using relationship words like *commitment* and *serious*.' She drawled each syllable as if it were poisonous.

'What's wrong with that?' Belle asked, putting the small slices of cake on a plate along with some star-shaped biscuits Isla had brought. Just once, she'd like someone to use those words about her. Just once, she'd like someone to put her first.

'We both know where *serious* leads,' Kenzy said with a frown. 'I'm not looking for that, Belle. I've had my mom on the phone today, calling from the beach house, complaining because Dad's decided to get married again. I think that's...' She spread her fingers and counted. 'Wife number seven. She told me my new stepmom's just out of diapers and only a few years older than me.' She rolled her eyes, but something dark flashed in their silvery depths. 'She's threatening to come to stay in Christmas Village to take her mind off it.' She shook her head. 'I wouldn't mind, but they've been divorced for over twenty years. I can't work out why she won't just let him go. But she says she loves him.' She shuddered, then put a hand against her forehead and rubbed. 'Am I getting frown lines?' She leaned closer to Belle and pointed. 'I'm sure all this stress isn't good for my skin.'

'No.' Belle finished cutting the cake and put the remainder back in the larder. She stood looking at Kenzy for a full minute before putting her hands on her hips. 'Are you scared you'll end up like your mam?' she asked gently. 'Feeling too much for someone?'

'No.' Kenzy jerked her chin. 'I'm terrified I'll end up married to some idiot who decides I'm no longer enough when he finds someone prettier, or younger. Treat them mean, keep them keen.' She tossed her head, but something about the arch of her eyebrow told Belle she didn't mean it. 'Don't fall in love and you won't get screwed.' She shook her finger, reciting yet another 'Kenzy mantra'. Belle had laughed in the past, but perhaps they weren't so funny after all?

Kenzy frowned at the slices of cake. 'Aren't we supposed to be making coffee?'

'And tea. I…' Belle blew out a breath. 'Do you think Logan, a man who's barely dated since he lost his wife, would treat you like that?' she asked quietly. 'I've always thought he was a bit like a barn owl, you know, mates for life?' She watched the emotions travel across Kenzy's smooth forehead, watched her consider the question before shaking her head.

'I'm happy, Belle. I just wanted to date Logan because…' She shrugged. 'He's gorgeous and he's there.' Her voice betrayed her confusion. 'But there's a whole world of men out there waiting for me.' She swept her hands out to her sides. 'Why would I settle for one?' When Belle opened her mouth to tell her, she shook her head. 'I'm not taking advice from a woman who hasn't dated in five months. Girl, you're no different from me. There's no space in your life for love. You're too busy saving the world. Why do you think Ted left?'

Belle frowned. 'Because he wanted to move to Australia?'

Kenzy shook her head. 'Or because he knew no matter how hard he tried, you were never going to give him what he wanted,' she said gently. 'Because you're too busy filling your life with everyone else's needs – too busy to fall in love. Too afraid…'

'Well, that's not—' Belle swallowed as Isla called from the top of the stairs.

'Need any help, lasses?'

'Aye,' Belle shouted up, wondering if Kenzy was right.

Jack slumped into a seat at the dining room table without looking at Tara. If there'd been a newspaper handy, Belle suspected he'd have buried his nose in it. Anything to signal he planned to ignore her.

'There are blueberry pancakes for breakfast,' Edina said cheerfully, smiling when he dug a fork into the pile and put three on his plate.

'I love pancakes.' He sipped some of the black coffee Belle had poured and something about his expression thawed.

'Ach, lad, you never were a morning person, even at the age of five. Do you remember, Tara? You used to tickle him to get him to wake up.'

Jack's mother nodded almost imperceptibly. Her eyes filled with emotion as she squeezed her mam's hand, then she watched her son dig into his breakfast. When he'd eaten one of the pancakes, he let out a contented sigh and turned to Belle.

'These are delicious, thank you.'

'You should thank your mam,' she said quietly. 'I was going to make porridge.'

Jack looked at the food again but didn't comment. Belle watched Tara swallow and straighten her rigid shoulders, clearly steeling herself to speak. 'They were always your favourite,' she said softly. 'I used to make them every weekend. Do you remember?'

Jack cleared his throat, his cheeks flushing. For a moment Belle thought he was going to relent and say he did, but his mouth stiffened. 'I remember Dad liking bacon.'

'Aye.' Tara nodded. 'I used to cook that for him too.' Her lips thinned and she sipped her tea. 'We always sat together at breakfast, it was the only meal Lucas could always do.' Perhaps encouraged that Jack had started to eat again, she tried to smile, but Belle could see how much effort it took. Jinx wandered over from where he'd been sleeping in front of the fire, gracing them all with a wide-eyed stare before winding himself around Jack's feet. 'You always had a connection with animals, even when you were wee,' Tara said timidly, her eyes shining. 'Do you have any pets now?' The question was tentative and a muscle in Jack's throat moved. It was as if he were holding on to something that wanted to escape. He put his fork on the table and shoved back the chair.

'Thank you for breakfast,' he said, picking up his half-full plate. 'But I've got some things to do. I'll put this in the kitchen and meet you at the front door in half an hour.' He looked meaningfully at Belle before marching across the room.

Tara stared after him with her heart in her eyes, and Edina placed a gentle palm on her shoulder. 'He sat with you and ate a pancake, lass, I'd call that progress,' she soothed.

'He's never going to forgive me.' Tara sighed. 'I don't blame him either, I'm not sure I could.'

'He's got a stubborn streak all right.' Edina smiled. 'Which just proves he's a Lachlan. You keep trying, lass, you'll get through.'

But as Belle watched Tara's face fall, hearing Jack come back from the kitchen, walk into his bedroom and close the door, she wondered if that were true. Was a man like Jack capable of forgiveness, of letting someone in? Because sometimes keeping people at arm's length was safer and much easier to do…

Chapter Sixteen

Belle led Jack through Rowan's Cafe, stopping now and then to say hello to the customers as she made her way to the main counter. She knew so many people in Christmas Village – so many wanted to stop her and chat, and he wondered if she realised what an integral part of the village she was, how many people's lives she was part of. 'Why don't you sit?' Belle pointed to a vacant table to the left of the shop. 'I'll get coffee and mince pies? I know we've only just had breakfast, but…' She shrugged, pointing to a glass counter that was filled with an array of Christmassy cakes and biscuits. 'I'll see if Rowan can join us in a wee while so we can quiz her about the parties at Evergreen Castle.'

Jack nodded and pulled out a chair, as Belle chatted with the older woman at the counter before placing their order. He'd been keen to get out of the castle after the awkward breakfast with Tara. He'd felt himself relenting, felt something inside him uncurl – a need he'd turned his back on years before. Leaving the room had been the only way to sever it – he wasn't going to let Tara inside his head and had no intention of listening to her excuses. His father had told him everything he needed to know.

He shifted in his seat so he could watch Belle. She looked beautiful. She'd put her hair up but ringlets hung around her face, and she wore jeans and a red sweater which clung to all the right places. He'd found himself tracing the contours of her body, each curve and dip, remembering how they'd felt when he'd kissed her in the kitchen. Had that really been almost a week ago? It was disconcerting how much he wanted to do it again. He dragged his attention up to her face as she approached the table and hung her jacket over the chair.

'Matt's going to bring the drinks and pies over in a minute; Rowan said she can join us in ten. Do you have your nana's list? I thought we could check where we are on everything?'

'Sure.' Jack reached into his pocket, pulled out the envelope containing Edina's Christmas list and put it on the table. Then, on impulse, he took out the two ripped pieces of envelope too. He'd searched his bedroom for them this morning, found them shoved into a drawer, and had decided to show Belle. He wasn't sure why – perhaps all her honesty had started to rub off? He wasn't used to showing his hand, but he wasn't used to feeling like the bad guy either. And after his encounter with his mother this morning, he'd started to feel like he was. Perhaps this would help make up for that.

Belle's eyes widened, and she picked up one of the torn pieces so she could read the handwriting. 'This is my Christmas list,' she whispered, her skin paling as her eyes drew up to search his. 'I put it in the bin in the kitchen.' She paused. 'You were washing up… you took the pieces out?'

'I wanted to see what you'd written,' Jack admitted. 'I didn't know you. I came to see Edina and found a stranger in her house.

I thought…' He shrugged. 'I wondered if it would give me some insight into your motives.'

Belle stared at him, then her shoulders softened. 'I understand,' she said quietly. 'That's no different from me suspecting you of being after Edina's castle, I suppose.' She folded her arms and stared at the ripped pieces of envelope, as a man brought two large steaming mugs and plates piled high with mince pies and giant slabs of chocolate cake to the table. 'Thanks, Matt,' Belle said, waiting until he'd walked away before continuing. Jack watched while she considered what she was going to say next. People were chatting around them and the low buzz of voices in the room was almost hypnotic. 'What did you learn?' she asked, chewing her bottom lip. Jack had been expecting anger, but the calm way she absorbed what he'd done left him feeling uncomfortable. Belle never did what he expected. There was no rule book, nothing to hold on to. Was that why she'd eased her way past his defences? Was it why he'd let her?

'Not much,' he admitted. 'You want your father home for Christmas – is he coming?' His eyes met hers and she looked away.

'No, he's busy – his work can't spare him this year. I'm a big girl, I don't need him.' There was a catch in her voice.

'My dad used to work a lot in the holidays,' he said softly. They'd been close, but their relationship had always been on his father's terms; it had only been since he'd died that Jack had begun to realise that. He pointed to the list. 'You started to write something by number six – "I want someone to" – and you scribbled the rest out. What did it say?' He was being nosy, but Belle knew so much about him now… perhaps he just wanted to even that up. Or maybe he wanted to know her – to understand what she really wanted.

'Why?' She looked surprised.

Jack shrugged. 'Because aside from wanting your dad home, there's nothing here for you. It doesn't add up,' he admitted.

'There's that lawyer again.' Belle smiled. 'Perhaps I have everything I need already?'

He leaned forwards and put his hand over hers. 'What did you want to ask for, Belle?' His voice was low.

She wriggled in her chair. Just the slightest movement, but he noticed. 'I... I don't remember.'

Jack leaned back and folded his arms. What didn't she want to tell him? 'You want someone to buy you diamond earrings?' he guessed, and she shook her head. What had Rosalind wanted for her last birthday? It had been a few months before they'd broken up. 'La Mer moisturiser, a Prada handbag?' Even as he recalled her wish list, Jack knew it would be nothing like that. But why wouldn't Belle tell him, what was she hiding – and why did it matter so much? He'd be leaving after Christmas and had no intention of letting this relationship progress...

Belle sipped her coffee. 'It's not important.' She picked up Edina's envelope and tugged out the letter, reaching over to take her list too, but Jack put his palm over it. He wasn't sure why he wanted to keep it; perhaps because he knew there was something important there. 'So the pink hair's checked off the Christmas list,' Belle said, saying nothing when Jack put her list back in his pocket. 'Feeling useful – your nana's enjoying helping with the nativity, so I'd say that's been done. She got her tattoo.' Her cheeks flushed and Jack wondered if she was remembering their kiss. Heat flooded him and he picked up his coffee and sipped. 'You took her to Christmas

Cairn.' Belle cleared her throat and tapped a fingertip onto the paper. 'Your mam's here already and—'

'The less said about that…' he murmured.

She jerked her head but didn't agree. 'Christmas dinner will be easy; I can cook and get everything ready,' she continued.

'Hopefully Tara will have left by then – she has her donkeys in Skye to get back to,' Jack said darkly.

Belle sighed. 'You were going to mend Edina's tiara.' She patted a fingertip onto the page again. 'You know it fell out of the drawer when she pulled it on top of her? I put the pieces to the left of her earrings so you could find them easily. There's a jeweller in Morridon I know. Do you want me to give you his details?'

'I…' Jack rubbed his chin. 'Do you want to call him? Perhaps we could go and see him together?' he said, wondering why he had. What had changed? *Trust no one.* His dad's words rung in his head – and for the first time he wondered what had made Lucas Hamilton-Kirk so suspicious. Was it his experiences with Tara, or was it just the way he was made? The only way he'd find out was if he talked to his mother, and he'd sworn he wasn't going to do that.

'I'd like that. I'll call him on our walk to school.' Belle smiled as Rowan came to join them.

She pulled up a chair and put the large mug she'd brought with her on the table. It had the words 'Warning: Plays with Knives' printed on it in large black letters – Rowan watched Jack read it and winked. Obviously word had travelled about the non-visit to the retirement home because he'd clearly been forgiven. 'Ach, it's been busy.' Rowan grinned as she looked around the heaving cafe.

'Are you off to the school in a minute to look at the space for the nativity scenery?'

'Aye,' Belle said. 'We're meeting Logan there. I wanted to pick your brains before we went.'

Rowan nodded. 'Pick away.' She sipped her coffee and leaned back in the chair, letting out a soft moan as she rocked her head from side to side. 'I've been decorating cakes all morning, I've got a crick in my neck.'

'There's a heat pad in Annie's house that'll help. I'll pick it up from Isla later,' Belle offered, before turning her attention back to the list. She was always helping people, Jack marvelled, feeling something inside him shift. 'When you first came to Evergreen Castle, you said something about not having been there for years. I heard Edina's family used to have parties – did you go?' Belle asked.

'Aye, lass.' Rowan nodded, her face creasing as she closed her eyes, transporting herself back in time. 'My granda was a good friend of Edina's da. I used to be invited to the parties right up until I was in my twenties. They were glamorous shindigs and the whole village got to go. But after Edina's da died and she married Reilly, they stopped.' She shrugged. 'That lad was a grumpy curmudgeon. I never knew what she saw in him but… love is love and opposites attract.' She smiled, her eyes shifting from Belle to Jack. 'Why do you ask, lass?'

'We thought it might be nice to throw a party on Christmas Eve in the castle.' Jack leaned forwards. 'A surprise. We want to do something special for my grandmother. I didn't even know she existed last Christmas,' he admitted. 'I feel bad about it. I feel worse that I haven't visited before now.'

He could feel Belle's eyes on him, feel heat skid across his skin. She'd worked her way into his head and was burrowing deeper. If he wasn't careful she'd get all the way in, and he wasn't sure if he was ready for those kinds of feelings. Wasn't sure if he was ready to be vulnerable and to open himself up.

'Aye.' Rowan nodded. 'A party on Christmas Eve.' She clapped her hands. 'Now that would be fun. I'll help you with it, lad. I can organise the food and there's a lot in the village who'd be happy to be involved.' Her expression turned wistful. 'Edina's da used to hire a band – there was dancing and carol singers. The old ballroom that's empty now used to be decorated and the villagers would fill it.'

'We could get a band,' Belle said. 'Couldn't we?'

Rowan nodded. 'You want to invite the whole village?'

'Yes,' Jack said. 'Everyone will be welcome but… we'd like it to be a surprise.'

Rowan patted his hand. 'You just leave that with me, lad, I'll speak to a few of the villagers. Matt plays in a band. I'm sure he can speak to them about performing and they could set up in the ballroom.' She tapped a fingertip on her chin. 'There used to be waitresses at the big parties and Father Christmas put in an appearance. Maybe Tavish will help with that? We usually had a reindeer arrive at some point in the evening. There's a herd that wanders the Highlands – last Christmas they were spotted in Lockton. Perhaps someone will be able to track them down.'

'Or the reindeer costume could be used,' Belle suggested. 'We're still short a donkey because Kenzy didn't manage to get those antlers off.'

'Aye, and she tried for most of the night.' Rowan chuckled.

'How about I put together a list of everything we need for the party, and we can divvy up who does what?' Belle suggested.

'Do you have time, lass?' Rowan looked at her carefully. 'Seems to me you've taken a lot on recently. You're looking tired, why don't you leave it to me?'

'Ach, I'm fine.' Belle shook her head. 'Everyone's been helping, and I'm happy to do it. Edina's been so kind.'

Jack watched Belle as she dipped her brow, wondering not for the first time exactly what it was that drove her to do so much for everyone. If he worked out the cryptic wish on her Christmas list, perhaps it would help him understand…

Chapter Seventeen

As they left Rowan's Cafe, Belle dialled the jeweller in Morridon just as Jack's mobile went off in his coat pocket. He picked it out and stopped on the pavement outside Tavish's Corner Shop so he could answer.

'Rachel?' Jack felt a small flutter of panic in his chest. 'Is Dave okay?' His friend's wife rarely called, and only if it had something to do with a surprise birthday party, dinner date, or something similar. The fact that she had, especially in the middle of their divorce, suggested something was very wrong. Belle finished her call and turned, and Jack waved a hand and mouthed that he'd join her at the school.

'He's fine.' Rachel sighed into the phone as Jack watched Belle walk away. He took a step to follow and forced himself to turn his back. 'I'm glad I caught you in between clients. How's the world of divorce treating you?' Rachel asked, her voice smooth. Jack knew she was joking, but Rachel had never made a secret of the fact that she hated what he did for a living. As an architect she was all about building things and had little time for those who, in her opinion, dealt in the dark art of dismantling relationships.

'Good.' In truth, he was enjoying the time away from the office.

'I *am* actually calling about Dave.' She let out a slow breath and Jack nodded, watching as a couple wandered into Rowan's Cafe. His feet were getting cold from standing in the snow and he wriggled them in his boots. 'I wondered if you could talk to him?'

'About?' Jack asked. There was a bench on the pavement not far from where he was standing, and he swiped snow from the seat and sat so he could tug a pen and pad from his pocket. He put the pad on his knee, ready to take notes.

'Our divorce.' Rachel's voice was flat. 'He's... the thing is...' She sighed. 'Dave's not listening to me. I know he talks to you all the time, and I wondered if you could... I don't know – translate what I've been saying into something he'll understand?'

Jack swallowed. 'I'd normally recommend you did this through your solicitor.' When Rachel didn't respond, he rolled his shoulders. 'Mediator?' His suggestion was met with more silence. *Priest. Friend. Dog?* the voice in his head pleaded. He could usually distance himself from things. But getting in the middle of his friends' divorce was difficult. He liked them both, had always thought they were the exception to his relationship rules and expectations.

'I've tried, believe me, but Dave keeps asking *why*.' Her voice filled with frustration. 'I've no idea where he's *been* for the last ten years. As far as I'm concerned, it's obvious.'

'Is it?' Jack asked, scribbling 'obvious' onto the pad, wondering what Belle would do in this situation – knowing already that she'd try to help. It irritated him how often his brain wandered to her, but at the same time he found himself circling back to the question. 'Tell me why it's obvious?' Iver, Tavish's dog, scampered over to sniff his shoes. Perhaps the older man had let him out for a quick wander while the shop wasn't busy? He didn't turn; he wasn't keen to see the scorn in the older man's eyes. When had he started to care about other people's opinions?

Rachel sighed again. 'Dave forgot my birthday last month. We've been together for twelve years, you'd think he'd remember the date by now.'

Jack pulled a face, making a note. 'One forgotten birthday is a divorceable offence?' He kept his tone light. He knew some people expected far too much from a relationship, although he'd never thought Rachel was one of them.

'Make that seven missed birthdays. Add in the fact that he has no idea when our wedding anniversary is either, despite my writing it on the calendar every year.' She paused and Jack heard her swallow. 'He cooks curry.'

Jack tapped his pencil on the page before sitting upright. 'That's good, right?' He'd known of plenty of marriages that had dissolved due to a lack of culinary equality. Okay, so there were a lot of other things wrong with those relationships, but it was a common complaint.

'I've recently developed an allergy to some of the spices used in curry. Even breathing them in can make me sick. I had to hide a stash and lock them away because Dave keeps insisting on cooking it. I've told him a hundred times, but he still ordered an Indian takeaway the other night – thought we could break bread and discuss the divorce over a piece of naan. I think that one moment summed up exactly what's wrong with our marriage.'

'Naan bread?' Jack joked, and wished he hadn't when it was met with a cool silence. He cleared his throat, watching Iver as he trotted back in the direction of The Corner Shop. 'Anything else?' The phone remained silent and Jack tapped his pen on the blank page. He knew it was hard for people to open up and while Rachel had called him, perhaps she was now regretting it. 'Tell me how I can help,' he asked softly, thinking of Belle.

She exhaled loudly. 'I just hit this point. This one moment. I was talking to someone at work and he was telling me how he'd booked to see this new sci-fi movie with his wife at the weekend. He hates sci-fi and she loves it, so he arranged this evening out for her. He put her first. I want someone to do that for me.'

'You want Dave to put you first?' Jack asked, wondering why the wish nagged at him.

'Yes,' Rachel continued. 'I realised in that moment what I was missing. It was like a thunderbolt – out of the blue. I've been unhappy but I didn't know why, and suddenly I did.'

'Why are you unhappy?' Jack asked, sensing his friend wasn't going to like him repeating this conversation. 'Tell me what Dave needs to know, aside from that you want him to put you first?'

She blew out a breath. 'He doesn't know my favourite film, or that when he's not around I crochet cushions, and that I've recently developed an addiction to boiled eggs. He doesn't know what I like to eat, or what I'm allergic to – *obviously* – and he keeps buying biographies for us to read, even though my favourite genre's crime. He doesn't know me. I'm not sure he ever did. And the fact that he's not prepared to listen— Perhaps that's the wrong word…'

'What is?' Jack asked.

'What I think I mean is, he doesn't want to *hear*. Which all adds up to something I don't want to live with for the rest of my life.

He's a good man in his own way and I love him in mine. But he's so wrapped up in his own head that he can barely see past his nose. He definitely can't see me.'

Jack wrote 'nose' and tapped the pen on the paper again, swallowing. 'You know he loves you?' he asked, feeling uncomfortable. Usually by this point he'd be discussing the division of assets. He was well out of his depth. Trying to fix something that was broken was a lot more difficult than helping something chipped to break apart. It was the first time he'd really appreciated how it felt to sit on the opposite side of a relationship. To hear the other side of the story.

'We were talking about listening,' Rachel murmured.

Jack nodded. 'I heard. He doesn't know you. I've got to say, after our conversation I agree.' It was clear from his recent calls with Dave that he didn't understand his wife at all. If he was married to his friend he'd probably be divorcing him too. 'And you want me to explain all this?' He grimaced, wondering how Dave would react to the news.

'I do…' Rachel let out another long breath and Jack slumped on the bench, ignoring the cold seeping into his fingers. She sighed. 'I know it's hard, but I want to put the house on the market so I can start again. I want the divorce to progress. It's…' He heard her swallow. 'Painful, and I don't want to make it any harder than it already is.'

'I can talk to Dave,' Jack promised, wishing he didn't have to.

'He's away for a few days,' Rachel said quietly. 'But I appreciate it, I know it won't be easy.'

Jack nodded. 'I… I'm sorry you're breaking up. I mean that. I've got to say, of all the couples I've met, I always thought you were the one that would last. I never expected…'

'Ah.' Rachel gulped and Jack could tell she was close to tears. 'Thank you. I'm sorry too. But a good relationship thrives on communication. Without it... let's just say, all kinds of things slip through the holes.' She paused. 'That can apply to so many things, you know... Dave mentioned your mother had come to see you.'

Jack swallowed. 'I'm really sorry, Rachel, there's another call coming in. I've got to go.' Then he hung up the mobile and slammed his notebook shut.

Chapter Eighteen

'Aye, it's a complicated fix because of the engraving.' Ernest Mac-Nally, Belle's jewellery contact, twisted Edina's tiara between his nimble fingers, examining the section where it had broken in two under a bright lamp. He wore a loupe on one eye which disappeared into the creases of his eye socket, and he was only a head and a half taller than the glass counter at the far end of the shop, which Belle was currently leaning on. 'This is a very valuable piece. I'd be interested if you ever want to sell…' He nodded curtly when neither Jack nor Belle responded. 'It's a true masterpiece. How did the band get broken?'

Jack shrugged. 'No idea. It's my grandmother's jewellery, I think she dropped it years ago.'

Ernest nodded. 'It'll be expensive to mend because of the complexity of the design – the workmanship is incredible and the emerald is just exquisite. Do you have a budget for fixing it?' He placed the tiara carefully onto a velvet bag which was lying flat on the counter, before glancing at Belle.

'Cost is not an issue,' Jack said gruffly before she could respond. 'Time is though. We'd like it before Christmas and I don't mind paying extra. How long do you think it'll take?'

The man tapped an index finger jammed with multiple silver and gold rings onto his chin. 'I know someone who specialises in jobs like these. I'll need to speak to my contact before I can confirm, but I'd hope to be able to persuade him to fix it within the week – weather permitting.' He looked behind them, out of the wide glass doorway into the high street. 'It looks like we could be in for a break from the snow which will work to our advantage.' It had been snowing when Belle and Jack had driven the twenty minutes from Christmas Village to Morridon earlier, but the roads had been gritted and clear. Since they'd arrived just half an hour earlier, the flakes had all but stopped – which meant the journey back to the castle should be uneventful.

Belle stepped away from the counter so Jack could discuss timings and logistics. She tracked across the red carpet which covered the shop floor so she could look in the glass case that lined the right-hand wall. She studied the jewellery on display. Earrings, rings, necklaces and bracelets gleamed – the red, green and gold Christmas lights and decorations someone had hung inside the case made the gems sparkle. She pressed her nose to the clear glass, wondering how many of her father's orphans could live for a few months on just one of those pieces. She'd never owned anything this beautiful. Her da had sold all her mam's jewellery soon after she'd died so he could buy supplies for the orphanage. Grief, she supposed, and a need to do something positive – but it still hurt that he hadn't thought of her or considered she might want the reminders of her mam. She didn't look up until she felt the warmth of Jack's body at her back and fought a shiver of awareness.

'Pretty,' he said gruffly, and she nodded jerkily. 'You like diamonds?'

Belle shrugged, wondering if the question was a trick. 'Doesn't everyone?' she asked lightly.

He frowned and stared into the cabinet. 'I know I asked about diamond earrings, but were you referring to any other jewellery on your Christmas list?'

Belle shook her head. 'No.' Her cheeks tingled as the flush crept across them. Why hadn't she chucked her envelope into the fire instead of putting it in the bin? Jack was going to ask again and again until she told him what she'd written – and she had no intention of sharing that with him. It was embarrassing and only fit for her eyes. She wasn't even sure why she'd written it. A moment of weakness when she'd been surrounded by the children in her class – when for an instant she'd felt an ache in her chest, a sharp stab of loneliness as she'd been reminded of how alone she was.

On the drive to Morridon, Jack had tried to guess what she'd crossed out again – with ideas ranging from a share portfolio and Liberty scarf to a reproduction Queen Anne chair. He'd only been half joking – which just went to show how little he knew her. What kind of childhood must he have had to be so cynical – was it just his mother leaving? 'Are you finished?' She glanced at the counter where the jeweller was now carefully placing the tiara into the dark velvet bag.

Jack nodded. 'Ernest said he hopes to be able to get it mended within the week – so Edina should have it in time for the Christmas party. Aside from us working out exactly how to make Tavish smile – and I'm convinced that's a lost cause – her Christmas list is pretty much complete.'

Belle noticed Jack didn't mention Tara or their reconciliation, which represented the main thing Edina had asked for. She knew it would mean the world to his nana to have Jack make up with his mother, but had no clue how she'd be able to deliver that. Especially if she kept her promise to Jack and didn't interfere. She sighed. 'There's a costume shop on the other side of the road which I spotted on our walk – I thought we could pop in to see if they have a donkey costume,' she said. 'Kenzy couldn't get the antlers off that reindeer head and she's given up.'

'Ach, the shop is closed. I know because it belongs to my friend. He only opens on Wednesdays, I'm afraid,' Ernest piped up from behind the counter.

Belle frowned. 'We'll have to come back.' Otherwise the nativity wouldn't feature a donkey at all.

'Shall we stop somewhere for dinner, before heading back to the castle?' Jack asked, opening the door of the shop and stepping back so Belle could walk through.

'You trying to avoid Tara?' she asked hesitantly. 'Because Edina told me she and your mam were going to Rowan's, so there's really no need.'

'Perhaps I'm hungry.' He shook his head. 'Perhaps I just want to spend an evening with a beautiful woman, discovering what she wrote on her Christmas list.' He paused as his eyes lit again. 'Pink Ferrari?'

She laughed.

'I saw a few nice restaurants on our walk from the car park. I thought it might be nice to eat out. It'll save us cooking.' Jack put his hands in his pockets. 'Unless you'd rather get back? I know you probably have a hundred things to do – a million, if I know you at all.' There was a vulnerability in his face and Belle found herself shaking her head. She could deal with her to-do list later.

'I like Italian.' Besides, eating out would save them cooking – and it would also mean she wouldn't find herself alone with Jack in the kitchen again, avoiding the temptation of the mistletoe which taunted her every time she walked into the basement. 'There's a small restaurant on the walk back to the car Kenzy's recommended to me a few times,' she said.

Jack gave her his trademark lopsided smile, making something in Belle's body fizz. 'It's a date.' He winked, and she wondered if agreeing to spend more time alone with Jack might just be a very big mistake.

It was still early – just past six o'clock – so the restaurant wasn't busy and the portly owner offered them a cosy table in the far corner of the dimly lit room, close to a roaring fire with a mantelpiece show-casing a collection of Father Christmas ornaments. Belle shrugged off her sweater as she sat, taking a moment to get her bearings while Jack glanced at the menu. 'What's your favourite dish?' he asked, leaning forwards and giving her his full attention. A waiter approached with a barrel of breadsticks, sliced fresh focaccia, olive oil and balsamic vinegar, and placed it on the table between them before whisking himself off.

Belle swallowed as the impact of being so close to Jack did odd, sizzly things to her insides. 'My godmother used to make lasagne. I've always thought of it as the ultimate comfort food. What do you enjoy?' she asked, picking up her napkin and sliding it into her lap, stroking the silky white material. She hadn't been out with a man since Ted had left for Australia and was out of practice with small talk.

'Squid.' Jack grinned. 'My father adored Italian food so he got me into seafood early. By the time I was seven, he made sure I knew how to cook. Calamari is a speciality of mine.' He considered her. 'Tell me about your parents and your godmother, Annie?'

'I'm impressed you remembered,' Belle said, meaning it.

'I have a good memory for names – it helps me at work, it's important to make people feel like you recollect their stories. No good me talking about someone's spouse and getting their name wrong.' He shrugged. 'We were talking about your parents,' he persisted.

'There's not much to tell.' Belle let out a slow breath as emotion stirred inside her. 'My mam died when I was eight.'

'That's tough.' Jack picked up a breadstick and bit into it. 'Was it… expected?'

Belle shook her head. 'A car accident. Faulty brakes – she drove into a boulder travelling back from a visit to the shops to buy some shoes, flipped the car.'

'Was she alone?' Jack asked quietly.

Belle shook her head. 'The shoes were for me, I'd been nagging her for them.' She swallowed. 'I was trapped in the back seat. It's why I'm not so good with small spaces.' Her voice was crisp and factual. It was easier to share when she rose above it, took the emotion out. Besides, it was years ago; she shouldn't feel this pinch in her chest anymore, the sharp ache of guilt. The fact that she did was annoying. 'We lived in Kenya at the time. She was a doctor and volunteered in an orphanage with my da.' She picked up the menu again and tried to study it but suddenly she didn't feel hungry anymore. Even now the feelings she had about her parents confused her. Guilt, grief, yes; but there was anger too. Anger she didn't want to process or examine. 'After she died…' Belle paused as a waiter came to fill their glasses with water and to ask if they were ready to order, but Jack waved him away.

'Go on,' he encouraged.

Belle stared at the menu but the words blurred. 'Da sent me to Christmas Village to live with Annie. She was my godmother and Mam's best friend from medical school. I think he thought I'd be safer here. He was probably right.' She could still remember arriving, being led to a small bedroom with pretty yellow bedding, wondering why she'd been exiled – if her da blamed her for what had happened to her mam. When she'd inherited the house earlier this year, Belle had given up her rented flat and moved in. But she'd changed nothing. She slept in one of the double bedrooms now – at least, she had until the MacGavins arrived – but it had felt wrong to redecorate. Because even after all these years, she didn't feel like she fully belonged in the home she now owned. She already felt more comfortable in Evergreen Castle. Perhaps because she felt needed there?

'Your dad didn't join you when you moved?' Jack asked, his voice low. There was no judgement there, but when she looked up she could see sympathy in his eyes and shook her head, because she didn't want it.

'You shouldn't feel sorry for me. I was well taken care of. Annie was a good woman. She was a doctor like Mam, and her patients lived across the whole of the local area. She clothed me and fed me, made sure I did my homework and went to school, was there if I needed advice.' She put the menu down and knotted her fingers.

'She loved you?' Jack asked mildly. It was as if he could read her – perhaps it was something to do with his job, having to dig deep and discover the truth. Uncover all the lies people told each other – and themselves.

'Of course,' Belle murmured, but even she could hear something sounded off. When Jack simply stared at her, her shoulders sagged. 'She loved me in her own way. The thing is…' She picked up her glass so she could sip some water, trying to keep her hands busy because she knew they'd betray the emotions now surging through her. How could you explain something you didn't understand? She hadn't put it into words before and had no idea why she was doing it now. Perhaps it was just time to acknowledge it. 'Annie loved everybody. She was there for her patients 24/7. In many ways she was exactly like my parents. She had so much to give to so many, but that meant sometimes she got spread a little thin. I didn't want for anything…' *Nothing tangible anyway.*

'And your dad, where's he now?' Jack asked.

'Still in Kenya – saving the world.' She smiled wistfully.

'While you're in Christmas Village, saving your bit of it,' he said faintly and nodded. 'A chip off the old block.'

Belle cleared her throat. 'I don't think you can compare baking cakes for local fundraisers, giving your nana a few things on her Christmas list, or putting on a nativity in the local primary school with what my da does.'

Jack pursed his lips. 'I'm not sure there's a scale for helping people, is there? If there is, I'd be at the bottom of it.' He pulled a face.

'You enjoy what you do?' Belle asked, putting her glass down and glancing at the menu again. She could see the waiter out of the corner of her eye. He was hovering now, and she suspected he'd be back soon to ask for their order.

'I've never thought about whether I enjoyed my job.' Jack picked up a spoon from the table and twisted it so the colourful Christmas lights dangling across the ceiling were reflected inside. 'It's what my dad did – what he wanted for me. I always felt that I was there to help someone when they were caught in a bad marriage. That I was around to rescue them, to make sure no one took advantage, but…'

'But?' Belle asked when Jack lapsed into silence.

'In my job it helps to work in absolutes – black and white, wrong and right, truth and lies. I have to pick a side. It makes things clearer. To be the best I have to be ruthless, I have to go for the jugular of whoever I'm not working for – whoever I deem to be on the wrong side. It's easy to lose perspective and…' He grimaced. 'I just… I don't know, I had a conversation with a friend's wife recently and I'm beginning to wonder if by not seeing the full picture, I'm distorting my view of the world. Look in this spoon.' He put it into the centre of the table so Belle could see. 'Twist it this way and you see one thing, but turn it another and the shapes morph and change. I only focus on one of these reflections. But I know that's wrong because there could be a lot of things in that picture that have been distorted. I've always thought that was right when it came to my job – I'm not there to make judgements, just to get the best result for my clients. But it does make me question some of my choices, and in turn the advice I give.' He was about to say something else, but then the waiter approached the table again and this time Jack focused on the menu so he could choose. Belle did the same and they ordered glasses of wine and food, lapsing into silence when the waiter left.

'Tell me about your da,' Belle asked eventually, wanting to explore a little more of the history of this man. Perhaps understanding his relationship with the person who raised him would help her understand him a little more... and she wanted to understand him.

Jack leaned forwards and steepled his fingers, resting his chin on the tips. 'Lucas Hamilton-Kirk wasn't a particularly kind man. He was critical, demanding, possessive, and it was hard to get on the right side of him. Even if you did, it was impossible to stay there for long.' He smiled and something in it made Belle's insides turn to jelly.

'You loved him?' she asked. It was obvious from the tone of his voice.

Jack nodded. 'He raised me after Tara left... it must have been difficult to take on the full responsibility for a five-year-old boy. But he never complained. He could have sent me away to school, hired nannies to care for me, but he didn't. He wanted to raise me himself. I had the best education money could buy and he pushed me to be the best. Wanted to mould me so I'd follow in his footsteps – which I did. He was my best friend, my biggest fan and my harshest critic. I wanted him to be proud of me and I think he was. I know he loved me.' His eyes met hers and held them. 'I had that. He may not always have shown it in the best way he could, but I knew.' He tapped a finger on his chest. 'Here.'

'Did he marry again?' Belle asked, wondering what that would feel like – knowing you came first for somebody. The waiter brought over two glasses of red wine, and Jack waited until he'd moved away from the table before answering.

His lips thinned. 'My father didn't trust women. He dated often, but he didn't let anyone get close. He always said having me in his life was enough. He never told me the full story of what happened with Tara, but I know it made him wary of relationships.' He picked up his wine and took a small sip. The waiter came back with their starters – fried calamari for Jack and bruschetta for Belle. She ate a mouthful, considering. What he'd just told her explained a lot. Perhaps she could even sympathise with him now.

'Did you ever think that you've only seen one side of that spoon when it comes to your mam?' Her voice was soft. 'Did you ever want to see things from her point of view?'

'No.' Jack's voice turned hard and he leaned back. 'I know what you're trying to do and as I said before, I appreciate it. How much you care for my grandmother, it's…' He shrugged. 'Impressive, even if I can't understand that need you have to help a stranger. But I think some things are best left in the past and my mother is one of them.' He scooped up some of his calamari. 'What about you? You wanted your da to come home for Christmas this year. Why isn't he going to make the trip?'

Belle shook her head. 'He's too busy…' she said, pushing the rest of the bruschetta around her plate.

'Did you ask him to come?' Jack asked quietly. 'Say you needed him?'

'I don't think that would be fair.' Belle's voice came out as a croak. 'He's got a lot of important things to do. An orphanage to run, children to take care of…'

'You're important too, Belle,' Jack said, frowning. 'I'm wondering if somewhere down the line you've forgotten that.'

Chapter Nineteen

Belle looked out of the window of the Land Rover as they made their way out of Morridon, taking the main road towards Christmas Village. She'd lost her appetite at some point during her conversation with Jack. Too many memories of her da, too many conflicted emotions. The food must have been good though, because Jack had finished his calamari and mushroom risotto, then he'd polished off the rest of her lasagne before working his way through a large bowl of Italian ice cream.

'Snow's starting again,' Jack said quietly, as a large snowflake hit the window and the windscreen wiper swiped it away – it was immediately replaced by another. Belle turned back to face the front. The weather was changeable in the Highlands and you couldn't always rely on forecasts – it was clear the mild weather was morphing into a blizzard. There were glittering banks of snow on either side of the road which hadn't started to melt – a build-up from weeks of heavy snowfall. Jack slowed the car as they took a corner. 'I'm pleased we've got snow tyres and chains,' he murmured, slowing a little more when those tyres bumped on a drift. 'You said Edina told you she was out tonight?'

Belle nodded. 'She went to Rowan's with your mam. If the weather carries on like this, they might be better off staying the night.' She pulled her mobile out of her bag and quickly texted Edina to say as much. No point taking risks in this weather. It wasn't a long journey but Rowan lived a few miles outside the village and there was a steep hill on the way back. Her screen lit immediately as Edina responded and she nodded. 'They've already decided to stay the night. Rowan, Isla and Edina have been drinking whisky so it means Tara can join them. Sounds like they're having fun. Apparently the costumes are all finished, so it's just the donkey to sort now.'

'Staying the night was a good call,' Jack said, hunching forwards as the blizzard thickened and it became more difficult to see out of the windscreen. They travelled a few more miles before Belle spotted a set of car lights shining in the distance. She knew this stretch of road, and knew there were no houses anywhere close by. Just fields – which in summer would be filled with grazing sheep and pretty, fragrant wildflowers. They were still a mile and a half outside the village and the snow was falling more heavily. Visibility was getting worse and Belle knew if someone was in trouble they'd need to stop.

'I think a car might have broken down, we have to help.' Belle put a hand on Jack's arm and he nodded.

'I see it.' He slowed the Land Rover as they drew closer, and Belle could just make out the figures of a man and woman standing by the edge of the road next to a large maroon truck. The vehicle was sitting at an odd angle.

'That's Bram and Moira from Christmas Pud Inn,' Belle said, feeling a little panicked as she took in the state of the car. Her stomach always pitched when she saw an accident, and as she grabbed the door handle her hand shook. She opened the Land Rover door before Jack had fully stopped and slid out onto the snow, pulling her coat tighter. She'd worn plenty, but the wind whipped at her hair and icy fingers bit into her cheeks, making her shiver.

'Thank goodness you stopped, lassie,' Moira said, stepping in front of her husband. She was immediately blasted by a gust of wind which thrashed hair around her face. She pushed it back and shouted, 'My da's in hospital – he fell at home and keeps slipping in and out of consciousness. His neighbour rang an ambulance and she called to say what happened, and that he's been asking for me. I need to get to him as soon as I can.' She looked terrified.

'What's happened to the car?' Jack asked, as Belle tracked up to the window, feeling her stomach uncurl when she peered into the back and relief flooded her. Lennie and Bonnie were slumped over in the back seat, wrapped in huge duvets – safe and asleep.

'Ach. The tyre blew,' Bram said, frowning at the car. Belle's stomach lurched as she fought back memories of her mam's accident. Of being trapped. This situation was totally different, she soothed, almost jumping out of her skin when Jack lightly squeezed her shoulder. Had he guessed how seeing the car would make her feel? 'We've been stuck here for twenty minutes,' Bram continued, as Jack left his hand lightly resting on the back of her neck. The contact was subtle but the link comforted Belle and she swallowed, surprised he'd realised how much she'd needed it.

'I'm frantic, lass,' Moira said. 'Scared something's going to happen to my da when I'm not there. I was afraid no one was going to come and help. Da's all on his own in the hospital, the neighbour couldn't stop – my sister can't get to him because she lives too far away and he's not making any sense. I left Logan in charge of the pub, we just grabbed the kids and ran.' She spoke rapidly and her chest heaved as she tried to slow her breaths. 'Bram called the AA but they won't be here for hours because of the weather. The hospital's just past Morridon and I want to get there as soon as I can. It's critical, lass.' She swiped snow out of her face, glancing at the Land Rover.

'Do you think you could give us a lift?' Bram jumped in.

'It'll be a squeeze,' Belle shouted. 'But we can't leave any of you here, you'll freeze.' She glanced at Jack. He was wearing a practical thick coat and boots – a far cry from the outfit he'd been wearing when they'd first met. 'Give me a minute, I have an idea,' she said to the couple, taking Jack's hand and leading him towards the Land Rover so they could talk privately. 'Can we give Moira and Bram the Land Rover?'

'What will we do?' Jack asked, and even through the howl of the wind, Belle could tell he couldn't believe she'd asked.

'Walk,' she said.

'In this?' Jack pulled a face, looking around as the gale battered the trees.

'Aye. I know a short cut, through that field.' Belle pointed right to a small gap in the hedge which lined the road. 'The snow's deep, but if we walk fast enough we could make it in half an hour. There's not much in our way. I used to walk that path when I was a wee lass.'

Jack grimaced. 'Couldn't we take Bram and drive to the castle so he can drop us off – then he could stop on his way back to pick up the others?'

'You heard Moira say her da's injured. He's got concussion. She's scared and there's no telling how long it'll take to drive there and back.' Belle looked up. 'Besides, the snow's getting worse. Christmas Village is in a valley – most years the main road gets cut off at least once. Last year it took just an hour of heavy snowfall to block the main highway, and it took until the next day for the ploughs to arrive and open it again. We can't risk it, Jack. Not with the wee bairns in the car and Moira desperate to get to her da.'

Jack squinted at Moira and Bram and swiped snow off his face. 'I don't like it. Are you wearing enough? Because it doesn't look like it.' He regarded her clothes critically.

Belle had dressed for inclement weather, but not for a hike in a storm. Her snow boots were fine, but she wished she'd worn an extra jumper and a few dozen underlayers, maybe a warmer pair of socks. She could already feel the chill from the wind searing through her coat, and her feet were freezing – but she wasn't going to admit that to Jack. Her need was less great than the McGregors' – besides, she'd be fine if they walked. 'There's another coat and a torch in the boot of the Land Rover – if we wrap up, we'll make it fine. We need to get moving though.' She nodded to the car and then back in the direction they'd travelled in. 'There's no telling if the road will get blocked further down if we wait.' Belle didn't wait for a response; she went over to Bram and Moira and told them the plan, then returned to the Land Rover and opened the boot, pulling out the thick coat she'd seen and a large torch, before handing the coat to Jack. There was a thin orange scarf tucked in the boot too – probably Edina's – and she wrapped it around her neck to protect it from the wind. 'Ready?' she asked, trudging to Jack and switching on the torch. They'd need it to guide them; the moon was hidden by clouds and the fields would be almost pitch black. 'Can we give Bram the keys?'

Jack stared at her for a few moments before taking the extra coat off and wrapping it around her shoulders. Belle could tell he was torn between giving in and trying to come up with another solution. In the end, he nodded and reached into his pocket to give Bram the keys. 'We should help move the kids,' he said softly, gesturing to Bram's car before pulling the passenger door open. He reached in and carefully picked up Lennie, making sure the duvet was wrapped around the sleeping child as he carried him to the Land Rover. Belle felt her chest fill – until that moment she wasn't entirely sure what kind of man Jack was. The kind of man who'd leave a family by the side of the road to fend for themselves, or the type who'd put himself in danger for others. Something clicked inside her – a feeling she knew signalled danger. The first step to letting someone in, to trusting them. A sure sign she was going to get hurt. She helped Moira pick up supplies from her boot – clothes in case they had to stay in Morridon and snacks for the kids – while Jack helped Bram to transfer Bonnie. Neither child woke and soon they were strapped in the back seat, wrapped in their warm duvets. The snow was getting thicker and Belle could feel the chill searing through her clothes.

'We need to leave,' she said to Jack, pointing to the field. 'Bram and Moira have to get going, and if we don't move soon we're both going to turn into snowmen.'

Jack nodded, looking unhappy. He turned to wave at Bram as the man thanked them again and climbed into the driver's side. They watched the Land Rover pull away and do a three-point turn before disappearing back the way they'd come. Then they walked towards the gap in the hedge and slipped through it.

Belle lit the ground with the torch – she was going to have to rely on all her senses to get them to the castle. The snow was so thick, even with the bright light it would be difficult to get her bearings. She knew if she followed the hedge that lined the field, they'd get to a kissing gate eventually – through that they'd enter another field, and they'd have to hike through one more before they reached the castle grounds. It would be faster to head directly across this field, but Belle didn't want to risk it. It would be too easy to lose her bearings and they might have to start all over again by following the hedge. They couldn't afford to waste time. Hypothermia was a very real possibility if they didn't keep moving. She shivered as another blast of wind swept snow into her face and some of it trickled through the thin layer of scarf before sliding down her neck. The dump of wet ice set off a torrent of goosebumps and an involuntary shudder racked her chest. Jack said something Belle couldn't hear because of the wind. He tried again, frowned and shook his head, grabbing her gloved hand so he could pull her along beside him. Belle shone the torch on the ground, lighting up about a metre of pure white. There were briars and small shrubs buried in the ice – twigs poked out at intervals which they had to dodge. Belle felt like she was picking her way through a minefield. She stumbled on a hard bump hidden under the layers of snow and Jack caught her before she fell into the cold. He squeezed her hand and she pointed the torch forwards. She had no clue how long it would take to reach the gate and tried to speed up, aware the faster they walked, the harder any fall would be – and the more it would hurt. They marched for what was probably only another few minutes, but felt like hours. Then Belle saw the kissing gate in the distance and tried to walk faster, but Jack held on to her hand, easing her back and slowing the pace.

They made it through the kissing gate and into the next field, which was identical to the last – snow and angular drifts dotted with shrubs and briars. There was a tree somewhere on their right – Belle knew it was there because she'd picnicked under it a few times, but she could barely see even a few metres ahead. 'We're going to have to walk through the centre of the field. I don't want to be out here any longer than we have to, and if we follow this hedge it'll take too long,' she shouted. Jack put a hand against his hood where his ear would be and she knew he couldn't hear. She pointed forwards with the torchlight and inhaled another blast of gale, trying not to choke on the snowflakes that swept into her mouth, riding the back of the storm. Her tongue was frozen and her eyelids were carrying around twenty pounds of snowflakes. She sped up and tugged Jack forwards, blinking, looking at the ground and praying she was leading them in the right direction. Would they make it, or were they lost? Belle began to question her decision to give Moira and Bram the car. Had she tried to do the right thing again and messed up? She chewed her lip as she realised she had no idea where they were. She could see nothing but snow – no markers, nothing to guide them, not even the slightest hint of the moon. She shoved the torch in her pocket and tugged her mobile out, suddenly realising she could check their location on a map. But the screen was blank.

'Your battery's probably dead – it's too cold.' Jack leaned over so he could talk in her ear. 'Mine's the same. We're going to have to rely on our sense of direction.'

'Good luck with that.' Belle grimaced, taking the torch out of her pocket again. That was fine if you could see where you were headed, but they were walking blind. Everything looked the same – the ground, hedges, fields. She stumbled, feeling sick. She'd put Jack in danger, convinced him she could do this, and now she had no idea where they were. There were no visible lights; everything was layered in snow. She stopped so she could swivel around, searching for markers, anything she might recognise. Then she heard a noise and jerked her head, expecting to find a yeti or a herd of wild reindeer about to charge. Instead she saw a small, plump, four-legged creature with pointy ears. Was that...?

Bob was staring at them, honking into the wind. Jack must have seen him too, because he began to walk towards him, tugging Belle. She could barely feel her feet and stumbled as they drew closer, losing her footing when one leg caught in a tangle of brambles, toppling head-first into a drift. Jack tried to hold on, but gravity was too strong and her glove came off in his hand. Cold burned her cheeks as she hit the snow at an odd angle and she swiped at the ice, grimacing as frost bit into her bare fingers. Her left arm hurt where she'd fallen on it. 'Eejit!' she grumbled to herself, annoyed she'd tumbled. She tried to get up and fell again – Jack knelt so he was close, his breath a welcome source of heat.

'You okay?' He helped ease her glove back over her freezing fingers.

'I'm fine, aside from frostbite.' Belle wriggled her hand as Jack helped her upright. 'How's Bob?'

'Better than we are.' He moved until he was close enough to pat the donkey on the back. 'Think he knows his way to the castle? I'm guessing he's the closest we have to satnav.'

'Aye.' Belle nodded. 'Come rain, snow or shine, he always makes it to his barn at mealtimes.' She watched as Jack leaned down so he could look into Bob's eyes. They must have had a moment, because the donkey dipped his head and turned.

'Do you want to ride him?' Jack asked. 'It'll save you falling.'

She shook her head. 'I can make it on my own.' Jack put his arm on Bob's back, holding tightly to Belle's hand. She wanted to close her eyes to stop the icy shards of snow from flying into them. But she'd fallen once and didn't want to risk doing herself a worse injury. Her arm ached but the pain wasn't serious. Her feet were numb, and she promised herself she'd buy better boots and warmer socks if they made it home.

'That way?' Jack asked, pointing to a gap in the hedge a few metres ahead.

'No,' Belle shouted, pointing forwards. 'That'll take you to the high street. We should keep going and follow Bob.'

They tramped for what felt like hours but was probably ten minutes. Then Belle saw a shimmer of light in the distance, and knew it came from the windows of Evergreen Castle because of the angle and height. She could barely feel her body now; it was as if the blood in her veins had slowed as she froze. A few metres more and Belle spotted a metal gate. She knew that gate, and knew it led into the castle grounds.

Once Bob was safely locked in his barn, tucking into his evening meal, Belle and Jack stumbled through the back door of the castle into the large boot room that led to the ballroom. It was freezing and Belle had to pat her limbs to get them to work, aware she needed to undress. Her teeth were chattering so hard she was scared they'd fall out. She tried to pull her gloves off, but it took a few attempts because her fingers wouldn't cooperate. It took even longer to undo the zip on her coat, and she only got it halfway undone before giving up. Jack stripped off his jacket and shoved it to the floor. His boots came off next, but Belle could see the bottoms of his trousers were soaked and wondered if his legs were as cold as hers. Exhaustion claimed her as she watched Jack undress, leaning her shoulder against a wall. She planned to push off her boots as soon as she could summon enough energy – then she'd crawl to the sitting room and wrap herself in Edina's warm tartan blanket. She closed her eyes, visualising the moment she'd fall onto the squashy sofa. Hopefully Jack would take over building a fire. She really had to move…

'Are you okay?' Jack pushed the hood from Belle's head and frowned when she didn't respond. 'Cold?' he asked, and her teeth chattered.

'T-too c-old to und-ress.' Her words must have made sense because Jack helped her unzip both coats and pulled them off along with the scarf. Snow had soaked her neck, drenching everything underneath.

Jack looked at her waterlogged clothes and shook his head. 'It's too cold for you to undress here, you're sopping. I'm going to pull off those boots, then I'll get a fire started in the sitting room. Can you walk?' His forehead creased when she didn't respond. He nodded then knelt and tugged off her boots while Belle gripped his shoulders. When he tried to put his arms under her legs, she shook her head.

'I'll walk.' A current of heat whipped through her as he stared into her eyes. Just as she was about to tell him she'd changed her mind, he rose, opening the door into the ballroom and leading her through it. Jack grabbed a blanket as soon as they reached the sitting room and wrapped it around Belle's shoulders before striding to the fireplace. She snuggled into the soft wool and slumped on the sofa, leaning back on the plump cushions and closing her eyes. The next thing she knew, Jack was pushing a glass of whisky into her hands and the fire was roaring – flickering giant orange and red flames. He'd dimmed the lights but put the Christmas tree on.

He ran a hand through his damp hair as he stared at her. Belle still couldn't feel her hands but didn't want to move closer to the fire – she didn't want to move full stop. She sipped the whisky, enjoying the heat as it slipped down her throat.

'You still look cold,' Jack said, studying her. 'And you're very pale. How do you feel?'

'I can't feel my feet – are they still there?' Belle asked, trying to inject some lightness into the oddly charged atmosphere.

'Let me check,' he murmured as his lips curved. 'If you're making jokes, you're not suffering from hypothermia, which is good news.' He grabbed the stool Edina used to rest her foot on and tossed the cushion onto the sofa next to Belle. Then he positioned it in front of her and sat, spreading his legs until he was comfortable. He picked up her right foot.

'You don't have to do that...' Belle tried to stop him, but Jack pushed her hand away.

'It's either this or I'm going to dump you in a hot bath,' he said softly. 'You look whiter than some of the snowmen I've seen the kids in the village building. You need help thawing out. I've been told I have magic fingers, guaranteed to warm even the coldest feet.' He wriggled each digit. When Belle snorted, he gave her another lopsided grin. A serious Jack was attractive, but a playful Jack was downright irresistible.

Belle leaned back in the chair, feeling her cheeks heat as Jack wrapped a large hand over the tips of her toes and begin to massage them through the sock. She wasn't used to accepting help from people – she was a giver, not a taker, and the sensation of having someone offer comfort was strange. She almost felt guilty. She tried to sit up but Jack mouthed the word 'bath' – the idea of sitting naked in a tub while he stood on the other side of the door filled her with a longing so strong it scared her, so she relaxed back onto the seat. 'This is soaked.' Jack whipped her pink sock off and placed it carefully on the floor. Belle's feet looked pale against his tanned hands and she watched as he pushed his thumbs into the pads. Pressing on the soft skin and working his fingertips into her muscles, he sent unexpected flickers of heat charging up the insides of her calves and thighs. Who knew a foot massage could be erotic?

Belle swallowed. 'You seem to know what you're doing.' Her voice came out husky.

Jack smiled. 'I had a girlfriend who taught reflexology; she showed me a thing or two.'

'What happened to her?' Belle asked. Idle chit-chat was good – it would keep her mind occupied so it didn't drift to wondering what those magic fingers might explore next.

'She left me for a massage therapist. He was more in tune with her needs, apparently.' Jack shrugged, not looking the least bit put out. 'But I learned how to do a few things before that. If I touch you here, for instance…' He pressed a fingertip into the arch of her foot and gently tickled the skin. 'You'll drink that whisky I poured you.'

Belle half snorted, half laughed in surprise. 'I will?'

He nodded and she grinned. Seduced by his playfulness, she picked up the glass and swallowed the rest. 'Told you I was good,' Jack said as he continued to work his magic, massaging each of her toes in turn, spending a little extra time on the smallest. 'And if I press this in exactly the right location, you'll tell me all your darkest secrets.' He rolled the toe gently between his fingers.

'I have secrets?' Belle tried not to giggle.

Jack's fingers pressed a little harder and she fought a groan as heat shot through her. He shook his head, his blue eyes lighting with humour. 'Obviously not,' he murmured. 'As I suspected, you're an open book. Aside perhaps from that one thing on your Christmas list… But I'm sure we'll get to that. If I tickle here…' He feathered his fingers across the sole of her foot, sending a spark of need through her.

Belle mimed zipping her mouth and Jack raised an eyebrow. 'A dare, I like it. You should never challenge a lawyer, we like to win.' His hand slid further up her foot, playing with her heel, his fingertips teasing the skin around her ankle, pinching and pressing, setting off fireworks up the inside of her leg. 'And we're not afraid of fighting dirty,' he murmured. Belle bit down on her bottom lip, forcing herself not to moan as the sensations ripped through her. She'd been to bed with people and been less turned on than she was right now. What was it about Jack – was it just those clever fingers, or something to do with him?

'Are you warm yet?' Jack asked. 'Your skin has a nice flush.' He scanned her face and Belle guessed he knew exactly what he was doing to her. He picked up her left foot and rested the one he'd been working on against the solid muscle of his left thigh. He tugged off her other wet sock and set gentle fingers to her skin, pressing and stroking, circling rough fingertips, finding erogenous zones Belle hadn't known existed. She just managed to stop herself from squirming on the sofa – or worse, from leaping off it and wrapping herself around Jack. What had got into her? Her nipples had hardened, heat pooled in her centre and if she tried to stand now, she'd probably melt into a puddle at his feet.

'You're shaking again.' Jack frowned, his fingers pausing their erotic dance across her soles. Belle opened one eye as he studied her. She pulled herself into a sitting position and tried to tug her foot back, but Jack held on. He stared at her, letting his eyes run from her cheeks to the damp sweater she was still wearing, stopping at her chest. 'Are you still cold?' he asked. 'You look cold – would you be more comfortable if you took off those wet clothes?' This time his voice had a husky quality and she swallowed.

'I'm…' Belle cleared her throat. 'Can I have more whisky, please?' Jack stared at her for a beat, then nodded and walked to his bedroom. The request had been a deliberate attempt to dampen the sexual charge humming between them. What had happened in the last twelve hours? Why had so much changed? They'd been for coffee, to a jeweller, for dinner, rescued a family – and now Jack was seducing her with something as simple as a foot massage. She normally kept men at arm's length, didn't allow or want them burrowing into her carefully constructed life. But tonight she'd revealed more about herself than she had in years, more than she ever had to Ted – and she wasn't sure why. She still wasn't sure if she could trust Jack: to tell the truth, or with her heart.

He came back from his bedroom with the bottle of single malt and refilled her glass before handing it to her, refilling his too and drinking it in one swift gulp. Then he dropped onto the stool opposite again. His trousers were still damp. He'd removed his coat and jumper, but the long-sleeved T-shirt underneath had moulded itself to his chest, highlighting solid planes of muscle. What would he look like under that shirt? Would his skin be tanned and firm? She chewed her bottom lip as her attention shifted lower. 'Aren't you cold?' she asked, finding her voice.

'Not anymore,' Jack said, his voice even huskier now. Belle looked up. He'd been watching her watching him. His eyes were filled with heat and a want she hadn't expected. 'I need to touch you,' he said. He sounded surprised and she wondered if he was.

Belle nodded, then she drank her whisky in one, put the glass on the coffee table and climbed into his lap.

Chapter Twenty

Jack had been expecting Belle to brush him off, or to leap up from the sofa, shake her head and disappear upstairs. He hadn't expected to find her warm, pliant body in his lap. He wasn't complaining but he was surprised, so it took him a few seconds to react. In those moments she must have decided she'd made a mistake because she started to back up, began to retreat, mumbling something that sounded a lot like an apology.

'Oh no,' he said, grabbing Belle's hand. 'This is exactly where I want you. I was surprised, that's all. It's not every day a woman throws herself at me.' He grinned, making it clear he was joking, and stroked a hand down the edge of her cheek. 'I told you I had magic fingers. This is exactly what I had planned,' he said tenderly, letting the tips of his fingers slide down the side of Belle's neck. Her skin was smooth but it felt cold and a shiver racked her body. The tartan blanket Jack had given her earlier had slipped from her shoulders when she moved and he wrapped it around her again. 'I think we need to get you out of those wet clothes,' he said again, dropping his eyes to her woollen sweater. He'd helped her remove the two coats and that silly orange scarf in the boot room, but had been too intent on getting her warm – and then on getting his hands on her – to consider whether she should take off anything else. Perhaps he'd been too worried she'd disappear upstairs into her bedroom and he wouldn't see her for the rest of the evening if he'd insisted she undress. And he'd wanted to spend the evening with her. Hadn't wanted it to end. The thought made him uncomfortable but he didn't want to think about that now. Didn't want to hear his father's voice in his head telling him he was a fool for letting any woman get so close. Physically, yes – but this one was burrowing deep into his head, making him question things he'd always believed. Showing him yet another side to the story, like Rachel had talked about. A side where people weren't just out for what they could get…

He dropped his fingers to the bottom of Belle's jumper and waited for her to tell him to stop. When she didn't, he lifted it up and over her head, then dropped it next to her socks. She wore a long-sleeved navy T-shirt with a V-neck. He'd seen it hours before in the Italian restaurant, but then it hadn't been damp and it certainly hadn't been clinging to her skin, highlighting the outline of her body and all those seductive curves. He swallowed as his eyes met hers. She looked pensive, but not conflicted – and he realised despite her obvious reservations that she wanted this to happen as much as him. She lifted the shirt without waiting for him and pulled it off, putting it down carefully. Her skin was paler than her pink cheeks and she wore a simple navy blue bra which perfectly highlighted the swell of her small breasts. Jack swallowed before reaching down to pull his shirt off too. Now they were the same – two half-dressed people staring at each other. Jack had been raised to keep a woman at arm's length, to protect his heart – and in turn his perspective – and to make sure no one ever got the better of him. But he knew he was out of his depth with Belle. Knew he had feelings he couldn't explain, rationalise or control. Which meant he should probably get up now, put her carefully back on the sofa and *run*.

Then Belle leaned closer and put her hand on his shoulder, triggering a wave of heat that coursed through his body, almost undoing him. She set her lips to his – a temptress now, exposing a side to her he hadn't known or expected. He liked it though – liked the fact that her need was obviously as great as his. In that they were equal and there was no misunderstanding the power of desire. Her kiss was tentative at first; she stroked her tongue against the seam of his mouth until he opened it and let her in. The kiss started slow – a tentative exploring of tongues, a gentle getting to know each other. The equivalent of kissing small talk, he supposed – and he was still in control so rejoiced in that one small thing. Because control was the lynchpin of everything his father had taught him – control he must preserve above everything else. When they'd kissed before in the kitchen, the feel of Belle's lips had imprinted itself onto Jack's brain – so when he ran his hand up the side of her neck and pushed his fingers into her long silky hair so he could deepen their kiss, he knew exactly what to expect.

But it still surprised him.

The heat was fast and as powerful as a force-ten gale – need swept through him like nothing he'd ever experienced. Belle's body was light and dainty but she packed a powerful punch and gave as much as she got. She leaned forwards and pressed herself into him, almost rocking him backwards off the stool. He just held on, wrapping an arm around her back as he tried to steady them both, tried to slow things down. If they continued like this, they'd be on the sofa and this would be over in a few fast minutes. But he wanted to savour her, wanted to enjoy the way it felt when she touched him; the way his heart thundered in his chest and his blood ran so hot he half expected steam to bubble from his ears.

'Bed.' He managed to say the word, breaking off from their kiss for a second, knowing he wasn't capable of more. Speech eluded him as desire turned into desperation, and he knew his legs would cease to work soon. He pressed a hand to the wooden coffee table beside him and managed to push himself upright with Belle still holding on. She wrapped her legs around his hips, pressing her warm centre to his core. He had to stop for a moment, to gather control, and then her arms sealed themselves around his neck and he knew he had to move. Jack shuddered as Belle pressed slow open-mouthed kisses to the edge of his neck. An inferno erupted inside him and he closed his eyes, trying to gain some semblance of control. Then it was all about speed as he stalked across the sitting room, still holding Belle tight. He launched himself into his bedroom, shutting the door and laying her down on the bed. She didn't let go of him so he tumbled over her as she set her palms to his chest, and they continued to drink each other in, losing themselves in a passion Jack had never before sought or felt. He was frantic, tortured, inflamed to a desperation that ripped at his control. Belle reached down between them, trying to undo the buttons on his trousers as she crushed herself into him. 'No,' he murmured. 'Not yet.' If he undressed now, he wouldn't be able to stop himself. He knew that with a bone-deep certainty and wondered how – he'd never lost control in his life. He'd never let himself.

Then his hands were on her waist, dragging her up so he could undo the clasp on her bra as her fingertips strayed to his jaw and she deepened their kiss, torturing his tongue with a ruthlessness he hadn't known she was capable of.

'Oh God,' she groaned, pushing herself up into his hips. He held on, dropping his head so he could guide his mouth to her perfect nipples, devouring her as she tried to lift herself up to meet him. 'This is crazy,' she whispered, but he didn't agree. This was way more than crazy – this need was paralysing. A loss of control he had no compass for. He couldn't wait any longer, so he reached down to shove at the zip on her trousers. But Belle took over, lowering her hands so she could do it herself, shrugging them to her thighs where they got trapped. They were still wrapped around each other so Jack pushed himself up, yanking at the buttons of his own trousers before yanking them off. Then he helped Belle tug off hers along with her knickers, tossing the bundle of clothes to who knew where. Now they were both naked, he eased himself over her again as the world around them dulled. He looked into the dark depths of her hazel eyes and drank her in, transfixed. He felt a tremor run through her, felt that same need mirrored in him. Then they were kissing again and her palms were at his shoulders and he was sliding slowly inside her, fighting for control. The feeling was surprising, exquisite, exhilarating as they rode each other – moved together as one. Jack could feel something loosening inside him, could feel emotions starting to emerge, and he fought them, fought to keep them tied down. Knowing, even as he did, that he was already lost.

Chapter Twenty-One

Belle felt her cheeks heat as Jack placed a gentle kiss on her lips before putting a fresh mug of black coffee in front of her at the dining table. Parts of her she'd forgotten existed ached this morning, and she had to fight back a contented smile. Jack was a sensual and attentive lover and she'd seen a whole new side to him last night. A side she liked far more than was wise. He'd be leaving for London in just over a week, and after that he'd probably forget she'd ever existed – which was the story of too many people in her life.

'Espresso machine?' Jack asked, sliding into the chair beside her and grabbing a slice of toast.

He'd insisted on making her breakfast this morning, giving her time to languish in bed. She was wearing PJs that she'd grabbed from her bedroom, while he'd thrown on a pair of low-slung jeans and a navy T-shirt which did all sorts of zippy things to her insides. The man was simply beautiful, and not just on the outside. She'd have to be careful if she was going to protect herself from getting hurt when she was left behind. 'Sorry?' Belle asked, sipping some of her coffee in an attempt to wake up. They hadn't got much sleep, which might explain why she had no idea what he was talking about.

His eyes sparkled. 'Your Christmas list – did you ask for a coffee maker?' He nodded at her drink. She'd all but devoured it and was ready for at least another three. 'Or a slave to keep your mug topped up?' He quirked an eyebrow.

'A slave would be nice.' She grinned back and he leaned in for another hot kiss which seared her through to the bones. 'I do have my eye on a gifted masseur – you know, the type who's guaranteed to curl your toes.' She winked and he poured more coffee. He seemed so much lighter this morning, as if a weight had been lifted from his shoulders. She liked this new Jack – his openness and teasing nature. He wasn't watching everything with his eyes narrowed, as if he expected someone to turn around and stab him in the back.

There was a sudden slam at the front of the castle, signalling they were no longer alone, and Jack placed another quick kiss on Belle's lips as they heard footsteps. 'Hello?' a voice shouted, and Belle sprang to her feet as Edina came zigzagging in using a cane for support. 'I'm fine, lass.' She waved a hand at Belle, indicating that she should sit. 'This wee cane Tavish brought from his shop makes life so much easier. My ankle's a lot better and walking's not as difficult as it was.' Tara followed her mam into the room, carrying a huge bag with a white sequinned sleeve poking from the top in one hand and Edina's sewing machine in the other.

'I wondered if you'd be up,' Tara said, giving them both a speculative look as she put the baggage down. Belle sipped more of her coffee, wishing for a clearer head. It was obvious Jack's mam had a good idea of what they'd been up to, and she felt her cheeks burn.

'Do you want something to drink?' Belle asked, but Edina and Tara shook their heads. Jinx appeared from underneath the sofa and ran up to Tara so he could brush himself against her ankles. When Jack cleared his throat, the cat looked torn.

'Nae, lass, Rowan fed and watered us before we left – I don't think either of us could handle another thing.' Tara's blue eyes fixed on Jack. 'Did you have a good evening?' she asked.

'Yes.' Jack's voice was clipped.

Tara put her hands in her pockets as her back stiffened. 'We finished the costumes.' She dipped her head towards the bulging bag on the floor. 'Making them reminded me of when you were three – I put a Spider-Man suit together out of a pair of my red dungarees.' Her face took on a dreamy quality. 'You wouldn't take it off, or let me wash it. I had to sneak it into the machine when you were asleep.'

'I don't remember,' Jack said abruptly.

Tara blinked. 'I suppose it was a long time ago,' she said faintly.

'I remember it, lad.' Edina gave Jack a disappointed look. 'You loved that suit – then your da took it from you one night because he said you were too old to dress up. You cried for two days.'

Jack frowned. 'I don't remember that either,' he said, but this time he looked surprised.

'Did you have a nice time last night?' Belle asked, determined to change the subject.

'Aye.' Edina dropped down onto the sofa and pulled over the stool Jack had been sitting on last night, resting her ankle on it. She rubbed a hand across her forehead. 'We may have consumed a little more single malt than I'm used to. But all the costumes are finished, aside from the wee donkey. I dinnae think even Santa would be capable of turning that reindeer outfit into anything else.' She glanced at her daughter. 'Tara thinks she might be able to persuade Bob to appear in the nativity. She's going to spend a little time with him later, see what she can convince the lad to do.'

'That would be brilliant,' Belle said, aware of the way Jack's body had stiffened as the conversation had progressed. Why couldn't he give his mam a chance, meet her halfway if she was prepared to make an effort? If she had just one afternoon with her mam or da, she'd relish every second of it. Maybe the saying was true – you didn't know what you had until it was gone.

'Perhaps you'd like to join me, lad… your nana says you have a rare gift.' Tara looked at her son. The hope on her face was tangible. He lifted his eyes to meet hers and he almost looked tempted. But then Belle saw the shutters come down and his expression harden.

'I'm afraid I don't have time,' he said gruffly, standing and gathering their breakfast stuff. 'We're going to the pub, then I promised Belle I'd help her with a few things. I told you that yesterday.' He turned and stalked back towards the kitchen, leaving the three of them staring after him.

Tara's mouth twisted and she looked at Edina. 'I tried. There's really no point, the lad doesn't want to know.' Her shoulders slumped as she leaned down to stroke Jinx. 'Who can blame him? I did leave when he was five. As far as he's concerned, I abandoned him – and in many ways, he'd be right.' She shook her head.

'That's not the full story. Don't give up, lass,' Edina said gently.

Tara let out a heavy sigh loaded with emotion. 'I don't know, Mam.' She glanced at Belle. 'I wouldn't go if you weren't being so well looked after. But the lad really doesn't want to listen and I'm making him unhappy.' She swallowed. 'If I pack now, I could be back at the sanctuary tonight. I've got a friend looking after the place as a huge favour, but I'm guessing he'd be happy to get back to his own house.'

Edina tapped her cane on the floor. 'You need to talk to Jack, lass. Insist he listens.' She took a deep breath and swallowed, perhaps so the next time she spoke her voice would sound less harsh. 'I know you don't find that easy. But if he doesn't know the full story, he won't know all the facts,' she soothed. 'Running away…' Her mouth pursed. 'You'll be doing the lad a disservice. He's a good boy.' Her eyes flickered to Belle. 'With a good heart. But you need to make him listen, you have to fight.'

Tara looked at her hands. 'Like I didn't fight for what I wanted thirty-one years ago, you mean?' she asked. 'Aye, I know. It's just not always so easy to… lay yourself bare.' She grimaced. 'To ask for what you want.' Belle found herself nodding in agreement as Tara stood straighter and stared into her mam's face. 'Okay – I'll try again. I'll tell Jack what happened. Once he knows everything, he'll be able to decide for himself.'

Belle decided to give Edina and Tara time alone and went to get dressed. Jack had returned from the kitchen and disappeared into his bedroom without a backwards glance, leaving his mam and nana staring at each other, looking grim. Belle had arranged to go out with Jack later – to head to Christmas Pud Inn to see how Moira's da was. She had no idea if they'd made it to the hospital and wanted to make sure everything was okay – and to offer help if they needed it. She wrapped a towel around herself as she got out of the shower and paused when she realised the mobile she'd rested on the bathroom floor was buzzing. She grabbed it and picked up.

'Thank God.' Kenzy's voice was filled with panic. 'I need you – please can you come to the salon?'

'When?' Belle asked, gathering her clothes and unlocking the bathroom door so she could pad the few metres down the hall to her bedroom.

'Now! It's an emergency,' Kenzy cried. 'Logan's supposed to be coming here in twenty-five minutes to give me another piece of the nativity set to paint. He can't see me. I need you to come.'

'Why?' Belle asked, quickly grabbing jeans and a pink sweater out of the huge oak wardrobe and shrugging them on along with her underwear, still holding the mobile to her ear. Her wet hair dripped down her back, soaking her clothes.

'There's no time,' Kenzy wailed. 'I'll explain when you arrive. Please be quick, ride on Bob if you have to!'

Twenty minutes later, Belle rang the doorbell at the front of The Workshop, panting hard as she waited, her hands pressed on her knees as she caught her breath.

'Belle?' Kenzy whispered through the intercom. She had a separate door to her flat which was around the back of the main building, but was more often than not found pottering around the salon. There was a blind pulled over the glass entrance so Belle couldn't see in. There were Christmas lights on in the shop though – she could just make out a multicoloured glow at the back.

'Aye, it's me,' Belle whispered, bending so she could get her mouth close to the letterbox.

'Are you alone?' Kenzy asked, and Belle heard footsteps approach the inside of the door.

She checked behind her. The high street was empty. It was early and only a couple of the shops opened on a Sunday. 'Yes. Let me in.' Belle patted her bobble hat. Her hair was still wet and cold wind blew through the wool, making her shiver. It was still freezing; flakes of snow had begun to slide from the sky as she'd half run, half sprinted to the salon from Evergreen Castle. Jack planned to pick her up later in his Audi, if he could make it down the drive. He wanted to get away from Christmas Village, he'd told her – after they'd visited the McGregors – but Belle had known he just wanted to get out of Tara's way.

The door swung open, and Kenzy grabbed Belle's arm and tugged her inside the shop before bolting the door and leaning on it. Her hair was tugged into a ponytail but her face was a mass of swollen blotches and spots, which had been painted with a layer of pink, gloopy cream. 'What happened?' Belle reached out to hug her, shocked. 'Are you okay?'

Kenzy shook her head. 'Shellfish allergy.' She pointed to her cheeks. 'I ate some on my date with that guy I told you about who lives in Morridon last night. He cooked for me and...' She shook her head. 'I've never had a reaction before. I used to eat shellfish all the time. Must be something to do with the sauce. I thought it tasted odd.' She scowled. 'I'm okay, but I'm covered. These spots are everywhere.' She marched up to a mirror hanging on the bright white wall of the salon and peered into it, whimpering. 'I look awful. There's no make-up brand in the world good enough to hide this.'

She patted her blonde hair which she'd swept up into a neat bun. 'Logan can't see me.' She turned, her eyes widening. 'He'd never be able to get this ugly vision out of his head – and there's no way I'll ever get him to agree to our date after that.'

Someone buzzed the intercom at the front of the salon and Kenzy jumped. 'That's him,' she hissed, running to the long white counter at the far right of the room so she could duck behind it. 'Just ignore it,' she said. 'I was going to get you to open the door and speak to him, but now I'm thinking it would be better if we pretend no one's here.'

'He'll know that's a lie,' Belle whispered. 'There's a light on and you're always working.'

'Kenzy,' Logan bellowed through the letterbox. 'I've made some chests for the gold, frankincense and myrrh, I finished carving them this morning. Are you okay?' He sounded worried and Belle saw the door handle turn as he tried to twist it. 'I know you're in there. I can see the light. Are you okay? If you can't open the door, lass, try to find a way to signal me.'

Kenzy poked her head up from behind the counter and mouthed, 'No!' when Belle took a tentative step towards the door.

'I heard something move,' Logan ground out. 'I can't risk that you're in there, lass, and unable to shout – I'm going to shove the door. I'll fix it afterwards so don't worry.'

'Stop!' Kenzy yelled, leaping out from her hiding place. 'I'm here. I just…'

'Let me in.' Logan still sounded worried.

Kenzy searched the room, then grabbed a white towel from a shelving unit so she could wrap it around the bottom of her face. There was a mass of irritated blotches on her forehead, but Belle didn't have the heart to mention that. Kenzy sighed, and her shoulders slumped. 'You can let him in. I'm going to turn the lights off – if I stay near the back, he might not be able to see my face.'

'What's going on?' Logan hammered on the glass.

'I'm coming,' Belle hollered, unlocking and opening the door. Logan was standing on the other side, holding a box filled with his creations, looking anxious.

'Hi,' he said, nodding at Belle with a surprised eyebrow arch before marching into the salon. It took him a couple of seconds to spot Kenzy, who was standing at the counter again, ducking her head behind the small decorated Christmas tree sitting on top. He frowned. 'What's wrong with your face, lass? Why have you covered it?'

'Stay back!' Kenzy held up a hand. 'You can leave the boxes, I'll paint them this evening. But please don't come any closer.'

Logan shook his head. 'I can't.' He paused. 'Are you hurt? Have you done something to yourself?' The man sounded genuinely upset and he walked to the counter, taking it slow. He placed the box of carvings on the counter and Kenzy backed up until she reached the whitewashed wall. 'What have you done, lass?'

'I'm fine – I'm just covered in spots, okay! I've had a reaction to some goddam crab.' She hovered a hand over her forehead, sounding desperate. 'I look horrible and ugly and…' Her voice broke and she turned so she could face the wall. 'I don't want you to see me. Please don't look…'

'Kenzy.' Logan advanced slowly and Belle hung back. For such a large man he was light on his feet and barely made a sound. 'I wouldn't care if you were covered in warts and dyed your hair green.' He laid a gentle hand on her shoulder and Kenzy flinched, her chest heaving.

'You're just saying that because you want to get me into bed. The minute you have, you'll be a hundred miles away. Dating someone younger and prettier with bigger boobs.'

Logan didn't say anything for a beat. He glanced over at Belle, and his eyes widened. When he turned back to Kenzy his voice had deepened. 'You know the thing I like about you most?'

'My eyes?' Kenzy asked, shrugging herself further into the wall. 'Or is it my arse?'

Logan took a deep breath. 'Someone did a number on you, didn't they?' he asked gently. 'I like how you moved to this village and didn't give a damn about what anyone thought. I like how hard you work, how you've grown this business.' He shoved his hands in his pockets and rolled back on his heels. 'I respect a person who knows the value of the life they have and the person they are – and you do. You know what you want and you know how to ask for it. You're funny, sassy, and you terrify me and most of the male population in Christmas Village. I like you because…' He shrugged. 'Of who you are. Not because of the way you look.'

'You don't like my arse?' Kenzy asked after a short silence.

Logan chuckled. 'I like it just fine, lass, your eyes too. Aye, your beauty is a bonus – but it's not the reason I want to date you.' His voice deepened. 'It's not why I want a *relationship*.'

Kenzy turned slowly and tugged the towel from her face. She looked pensive as Logan took in the ointment, swelling and spots.

'Fancy me now, do you?' Her voice was deceptively light. 'Because I can see that look in your eyes and it's definitely not lust.'

'No. It's sympathy, lass.' Logan reached out to put a fingertip under Kenzy's chin. He angled her face so he could examine each of her cheeks. 'That can't be comfortable,' he said gently.

'It itches.' Kenzy blinked. She stared at Logan for a moment, her eyes wide, and Belle thought she was going to reach out. Then her expression changed. 'You've seen me now – I think it's time for you to leave.' She swallowed. 'I'll paint the props and give them to Belle...' Her voice cracked. 'Soon...' Logan started to say something else but Kenzy shook her head. 'Please go. Just... please...'

He exhaled slowly. 'Still not ready...' he said, before turning and walking out of the shop.

Chapter Twenty-Two

'Fancy a coffee?' Jack asked, as Belle followed him into the bar of Christmas Pud Inn. It was still early, too early for drinking, and she wanted to head to the school in a while to double check that the pieces of newly painted scenery had been set up in the correct locations. She'd left Kenzy in The Workshop. Her friend had put a sign over the door declaring herself too sick to work, and had decided to go to bed until the spots and blotches had either faded or disappeared. Belle had wanted to stay and help, but Kenzy had insisted she leave. Logan had definitely got to her and Belle suspected Kenzy needed to regroup.

'Morning, you two! Bram's in the car park behind the pub giving the Land Rover a quick check over,' Moira said, her rosy cheeks beaming as she headed out from behind the counter to give Belle and Jack a hug. 'You're both angels,' she said, untangling herself from Jack. 'I can't thank you enough for what you did. The road was almost impassable by the time we got to Morridon – it took the snowplough three tries to clear it this morning in the early hours.'

'How's your da?' Belle asked.

'Ach, better. It was a tonic to see him. He didn't have concussion after all, just a bad bump. We stayed with him most of the night and they let us bring him home.' Moira pointed a finger at the ceiling. 'He's resting and he'll be staying with us until after Christmas. Rowan gave me an invite to Edina's Christmas party – is it okay if Da comes?'

'Aye, the more the merrier,' Belle said, grinning.

'Can we have two coffees, please?' Jack asked, and Moira nodded.

'On the house – the world needs more people like you. Truly.' She grinned.

'Can't say I hear that very often,' Jack said, so quietly Belle almost didn't hear.

'Find a table and I'll bring your drinks over with some of Rowan's chocolate cake. She heard about Da and delivered enough slices this morning for the whole pub,' Moira said.

Jack and Belle found a table by the fire. She was finally warming up after her run to get to Kenzy's, so she shrugged off her coat. 'You okay?' Jack asked, studying her.

'Belle!' Isla came wandering into the bar before she could respond. 'I popped in to see Edina and she told me you were here. I wondered if we could talk?' She nodded hello to Jack as Belle pulled out a seat for her.

'Do you want a drink?' he asked.

'Nae, thank you,' Isla said, leaning forwards, looking upset. 'My uncle's decided to visit Mam for six weeks after Christmas. He lives in New Zealand and she's not seen him for almost ten years.' She gulped. 'It means we can't move in with her until the middle of February because he'll be using the spare room. Clyde and me...' She grimaced. 'We're still looking for places to rent.' Her forehead squeezed. 'But if nowhere comes up, well...'

'Ach, I'm sure Belle can stay with Edina,' Moira interrupted, placing two mugs of steaming coffee onto the table along with giant slabs of chocolate cake. 'I spoke to Rowan this morning and she said Edina's never looked so happy. I've rarely seen her over the last twenty years, but I can tell you now she's transformed – and it's all thanks to this poppet here.' She nodded to Belle, then turned to look at Jack, beaming. 'Edina told Rowan she wished Belle could stay with her forever.'

'Well, I…' Belle looked up. Jack picked up his coffee and sipped a little before looking around the pub – anywhere but at her. Was he angry? She couldn't read his expression.

'I'm sure I could find alternative accommodation,' she began. Kenzy only had one bedroom, but she could sleep in her sitting room at a push.

'Sounds like that won't be necessary,' Jack said quietly, as Isla beamed and threw her arms around Belle.

'If you want to throw us out at any point, you just need to say. I know we haven't been able to find anywhere close to Christmas Village, but we'd figure something out. I know I've said it a hundred times, but I don't want to shove you out of your home.' She leapt to her feet. 'I need to go, sorry. Clyde's waiting outside, I wanted to find you to tell you the news and to make sure it was okay if we stayed on a bit longer. See you at the nativity.'

The table fell silent when she'd left and Belle sipped some of the coffee, trying to meet Jack's eyes. 'I'm sorry,' she murmured. 'I know I was supposed to move out, but…'

'I'm sure my grandmother will be delighted to have you,' Jack said lightly, smiling, although she could tell something was definitely off because his eyes dulled. 'Besides, there's plenty of room. There'll be even more after I leave.'

'Of course.' Belle picked up a fork so she could nibble some chocolate cake, but she'd lost her appetite.

'I've got things I need to do. Things I forgot about,' Jack said, drinking down the rest of his coffee and quickly devouring his slice of cake. 'If I take the Audi, do you want to drive the Land Rover home?'

'Oh, aye,' Belle said, swallowing the ache in her chest. 'I thought…' She shook her head when his eyes met hers. 'Doesn't matter,' she murmured, wishing she could ask Jack what was wrong. 'I'll see you later,' she added, frowning.

'Great,' he said, standing and giving Belle a quick peck on the cheek before disappearing out of the pub.

Belle was halfway down Evergreen Castle's drive when she spotted Tara and Bob. They were standing to the right of the driveway under a huge fir tree surrounded by banks of sparkly white snow. Belle had hung Christmas lights and baubles on most of the trees a few days before in an effort to make the grounds more Christmassy, but it was still light so none of them had flicked on. Tara was feeding Bob carrots but his ears pricked up when he saw the Land Rover, and he took a couple of small steps towards it. But when Belle switched off the engine, opened the door and climbed out, the donkey honked a couple of times before turning back to his snack, clearly not as interested now he knew Belle wasn't Jack. She crunched through the snow towards Tara. She didn't know why, except the woman was probably hurting and she wanted to help.

'How's it going?' Belle asked as she approached. Drawing closer, she noticed Jinx winding himself around Tara's feet.

'It's going well.' Tara stroked Bob as he nibbled on the carrot, her face lighting as the donkey turned and nuzzled her. Tara had barely smiled since arriving in Christmas Village and the glitter in her blue eyes suddenly reminded Belle of Jack. 'Bob stayed with me for a couple of years before coming to live with Mam. He remembers me…' She scrubbed a hand over his head. 'He's made friends with Jinx.' She glanced at her feet. 'I found the cat wandering in the grounds near to the barn. He's out here quite a lot.'

Belle looked at the cat, surprised. As far as she knew, Jinx spent most of his time under her bed, only coming out when Jack was about. 'He misses my godmother, Annie – I didn't think he'd settled into the castle that well.'

'Watch this,' Tara said. Belle's jaw dropped as Tara lifted the cat onto the donkey's back. Bob honked, then nuzzled Tara's hand, obviously scrounging for another carrot. Jinx blinked and stretched, then slowly settled himself onto Bob, wrapping his legs under him to make himself comfortable.

'How did you know he'd be okay with that…?' Belle gaped.

Tara shrugged. 'I've got a donkey in my sanctuary who's a little shy but she loves cats. I guessed they might be good for each other.'

'That's… amazing,' Belle said.

Tara shrugged. 'Animals are easier to understand than people. I never was good with the human race.'

Belle reached out and rubbed a hand over the rough donkey fur before stroking Jinx. The cat was purring and Bob seemed happy with the arrangement. 'You're talking about Jack?' Belle guessed.

'Aye.' Tara's shoulders slumped. 'And his da.'

Belle folded her arms and looked around at the field. How should she approach this? She didn't want to upset Jack's mam, but if she didn't say something they'd be stuck in the same situation – reliving it over and over again. 'You promised Edina you'd talk to Jack. What do you want from him?' she asked softly.

Tara shrugged, but when Belle remained silent she shook her head. 'I came to the castle because I wanted to see my son. It was the first time since I left him that I've had the opportunity. If I'd tried when his da was alive...' She sucked in a breath and her face crumpled. 'Let's just say he'd have made it impossible. But I thought... hoped...' Her forehead crunched. 'Jack would find it in his heart to at least listen to what I had to say. I was stupid – I should have stood up for what I wanted when he was five – but it was a long time ago. I want to find a way of making it up to him.' She shook her head. 'But Jack doesn't want to spend even a moment in the same room as me. How am I supposed to explain my side of the story if he won't listen?' Bob nudged Tara's hand and she fed him another carrot.

A little cold now she was standing still, Belle shifted from foot to foot. 'I've seen you talk to Jack about spending time together. But have you ever just asked him to talk?' She held up a hand. 'I mean, really asked?'

'No.' Tara shook her head. She wore a bright red bobble hat, and strands of dark hair dangled from underneath it. She had the same angular face as Jack and their eyes and hair were the same colour, but the resemblance ended there. Tara was much smaller than her son, almost delicate, definitely wounded – she had an air of suffering about her, whereas Jack was all about barriers. Where Jack fought, Tara retreated. Belle wondered if it was because of how badly Jack's da had hurt her, or whether it was just the way she was. 'He doesn't want to know…' Tara paused. 'I'm not sure I blame him.'

Belle thought about her da. She hardly knew him. Had it been easier for him to make her leave Kenya because he couldn't face something happening to her too, or had he thought it was what she wanted? Belle had never asked, she'd never been brave enough – she wasn't sure she ever would be. She frowned. 'Perhaps you need to tell him it's time you told your side of the story. Time for him to listen to you.'

'I don't really like talking about it,' Tara said, stroking Jinx. 'I'm not proud of what I did – what I let happen.'

'I'm not asking you to tell me,' Belle said, feeling frustrated. 'That's a private story for your son. I am saying you're here now – isn't it time you insisted? You walked away once, are you really going to do it again? It might not change anything, but at least you'd have done everything you could. If Jack has the facts, he'll be able to make an informed decision.'

'He hates me.' Bob grabbed the final carrot from Tara's hand and she wrapped her arms around herself. 'It's difficult to live with, and easier to walk away from. I know that makes me a coward. Perhaps I'm just a person who takes the easiest route.' She looked at Bob. 'Animals love you whatever your flaws. However badly you mess up.'

'They don't talk back either.' Belle nodded. 'I get that. But let me ask you a question. Are you really prepared to walk away from your son for a second time? Because I suspect if you do, there'll be no going back.'

The words must have hit deep, because something fluttered across Tara's face. 'No.' She shook her head. 'No, I'm not.' She sighed. 'I'll talk to him. I'm not going to walk away again.' She screwed up her face. 'If he won't listen though, there's nothing I can do to make him. If he asks me to leave, this time I will.'

Edina was sitting in front of the fireplace when Belle returned to the castle. A fire was roaring in the grate and lights shone on the tree. Strange how in just a few short weeks the atmosphere of the building had altered. What had once been grey and cold now felt cosy and warm. Belle guessed after his reaction today that Jack didn't want her to stay in the castle after Christmas, and she had no intention of outstaying her welcome. But she'd miss it; she'd miss that feeling of belonging and she'd definitely miss Edina. Her friend had blossomed since the accident – she was animated and seemed to laugh all the time. Belle also suspected she'd have a new regular helper in her class at school once Edina's ankle had healed.

'Ach, lass, I hoped I'd see you,' Edina said, almost bouncing on her seat as Belle entered the sitting room. 'Tavish just left. He popped in to make sure I had enough firewood – he knows Logan keeps me topped up so I'm not sure why he's bothering. The bampot still won't show me his tattoo, no matter how many times I ask. I thought we were friends…' She huffed. 'How's the stage for the nativity looking?'

'Brilliant – we're all set.' Belle had popped into the school straight after she'd been to the pub. Logan had obviously been working hard to set everything up. There was now a backdrop on the small stage in the school featuring a barn, desert and night sky. Kenzy had painted the tiny crib and that had been positioned in front of the picture of the barn, ready for Nessa to place the 'Baby Cheeses' inside. Logan had hung silver stars from the ceiling and the whole stage had sparkled – once Kenzy had painted the three boxes for the kings to carry, everything would be ready. Along with the costumes Isla, Rowan, Kenzy and Edina had made, Belle suspected this would be the most professional-looking nativity at the school for years – rivalling even London's West End. During rehearsals the week before, the children had been so excited about trying on the new costumes. They had a full dress rehearsal planned tomorrow and a couple more during the week, and the play would be shown to the parents on Friday evening, which was the last day of term.

'I can't wait. Tara's somewhere in the grounds trying to see if Bob can be persuaded to behave,' Edina said.

'Aye, I chatted with her on my way here. Bob would make a big splash – I can only imagine Robina's face.' She grinned, taking a seat on the sofa opposite.

'Where's Jack?' Edina asked, glancing behind her towards the hallway.

'He had to make some calls,' Belle murmured.

'Avoiding his mam, you mean?' Edina sighed. 'The lad's stubborn. Then again, he might get that from me.' Her forehead wrinkled. 'I hope Tara will talk to him. She always was a shy one.' She shook her head. 'Too afraid to stand up for herself – not good at focusing on her own needs, always so concerned about other people.' She gave Belle a sly look. 'She has a gift with animals though, like you do with the wee kids.' She beamed. 'Jack seems to have inherited

Tara's gift – as much as he doesn't want to admit it. The lad doesn't want to acknowledge he has any of his mam's genes.'

Belle nodded. 'He's stubborn but I'm sure he'll come around in time.' She hoped so anyway.

Edina lifted an eyebrow. 'I hope so, lass. Depends if he's got too much of his da in him to listen to anyone else.'

Belle put her hands on her knees. 'What was his father like?'

Edina frowned. 'He was a hard man. I never knew what Tara saw in him. He was handsome enough.' She nodded. 'On the outside. But he wanted everything his own way and he trusted nobody.' She shook her head. 'Once they had Jack...' She puffed out a breath. 'It was like nothing else mattered – he couldn't see anything else.' She shrugged. 'After that... the story's too long for me to tell and it really should be Tara explaining things to Jack.'

But would Tara find it in herself to persuade Jack to hear her side of the story? Belle wondered. And if she did, what would it change?

Chapter Twenty-Three

'Is Jack here yet?' Belle asked, putting a hand against her stomach, trying to fight down the nerves bubbling inside. Her head was thumping and she tried to suppress a sneeze. She'd been feeling run-down for the last few days, but there was no time to be sick. It was Edina's party in a couple of days and there were still a lot of things to organise – although Rowan had handled most of them. Jack had travelled to London on Sunday soon after leaving Christmas Pud Inn, citing an emergency with a client. They'd spoken on the phone a couple of times but he'd sounded odd. He'd promised to make it in time for the nativity this evening though, and as Belle regarded the sparkling stage and the hall filled with chattering parents, she hoped he would. Not that she'd told him. He had enough pressure from work and Tara, without her adding any more with a load of demands.

Edina waved as Belle did an extra check to ensure everything had been set up properly on the stage. She was sitting in the front row of the audience next to Tavish, with her foot propped up. Tara was in the bicycle shelter at the back of the school playground, waiting for Bob to make his grand entrance. Edina had brought her tiaras to the school this morning for the children playing kings to wear.

Belle had put Kenzy in charge of keeping track of them, knowing she'd probably forget who had them in all the excitement.

'Miss Albany.' Nessa came to tug Belle's hand. Dressed as Mary, she wore a pretty blue dress which Edina had made from sections of unused curtain. She'd added sparkles around the skirt which had made the little girl squeak in delight. It wasn't traditional, but Nessa obviously loved the look. 'Lennie's frightened. He wants you.'

'He's scared – of what?' Belle asked, following Nessa into the dining room, where Kenzy was waiting. Her friend had volunteered to help supervise and organise the kids for the evening now that her spots and blotches had mostly faded. She was still subdued, and despite Belle trying to get her to open up about her feelings for Logan, she was reluctant to talk.

All the kids were in Belle's classroom with a couple of parent helpers who were assisting with dressing and make-up, along with Robina who was admiring all the new outfits. 'Ach, lass, I can't believe how professional the children look,' she declared, clapping her hands in delight. 'I'll be telling Benji he can organise something else next year – I think the nativity will be yours permanently after tonight.'

'Oh, really?' Belle tried to smile as her stomach sank. She wasn't sure she wanted the responsibility every year. Then again, the kids loved it and it wasn't like she had anything else to fill her life. She walked past Adam, who was dressed in his furry sheep costume. The child was on all fours, sniffing the legs of the tables and chairs in the classroom. 'Okay, Adam?' Belle asked.

'*Baaaaa*,' he replied, giving her a toothy grin before sniffing another chair leg.

Lennie came loping over, and one of his blond curls flopped over his right eye. 'Miss, I've got stage mice,' he whispered, tugging the bottom of her jumper until she crouched so they were the same height. 'Granda told me about them last night.' He pressed a hand to his stomach and rubbed. 'There's something running in my tummy making everything feel weird.' His blue eyes widened and Belle smiled.

'You're just nervous, lad, there's nothing there except a few bubbly nerves – and I promise, they're perfectly normal.' She patted a hand on his back.

'Are you sure?' Lennie didn't sound convinced.

Belle nodded. 'Once you're up on that stage, those mice will disappear and you'll enjoy every minute.' He would too; Lennie loved being centre of attention like his sister Bonnie, and he was going to make an amazing Joseph. 'Remember how well you've been doing in rehearsals and just look at that outfit!' Edina had created a blue flowing cape costume for Lennie. She'd added gold edging about the neck and sleeves. The little boy had shrieked in delight when he'd first tried it.

'Will Bob arrive in time?' Lennie looked worried. They'd done rehearsals with him on Monday and Wednesday and the donkey had behaved impeccably – possibly because Jinx had also turned up. Although the donkey had tried to nibble the collar of Lennie's costume a few times.

'Aye, Ms Lachlan will be bringing him in just before you go on. Remember, you need to hold on to his reins because we won't want him running off.'

Lennie nodded, looking serious. 'Ms Lachlan told me I have to be firm with him.'

'Err, Belle – Miss Albany?' Isla knocked on the door.

'Aye?' Belle turned as Lennie got distracted and started chattering with Angus, who was being helped into one of the sumptuous velvet king outfits.

'Logan's outside – he wants to speak to Kenzy. I said I'd take over helping with the kids, if that's all right?' Isla asked.

Kenzy looked stunned and she shook her head. The blotches on her face and body had mostly disappeared since Sunday, but there were still tinges of red and a couple of small spots on her cheeks. Kenzy had tried to cover them with make-up but Belle knew her friend felt self-conscious about being seen – she'd already asked if she could sit at the back of the hall during the nativity and only planned to sneak in when the lights were dimmed. 'I'm too busy, I'm sure it can wait.' She folded her arms. 'Tell him I said no.'

'Logan's, well…' Isla stammered. 'I think you need to see him – he's done something to his face.'

Kenzy paled and took a step towards the door, before she obviously thought better of it. 'I can't.' She grimaced. 'Is he hurt?'

'Um…' Isla shrugged. 'I'm not sure. I've not seen anything like it. He's in reception – I told him he should see a doctor or go to the hospital, but he said he had to speak to you first.'

'Hospital – you think he's hurt that badly?' Kenzy took off at a run, which wasn't easy considering how spiky her red heels were. Belle followed her into the school dining room, tagging along as she sprinted towards where Logan was waiting. Belle knew she couldn't be long, but if Logan was sick or in need of assistance, she wasn't going to leave her friend to handle the situation alone. When she reached the doorway leading to the main reception area, Belle paused.

'Goddam it, Logan, what have you done?' Kenzy yelped, skidding to stop as he stepped out of the far corner of the dim room. Belle couldn't see his face from where she was standing but heard Kenzy's shocked gasp. 'Why are you here and not in hospital – and what the hell have you done to your gorgeous face?' Belle watched as her friend carefully cupped the edge of his cheek. 'Is that… blood?'

'You think my face is gorgeous, lass?' Logan reached up to take her hand.

'What is it – an allergy?' Kenzy watched as he linked his fingers with hers. Her back stiffened and Belle wondered if she was going to pull away. 'Did you get attacked by an animal or eat something that didn't agree with you?'

Logan moved further into the light which was pooling from the ceiling, until Belle could see his face properly. His cheeks and chin were covered in blotches and spots – a mass of red lumps similar to the ones Kenzy had had. 'No, lass,' Logan murmured, smiling. 'I think it might have been bewitched.'

'What are you talking about?' Kenzy frowned. 'Did you bang your head?' She put a palm against his forehead. 'You've not got a temperature. Tell me your symptoms.' She spoke rapidly, the fear in her voice tangible. 'You have to see a doctor – *now*, Logan.' She pressed a hand to his chest, shoving him back towards the entrance.

Logan shook his head. 'I'm sorry, lass, I didn't do this to scare you. I was trying to make a point. Badly, it seems… You dinnae have to worry.' He rubbed a finger on his cheek and one of the spots smudged, smearing a layer of pink the size of a two-pence coin. 'I'm okay.'

'Make-up?' Kenzy swiped a fingertip across his chin too, smudging another circle of pink. 'Are you trying to trick me?' The fear in

Kenzy's voice quickly morphed into anger. 'Is this some sick way of getting me to go on a date with you?'

'Nae, lass.' Logan blew out a breath when Kenzy unlinked their fingers and started to pull away. He took hold of her forearm, gently turning her again so he could look into her eyes. 'I'm trying to show you looks aren't important. I was trying to…' He shrugged, clearly frustrated. 'You didn't give a damn how I looked just then. But you were worried. It was the first real emotion I've seen from you since you moved to Christmas Village. The first time you've let your guard down. You told me all I cared about was the way you looked, and that wasn't true. I honestly thought if I came here tonight, sat in that hall next to you looking like this, I'd be proving something.'

'What?' Kenzy asked, tugging her arm away from Logan and taking a long step back. 'That you've lost your senses?'

He sighed. 'That looks don't matter. You don't have to protect yourself from me, I'm not going to hurt you.'

'I don't know what you're talking about,' Kenzy said, turning away again.

Logan let out a long sigh. 'I'm sorry, lass, I'm pushing you. That wasn't my intention.' He wiped more of the paint off, smearing it over his cheekbones, and Belle had a sudden urge to reach out and intervene but held herself back. 'I'm an eejit. I knew you weren't ready. I said I'd wait and got impatient. That wasn't fair.'

'You look ridiculous,' Kenzy grumbled, glancing around the room. There was a box of tissues by the reception desk and she grabbed some, handing the bunch to Logan before dabbing his cheek. 'This was a stupid idea,' she said. But she didn't sound angry now. 'I don't understand you…' Kenzy swiped at his nose, cleaning off another layer of make-up, revealing more unblemished skin. Logan stood with his arms by his sides, holding on to the tissue, obviously doing his best not to upset her. It was as if he didn't know what to do. If he reached out and touched her, would she run? Belle wasn't sure either. This was new territory for her friend. 'I don't know what to do about this…' Kenzy stood back when she finished cleaning Logan's face. 'Most men would be content with a wild fling… no strings, just fun.' She hissed a breath between her teeth.

'You're kidding yourself, lass,' Logan said. 'And I'm not most men. We've been through this. You know what I want.'

'No one's ever tried to date me by making themselves look uglier.' Kenzy shook her head but a slight smile materialised at the edges of her lips. 'They usually give me flowers or jewellery – chocolates have been known to work…'

'Aye.' Logan nodded, and he gave her a wry smile. 'I suppose I could try that – making a fool of myself hasn't worked.'

Kenzy stared at him for a few moments, then shook her head. She went up onto her tiptoes and gave him a peck on the cheek, before heading back towards the dining room and Belle.

Just before she got to the door, she turned to stare at Logan. 'I don't want those things from you,' she said gently. 'You're…' She sighed. 'I need to think about what I do want.' With that, she marched into the dining hall and headed back to Belle's class, leaving him staring after her with hope in his eyes.

Chapter Twenty-Four

'Sorry I'm late.' Jack leaned down to give Belle a quick kiss as he swept into the school, and her stomach jumped at the contact. 'I got stuck in traffic on the motorway on the way up from London – I haven't missed anything, have I?'

'No,' Belle soothed, guiding him from the main entrance through the dining room and pointing to the empty seat in the front row of the audience next to Edina. 'The nativity's about to start. If you want to take a seat, it won't be long.'

Jack sat next to Edina as the lights went down. As he did, Belle saw Kenzy walk to the door and skim the crowd until she knew where Logan was seated. She stared at him for a moment with a puzzled expression, then took a seat at the back. Robina sat in front of the large black piano to the right of the stage and began to play – the audience hushed. Then the line of children who'd make up the chorus, all dressed in white, filed into the main hall. They wore crowns and halos which Belle knew they'd made in their art classes. The children took their places at the front of the hall to the edges of the stage, with the taller kids at the back and the smaller in front. The youngest class sat cross-legged on the carpet. As the audience settled, Mazey Taylor – one of the oldest children in Belle's class – began to narrate.

'Good afternoon, ladies and gentlemen,' Mazey boomed. 'We have a special tale to perform for you this evening, which you probably all know quite well. Please make yourselves comfortable so we can tell you the story of the nativity.' She bowed her head as the children in the chorus began to sing, their voices a sweet melody which filled the hall. Belle heard the tap of hooves and saw Tara standing at the far edge of the room. Then Lennie slowly ambled through the entrance, guiding the small grey donkey. Nessa followed, her eyes sparkling as she held on to the shiny leather saddle that Tara had insisted Bob wore. The donkey stopped halfway when he spotted Edina and let out a loud honk. Lennie tugged his reins and Bob started to move again, following the children to the main stage.

Then Bonnie entered the hall. The little girl looked radiant; she wore a bright white gown with a fluffy white cape and a star-shaped hat, which Isla had made from cardboard and Rowan had decorated with sparkly sequinned material. She meandered towards the stage, stopping for a moment to wave at Bram and Moira who were sitting in the audience, next to Moira's da. 'Mam, can you see me?' Bonnie whispered in her loudest voice, and the audience began to laugh.

'Aye!' Moira blew Bonnie a kiss and waved her along. When Bonnie reached the stage, the fairy lights Edina and Rowan had sewn into the edges of her cape suddenly switched on. There was a collective '*ooooh*' and '*ahhhh*' from the crowd, who began to applaud – a few of the children leaned across each other so they could get a better look.

'You look beautiful, lass!' Edina cheered, and Bonnie beamed.

Belle watched with her heart in her throat as the rest of the nativity progressed without incident. The children were brilliant and the audience laughed in all the right places. Belle could see Edina bouncing up and down on her chair, enraptured as she watched the performance unfold. Would she have been sitting alone in her castle this time last year? So much had changed and Belle knew she'd played a small part in that. She was just happy she'd decided to get Edina to write a Christmas list – even if she hadn't been able to give her everything on it. Her attention drifted to Jack, who was sitting next to his nana. He was laughing, his face a picture of pure delight – and as Belle watched him, something inside her clicked once more and her stomach fell away. Because she had feelings for Jack, strong feelings, and she had no idea what to do about them…

'I'll take Edina back to the castle,' Tavish said gruffly a few minutes after the play had ended, dodging parents who were slowly filing out of the main hall, hand in hand with their children. He helped the older woman to her feet. 'I can see you've got clearing up to do.' He regarded the hall with a grimace. There was a lot to put away on the stage. Logan had already started to dismantle the scenery, helping the caretaker who was tackling the larger pieces.

'Aye, I'll see you later,' Belle promised, taking a moment to drop a quick kiss on Edina's cheek and watching as Tavish guided her out with one arm ready to catch her if she tripped. Belle gathered up a few stray props from the stage. Today had been the last day of school and they had a couple of weeks off now, so she wanted to leave things as tidy as she could. She also wanted to make sure she knew where everything had been tidied away to so nothing went missing next year.

'Jack, I want to speak to you,' Tara said suddenly, marching up to where he was quietly stacking chairs. Belle watched as Jack took a step away from his mam and folded his arms. 'You need to hear my side of the story.'

'We've been through this; there's nothing you can say that I want to hear,' he said. 'My dad told me what happened – I'm not interested.'

Tara swallowed, but instead of backing away as she had before, she stepped forwards. She glanced over to Belle and nodded: a clear message that she'd meant what she'd said. 'How will you know that, lad, unless you listen? Don't you know there are always two sides to any story?' She folded her arms, mirroring him as the last dribs and drabs of children and parents walked out of the exit.

'I know all about stories.' Jack's voice was hard. 'I hear them every day. I know you left when I was five. I know my dad gave you money so you'd never contact me again, and I know you took it.' His eyes were cold. There was no emotion in his voice, no connection, and Belle wondered at how easy it was for him to shut off. Could he do the same just as easily with her – just like her da had done?

'I did, lad,' Tara said faintly. 'I've regretted that moment ever since, but if you knew why…'

Jack pressed his lips together. 'I know everything I need to already.' He started to turn away and Belle found herself putting a palm on Tara's shoulder, found herself standing side by side with her. Two women ready to do battle with the man they cared for.

'Listen to your mam, Jack,' she implored. 'I know you're furious. But sometimes it's important to move past that.'

'You need to stay out of this,' Jack said, his face clouding.

'I can't,' Belle said. 'I've watched you wrestle with how you feel – I know how angry you are, but I know if you don't listen you'll never know the facts. Perhaps you could forgive your mam.' She glanced at Tara – she looked pale. 'Remember the spoon in the restaurant... remember how things can be distorted,' she added desperately. 'That there are always two sides.'

Jack's face shuttered. 'Throwing my words back at me is a clever trick, but it's not going to work on a lawyer. I'll eat you for breakfast, twist you in knots and spit you back out. Are you prepared for that, Belle?' His voice was dangerous and she felt something inside her knot. Was this the real Jack? All barriers and hard edges? Had the softness she'd seen been a lie?

The lights above them flickered on, jerking Belle back to her senses. 'Bye, lass.' Robina waved from the doorway, mouthing 'Happy Christmas' before turning to leave.

Belle tightened her hands into fists and turned back to Jack. 'Your mam's in pain – you are too. Talk to her, or at least listen...'

As Jack started to argue, Tara held up a hand. 'Stop. Both of you,' she yelled, then lowered her voice. 'I didn't come to cause problems between you. I never expected I'd make you unhappy. I'm sorry, I shouldn't have pushed.' A tear tracked down her cheek. 'Jack's right, Belle. I know I said I'd try, and I have, but it's obviously too late. He doesn't want to know. If I was him, I wouldn't either. I'll go.' She nodded at her son. 'I'll leave tonight like you asked. I'll take Bob back now and pack. You'll never see me again. I'm sorry.'

'You said you'd fight,' Belle shouted after Tara, but she'd already run from the hall. Belle turned to Jack again, feeling her temper heat. 'Couldn't you have listened?' she asked. 'Was it that hard?'

'You said you'd stay out of it.' His voice was cool. 'You told me you were sorry you'd asked Tara to come and you wouldn't get involved. Was that a lie, Belle? Because I thought you were all about truth.'

She stepped closer, unnerved by the coldness in his expression. 'I couldn't – I'm not built like that,' she admitted. 'I can't believe you'd turn your back on your mam.' She shook her head. Was this man really as cold as he seemed?

He nodded but didn't smile. 'I know you have this insane need to help everyone. In some ways I admire it. But this isn't your fight and it's not your business. I told you that when I arrived.'

'I care about you,' Belle said, reaching out to touch his face, but he jerked his head and she dropped her hand.

'Don't try to manipulate me…' he murmured. 'I know what you're doing.'

'I'm not one of your clients,' Belle fired back. 'I'm just asking you to hear another side of the story. I'm asking you to open your heart. You're so much better than this.' Something in her chest was pounding and she breathed in, trying to calm herself.

'This is exactly who I am,' Jack growled. 'I think for a while I stopped seeing that.'

'What – a man who won't listen to his mam, a man who won't trust? Someone who's as closed down as his da? Is that really who you are?' Her heart leapt when he looked uncertain, then his face clouded. 'Just talk to Tara,' Belle pleaded. She didn't know why it was important, why she had to convince him. But there was something about his mother's need to confide, to tell all and lay herself bare, that touched her. She was hurting and Belle couldn't bear that.

Jack's mouth thinned. 'Like you talk to your dad, you mean?'

'What?'

He shook his head. 'You wrote that you wanted him to come for Christmas on your list – did you tell him?'

'No,' Belle whispered. 'He can't. He's too busy. What's that got to do with anything?'

He raised an eyebrow. 'Did you ask?'

She swallowed. 'It's not like that. You don't understand. He's got more important things to worry about than me.' He always had.

'Or are you afraid to ask – scared of what he might say because you don't think you matter to him, or he might reject you?' Jack asked, his voice harsh. 'Same as you're afraid to tell me what else you wrote on your Christmas list. What do you think I'll do – laugh, judge you because of it? What did you write, Belle?'

She shook her head. Telling him would expose far too much.

Jack rubbed his chin. 'You're as closed down as I am, Belle. You help people on your terms, but you don't let anyone in either. It's so much easier to fix everyone else, to fill your life up helping out, than it is to focus on what you need. Don't think I haven't noticed.' His eyes glittered and he nodded before turning and marching away, leaving Belle with a lump in her throat, wondering if he was right.

Chapter Twenty-Five

'Is Tara with you, lad?' Edina greeted Jack as soon as he walked into the castle. He was still angry; something inside him burned as a jumble of emotions swirled around his stomach, making him confused and out of sorts. 'I tried her mobile, but it's still here.'

'She left before me,' he snapped, instantly regretting it when his grandmother's face dropped. 'I'm sorry. We argued, she told me she was going back to Skye. I assumed...' He glanced towards the front door. He'd gone for an aimless drive in the Audi after his row with Belle so he could think, then turned round when the snow had started to thicken and his tyres had slipped. 'She probably shouldn't travel in this,' he admitted, wondering why he cared. His mind slid to Belle – to the hurt on her face when he'd stormed out of the school – and he pushed the emotions away. He'd been right to be angry. So why did he feel bad?

'Tara was supposed to be making her way home from the school with Bob.' Edina's face paled as Tavish wandered into the room, shaking his head. 'It surely couldn't have taken her this long to walk.'

'I can see the barn from the back door, lass. It's open and the donkey's not back.' Tavish picked up his hat and put it on, then shoved his jacket onto one arm.

'How could she be lost?' Jack asked, as something in his stomach squeezed. 'It's not a long way. I didn't see her when I drove down the high street, I assumed she was ahead of me.' He checked his watch. 'It's over forty minutes since she left the school.'

'She might have taken a short cut,' Tavish murmured. 'Or maybe Bob decided to go another way. He can't read maps and he's a stubborn eejit.' A gust of wind howled through the chimney, and Edina grabbed her cane and started to get up.

'We need to look for her.' She glanced around the room. 'I could call Belle.'

'Where is she?' Jack asked, his voice thickening. Her car hadn't been parked where he'd expected, but he'd assumed someone had given her a lift.

'She texted to say she was going to spend the night at Kenzy's, I didn't get the details,' Edina said, clearly distracted. 'She'll come in the morning to pick up fresh clothes.' Her eyes jerked up as she took in Jack's face. 'You didn't fight with her too, did you, lad? I thought it was odd that she didn't come back here.'

Jack opened his mouth to respond, then closed it. Edina wouldn't understand why he'd been angry.

'We need to look for Tara,' Tavish jumped in, as Iver hopped around his heels. 'You stay with Edina.'

'No, I'll go,' Jack said, striding ahead. He heard Tavish grumble something, but was almost by the door. He was still wearing his thick coat and boots, but the cold wind bit into his body nonetheless as he stepped outside, and the force of it was a shock. He marched around the castle past Bob's barn and saw it was empty because the door swung open – the light was on and the pictures

Belle's class had drawn billowed as the wind caught and slammed it shut again. He trudged left, remembering the short cut Belle had pointed out when they'd been lost a week before. How much had changed since that evening – and how much of it was his fault? He was confused – by his fight with Belle and the odd tightness in his chest when he thought about Tara. Not just that, his father's words kept racing around his mind – a lifetime of warnings, life lessons and rules. *Trust no one.* For the first time, Jack wondered if that included Lucas Hamilton-Kirk…

He searched the ground as he joined the track at the far end of the castle grounds, fighting the barrage of snow that flew into his face. There were no prints visible, but Jack suspected if any had been there, they'd already be buried under a layer of snow. He could barely see through the flakes, and almost jumped out of his skin when Jinx launched himself into the centre of the pathway.

'What are you doing out in this?' Jack bent so he could scratch behind the cat's ears before pointing back towards the castle. 'Get yourself inside.' Instead of doing as he was told, Jinx's ears pricked, then he turned and trotted down the same trail Jack had joined. The cat didn't look cold but Jack pulled his coat tighter, wishing he'd added at least one extra layer. He tramped slowly, swiping ice as it settled on his face, keeping his eyes straight ahead as he followed the cat. He could barely see anything beyond a few feet now, could hear nothing above the howl of the wind. What if Tara had tripped, or was hurt? Something gripped his chest. Fear, concern?

Then Jack found the gate he and Belle had slipped through and tramped to the right, only finding the gap in the hedge because Jinx glided through it first. 'Where are you going?' he shouted, knowing it was pointless. But the sound must have travelled on the wind because somewhere in the distance, an animal honked. He sped up, trying to run as his stomach tightened, searching the ground for some hint they were going in the right direction. The cat found the donkey first. He was standing under a tree and Tara was kneeling next to him, tugging at his hoof.

'Help me, you eejit!' she shouted, looking up when Jinx rubbed himself around her knees. Jack saw the moment she spotted him too, because her eyes widened. 'What are you doing here?'

'Looking for you,' Jack shouted. He could see she was cold because she'd started to shake. 'What happened?'

'Ach.' She frowned. 'The bampot donkey's got his leg stuck. I gave him some time to free himself, but he's a stubborn thing and didn't want to help himself. I wasn't going to leave him.' She looked down, then picked Jinx up and popped him onto Bob's back. As soon as she did, the donkey tugged at his leg, immediately liberating himself. It was as if he'd been waiting for them to arrive. Bob honked once, then skirted around Jack and joined the pathway. Jinx stared forwards as they went, folding himself tightly onto his friend, looking perfectly content despite the battering wind. Tara nodded at Jack and began to follow too. He watched her for a beat before catching up and matching her pace, walking so they were side by side. She didn't try to talk to him and didn't complain, even though Jack could see she was still shivering. On impulse he grabbed the scarf from around his neck and handed it to her, feeling something move inside his chest when her eyes filled.

It took ten minutes to get to Bob's barn. As soon as the donkey wandered in, Jinx leapt down and scampered towards the castle, his job clearly done. Jack waited with his hands in his pockets while Tara scratched the donkey's back, removing his saddle before making sure he had enough food in his trough. She was patient and gentle, and watching her triggered a rush of memories. Of her helping him tie his shoes, reading to him, cooking pancakes and laughing. That woman was nothing like the image he'd built in his head. The image his dad had helped to paint. As Tara stood, she pointed to one of the drawings pinned to the wall and she smiled. 'I love the picture – they're down to Belle, right?'

Jack nodded.

'Aye, she's a good lass,' she said, sighing. 'She cares for you. I'm glad you found someone.'

'Who do you have?' Jack cleared his throat. He didn't know why he'd asked, but he couldn't shake the way he'd felt when he'd been looking for her. It had been the same feeling he'd had when she'd left. He recognised it, though he thought he'd moved on…

'I have my donkeys, lad.' Tara scratched a hand over Bob's back. 'They're funny creatures – stubborn, affectionate, curious. They give a lot back.' She glanced at the door. 'I need to go, this weather's getting worse and I've a long drive ahead.'

'Why did you leave?' Jack wasn't sure why he'd asked. Perhaps they'd been moving towards this moment since Belle had invited Tara to Evergreen Castle. Perhaps he finally understood what Rachel had meant. He hadn't wanted to hear another side of the story, hadn't wanted to have his father proved wrong. Perhaps because it kept him safe? Stopped him from letting anyone close, from getting hurt again? Wasn't that why he'd rejected Belle last week and made an excuse to go to London? Because he'd been falling for her?

Tara sighed and wrung her hands. 'I've wanted to tell you for a long time. Now I have the chance, it's more difficult than I expected. I'm not sure any reason would be good enough. You have to remember, I was young and… afraid to stand up for what I wanted.' She stared at the ground. 'Your da adored you. You should know that.'

'I do.' Jack nodded. 'But I'm wondering if perhaps he cared too much?'

Tara's eyes met his and he saw hope in them. 'Yes, that's exactly right,' she said rapidly. 'He did care too much. Lucas was larger than life. I fell in love with him almost immediately and we married within weeks.' She pulled a face.

Jack put his hands in his pockets. 'Larger than life, that's exactly right.'

Tara jerked her head. 'I was obsessed. He was beautiful, smart, rich – everything I'd ever imagined I wanted. And he loved me. At least, I thought he did.' She frowned. 'It took months but he began to change. What I'd thought of as attentive, I realised was possessive. He wanted to control everything I did – what I wore, who I spoke to, what I said.' She looked into his eyes, her expression vulnerable. 'I'm not speaking ill of him, or trying to turn you against him, I'm just trying to explain…' She flushed and went to stroke Bob again.

'Go on…' Jack said. This wasn't easy to hear, but he had to listen, had to hear Tara's side of the story. If he didn't, how would he ever know what had happened? Besides, these were sides to his father he recognised. Sides he hadn't particularly liked.

She nodded slowly. 'I didn't have a lot of confidence, but what I did have was gradually eroded until I could barely muster an opinion on anything, even things as simple as what clothes to wear.' She winced, clearly embarrassed. 'Lucas stopped finding me fascinating and instead found me frustrating – but he adored you. As soon as you were born, he went a little crazy, couldn't bear to be parted from you. After those first few weeks, he didn't really want me involved at all.' She grimaced. 'He told me I wasn't good for you, that I'd hold you back. I didn't believe him at first…' She let out a sigh, scratched Bob's ears again before turning to face him. 'We'd been married almost six years to the day when he told me he was going to divorce me. I was so unhappy, I honestly didn't know what to do for the best. At first I thought it might be better for all of us.' Her eyes flashed. 'Until he said he wanted me out of your life.'

'You agreed?' Jack asked, as anger and hurt stirred inside him.

'No,' Tara snapped. 'I told him I'd fight it.' Her face filled with emotion. 'But he was a lawyer – a damn good one.' Jack nodded. His father had been one of the best. 'He told me he'd destroy me if I tried to fight him. That he'd go after my parents – and if that didn't work, he'd do everything in his power to ruin your life. That was the ultimate threat – if he couldn't have you for himself, he'd destroy everything you could be.' Her voice dropped to a whisper. 'I had no idea what to do. I was terrified, I had no confidence, no real job. I felt useless, like I was nothing. You were so special, so perfect, and you adored your da – how could I put you through that?' She shrugged. 'So I took the money and left. Hid myself away with my donkeys. I tried to contact you a couple of times when I began to see more clearly, and he told me I had no chance of ever seeing you again. That if I didn't stop, he'd go after the sanctuary. Take that from me too. He had friends who could have objected to the use of the land.' She shrugged. 'I don't know if it would have worked. But I was too afraid of him to take the risk. I knew by then that whatever happened, he'd never let me see you…'

Jack tugged his hat off and scrubbed a hand through his hair. It was a whole other side to the story – a new reflection in the spoon. One he didn't particularly like. He'd known his father could be ruthless, but he'd never expected him to be cruel.

'I will say if I had the same choice now, I'd choose differently,' Tara said, her eyes shining. 'That I'd fight. But I have to live with what I did. You've grown into a good man with an incredible career. I have to be content with that…' She began to move past him, had almost reached the door when Jack opened his mouth.

'Stay,' he said, thinking perhaps Belle and Rachel were right – seeing the world from another perspective might just change things after all.

Jack tried Belle's mobile for the fourth time, giving up when it switched to answerphone. He grabbed her Christmas list out of his pocket and stared at it, willing the words she'd half written and then scribbled out to appear.

What did Belle want? And why did he want to give it to her? He shook his head and shoved the envelope into the pocket of his trousers just as his mobile began to vibrate. He snatched it out, hoping to see Belle's name.

'You spoke to Rachel?' Dave snapped, and Jack reached for the bottle of whisky on his desk and poured himself a large glass. 'I just returned from my conference and she said I had to talk to you. What did she say?'

Jack swigged some of the amber liquid, feeling the warm burn slide down his throat. He began to pace the bedroom. 'She—'

'Because Rachel's not talking to me and the divorce is still going ahead.' He paused. 'I bought her two new biographies and she rolled her eyes. I don't understand, but she told me you would.'

'She reads crime.' Jack swallowed the rest of his drink. 'And she's allergic to curry.'

'No, she's not.' Dave snorted. '… Is she?'

'You forgot her birthday.'

'Once…' Dave growled.

'Seven times,' Jack corrected. 'She's obsessed with boiled eggs. That doesn't mean she couldn't cook if she wanted to.' Jack waited while his friend processed the information. 'She says you don't know her…' He picked up his glass and tried to stare through it – the room was altered, distorted somehow. Different sides to a story – a whole new way of seeing the world. How come he'd missed the importance of that for so many years and only seen the world through his dad's eyes? 'That's why she wants a divorce,' he said.

'You're telling me this now?' Dave's voice rose.

Jack nodded. 'I've had an epiphany.'

'Congratulations – perhaps you can get a prescription for it.' His friend cleared his throat. 'So what do I do now?'

'Fire your solicitor. Talk to Rachel,' Jack said. 'Then listen to her side of the story. Give me a call when you have.'

Chapter Twenty-Six

Belle woke and immediately groaned as she tried to stretch, but the sofa in Kenzy's sitting room was tiny and her back ached. Her friend had offered her half the double bed the night before, but Belle had known she wasn't going to sleep that well and didn't want to keep Kenzy up. She stared at the Christmas tree in the corner. The lights glittered but she couldn't summon a smile. Her mobile buzzed on the glass coffee table in front of her and she picked it up. She'd left it on the evening before, hoping Jack would call. But when he had, she'd left it ringing. She grabbed it now and read the text. *What do you want, Belle?* She started to reply and stared at the screen, her thumbs hovering.

'Coffee?' Kenzy asked, wandering out of her bedroom and taking in Belle's expression as she put the mobile back on the table. 'Don't worry, I'll give you a facial later, get all those grumpy toxins out of your skin.'

'I'm fine,' Belle snapped, as Kenzy went to busy herself in the small kitchenette. She ground beans and boiled water before wandering back with a cafetière, milk jug and two mugs. She slumped next to Belle and poured them both a drink.

'So, what are you going to do about Jack?' The direct question was typical of her friend, so Belle had been half expecting it.

'What are *you* going to do about Logan?' she shot back, picking up her mug and taking a long sip of coffee. It was hot and bitter and exactly what she needed. She closed her eyes.

Kenzy huffed. 'I… don't know.' She'd put her hair up in a bun and wore silk pyjamas decorated with love hearts. She was the only person Belle knew who could have graced a catwalk immediately after getting up.

'If I had a man that crazy about me, I'd go for it,' Belle murmured, thinking about Jack's face last night, the way he'd looked at her. All that rage and bitterness. All the things he'd said… *You're as closed down as I am. You help people on your terms, but you don't let anyone in either.* Was it true?

Her eyes drifted to her mobile. *What do you want, Belle?*

Kenzy got up and picked up a frame from a white shelving unit set to the right of the sofa, bringing it back and placing it on the glass coffee table in front of them.

'You're not your parents,' Belle said, staring at the photo. It was of their wedding day – she didn't understand why Kenzy kept it. The marriage hadn't lasted long and her friend had been the one good thing to come out of it. 'Logan's not your da.'

Kenzy chuckled. 'Too right – I was just trying to imagine him making up his face with spots so he could woo his latest wife-to-be.' She snorted, then frowned. 'I have to be brave, don't I?'

Belle nodded. 'So do I.'

'You're going to talk to Jack?' Kenzy asked, sounding pleased.

'No,' Belle said firmly. 'I'm going to call my da.'

*

'Are you okay?' Hunter Albany sounded stressed, and Belle fought the desire to tell him she'd call back as Jack's words rang in her head again. *What do you want, Belle?*

'I'm fine,' she said, straightening her shoulders. 'I wanted to talk to you.'

'Thank you for the money,' he said quickly. 'I got the wire – we bought mosquito nets. Sorry, I meant to email.'

Belle inhaled deeply. 'Why don't you ever come home? Why did you send me to live with Annie? Why does everyone seem to matter, except for me? Do you think it was my fault Mam died – are you angry with me?'

'Sorry?' he spluttered.

'I know we were only in the car because I wanted those stupid shoes…' The words spewed out, set free after years of being chained down. All that need and guilt she'd been suppressing. The reason she'd never felt like she mattered or belonged. She'd spent a lifetime trying to make up for it, only to feel like she'd failed.

It took a full minute before her da responded. 'What shoes? I… I wanted to keep you safe. I never blamed you for anything. I… I stayed because I felt so much closer to your mam here. But, Belle, I'm sorry you felt like that. You've always been so independent. Never needed anyone. If anything, you looked after me. I…' He paused. 'Of course you matter. I never came because I thought you didn't want me to.'

'Why?' Belle asked, surprised.

'Because you never asked,' he said.

Chapter Twenty-Seven

Belle took a quick walk through the sitting room in Evergreen Castle as the band finished a practice song in the ballroom. She'd come over early this morning to help set up. Jack had taken Edina to see her friend Duncan at the riding stables just outside Christmas Village. Rowan had arranged the distraction with him days before, and Belle was pleased to have some time in the castle without him. She hadn't talked to Jack despite multiple visits and messages, and she hadn't answered the text. *What do you want, Belle?* What would he say if she told him?

'Matt's put all the food downstairs and we've been laying snacks out on the big table. There's a bar at the edge of the ballroom and he's got some friends to serve drinks,' Kenzy said as she entered the room and joined Belle. Instead of a tight slinky dress, which would have been her usual attire for this type of event, she'd worn a pair of jeans and a jumper with a snowman on the front. It had been a joke present from one of Kenzy's father's ex-wives – but it would be a good final test, she'd decided, for Logan.

'What about the band?' Belle asked, as Rowan swept in from the ballroom, wearing a sparkly black pantsuit and glittery Santa earrings.

'It's all set up, lass.' She patted Belle's hand. 'Nothing for you to do – we loved the nativity on Friday. You're a credit to this village.' Belle smiled, a little overwhelmed.

'Where's Tavish?' The older man had been persuaded to dress up in a Santa costume so he could give presents to all the children later. He'd promised, but Belle wasn't entirely convinced he'd follow through.

'He's out with Tara, in the barn with the donkey,' Isla said, sweeping into the room with a cake and putting it on the table next to a huge spread of food. The villagers had obviously been cooking and baking all weekend because there were cakes, mince pies, sausage rolls, sandwiches, sweets and a hundred other temptations. Belle had offered to make something too, but Rowan had told her she'd done enough.

'Tara's still here?' Belle asked, frowning. 'I thought she was going to leave?' She hadn't seen her when she'd arrived at the castle and no one in the village had mentioned a thing – not that she'd left Kenzy's flat since Friday evening.

'No.' Rowan shook her head. 'She's been here the whole time helping get things ready for the party. They're trying to see if Bob will help to pull the Rolls-Royce out of the garage – Jack thought Tavish could arrive in it.' She winked, grinning. 'Sure beats a sleigh.'

'What else needs doing?' Belle asked, as the band began to play and the doorbell at the front of the castle rang.

'Nothing. I told you before. You need a drink!' Rowan said, as Isla walked up and handed her a glass of wine. 'Now, relax and have fun, it's time for us to take care of you.'

Everyone from the village arrived in the next ten minutes and soon the castle was filled with people and music. As they waited for Jack to bring Edina back from Duncan's stables, Isla caught Belle as she was admiring the cake. It was shaped like Santa and had been decorated with layers of silver baubles and sweets. 'Like it?' she asked.

'Aye – did you make it?' Belle smiled when the woman blushed.

'I've made you something similar – it's back at your house. I've got good news.'

'You have?' Belle glanced distractedly towards the door. When would Jack and Edina arrive? What would she say to Jack when they did?

'We've rented somewhere for us to live.' Isla did an air punch and grinned. 'It's just come up and it'll be free a few days after New Year, so you can move home. Rowan told us about it actually; one of her neighbours is relocating for work for a year and needs a caretaker. The one he had lined up just fell through. He has horses – and sheep. Adam's ecstatic. He wanted to put his nativity costume on the minute we told him.'

Belle chuckled. 'He's welcome to keep it. I'm sure Edina will make us another.'

'Thank goodness.' Isla did a mock gasp. 'Seriously, I wanted to thank you again. It couldn't have been easy giving up your home like you have.'

'Ach.' Belle felt her cheeks flush. 'I think you did us all a favour.' She glanced around the room. 'If you hadn't moved in, I wouldn't be here. Perhaps we wouldn't be having this party.' Because Edina wouldn't have written her Christmas list. Then again, neither would she – then she'd never have talked to her da, never met Jack…

'Oh…' Belle heard Kenzy let out a sudden surprised gasp behind her, and saw the moment Logan spotted her. He'd just walked into the room behind Tavish, who was dressed in his usual dark trousers and Aran jumper, so Belle guessed he planned to change into the Santa outfit later. Tara and Logan followed – and he only had eyes for Kenzy. He stalked up to her as Isla made her excuses and went to help Rowan hand out drinks.

'You look pretty, lass,' he said quietly, as Belle took a step away to give them privacy.

Kenzy flushed but met his eyes. 'What, this old thing?' She pulled the bottom of the jumper out and shook it until the snowman's nose wobbled. Logan chuckled and beamed, which must have been the right reaction because Kenzy's face softened.

'I like you better without the spots,' she said after a pause. 'But I like you with them too. I know what you were trying to tell me…'

Logan reached out and stroked her cheek. 'Does that mean you're ready now, lass?'

Kenzy blushed and nodded. 'Will you come for dinner later?'

'Nae, lass.' Her face dropped and he grinned. 'You can come to mine.' Then he leaned down, swept an arm around her waist and gave her a long, slow kiss.

'Jack texted before he left Duncan's. They should almost be here!' Tara shouted ten minutes later, and everyone in the room hushed as the lights were dimmed. Belle heard the front door open and close, the tap of a cane on the wooden floor. Then Edina entered the room, and the lights went up as all the villagers waved and cheered. Belle had never seen so many of them in one place and the atmosphere in the room was electric.

'Oh!' Edina gasped, as she took in the crowd of old and new friends who'd gathered to welcome her. 'A Christmas party!' She beamed and her eyes filled with happy tears as she made her way further inside. As she did, the lights from the Christmas tree sparkled, picking out the emerald tiara tucked into her hair: the same one Belle had taken to Morridon with Jack to get fixed. Had he picked it up and given it to his nana?

Before she could ask, Rowan ran up to join Edina, Isla gave her a glass of punch, and Tavish repositioned her chair with the trusty stool so she could sit by the tree, facing out so she could see everyone. 'Aye, and Santa will be here later!' Rowan bellowed, and there was a roar of excitement from the assembled children.

Edina's eyebrows lifted and she glanced over at Belle, before seeking out Jack and Tara. They were standing next to each other, not exactly hugging, but even from here, Belle could see there had been some kind of thaw. Had Jack finally listened to his mam and forgiven her? Her stomach turned over – what did that mean?

'I'm not sure I need to see Santa. I've got everything on my Christmas list this year already,' Edina said loudly, her eyes misting as she looked at Jack and Tara. 'Aside from one small thing.' Her attention shifted to Tavish.

'What's that, lass?' he asked, as his dog Iver trotted up to nuzzle her hand. The older man followed and crouched so he could look into Edina's face.

'That's not important, but while you're there, will you finally show me that tattoo?' she demanded. Tavish huffed and bristled, but this time he rolled up his sleeve.

'You'll keep asking until I do, and I suppose it's almost Christmas,' he grumbled, thrusting the inside of his wrist under her nose.

'"Never Get a Tattoo When You've Been Drinking",' Edina read, before snorting and bursting into a torrent of giggles. 'What does that mean?' she spluttered, still laughing.

Tavish shook his head, but his shoulders shook as he began to laugh too. His smile broadened, making him look years younger. 'Damned if I know, lass, I don't even remember getting it! Why do you think I didn't want to show it to you?'

Belle smiled. Aside from Christmas dinner tomorrow – which was mostly prepared, courtesy of Rowan – the final thing had been ticked off Edina's list. Was her work done? Should she leave? She glanced towards the door and saw Jack standing alone. He was watching her and he wasn't smiling.

She took in a deep breath, then walked over slowly to join him and he swept a hand towards the hallway. The location of the first place she'd seen him in the flesh – would it be the last place she'd ever see him too? He looked handsome today in a soft blue shirt and dark trousers. She tried not to look at him and studied the floor, waiting for him to speak. When he didn't she glanced up, her stomach a jumble of nerves. 'You talked to your mam?'

'Yes. There are a few more things we have to work out, but we've got time – she's staying for Christmas.' He stared at her, his blue eyes dark. 'You talk to your da?' he asked gently.

She jerked her head. 'He's coming to visit in January.'

He nodded.

'I'm sorry,' she rushed. 'You were right. I've been pushing people away since Mam died. Since Da made me move to Christmas Village.' She glanced at the crowd in the sitting room. 'I thought he didn't want me, that he was angry about Mam, but he just wanted to keep me safe…' She heaved in a breath. 'He thought I was happy, thought I didn't need him. All these years…'

Jack nodded. 'Of only knowing one side of the story because you were afraid to ask for the rest?' She nodded. 'I learned the same lesson myself – and today I found out my best friend Dave has reunited with his wife because of it.'

'That's… amazing.' Belle swallowed, her eyes filling – was everyone getting their happy ending except for her? 'When are you going back to London?' she asked, staring at the floor.

'After the party,' Jack said.

'What?' Belle jerked her face up to meet his. 'But I thought—'

'To collect my things. I'll be here for Christmas, then I plan to take a couple of weeks' holiday. I talked to the other partners in the law firm yesterday. I know it's the weekend, but I couldn't wait.' He looked at her, unblinking. 'We discussed opening an office in Morridon. I'll move into the castle for a while, maybe visit Skye…'

'You're staying?' Belle asked, shocked.

'Yes.' He stared at her and the silence stretched. 'I've learned a lot since I came to Scotland and met you. I learned about giving and I learned about listening and I learned about opening myself up.' He gave her a lopsided smile. 'I learned my father was wrong about a lot of things. That there really are people in the world like you… I still love him, but there's room in my life now for my mother too. Because I listened to the other side of the story – and now I want to hear yours. What do you want, Belle?' he asked again, and she felt warmth flood her to the bones.

'I…'

'Because I think I know.'

'It wasn't jewellery,' she said roughly.

He chuckled. 'It wasn't a pink Ferrari either. It's been under my nose the whole time,' he added. 'You do so much for everyone, fill your life with good deeds.'

'I don't mind,' Belle said, frustrated. 'It makes me happy.'

'I know.' He nodded. 'The same as your mam and da.'

'I suppose…' she agreed. Someone cheered in the other room but Belle didn't look away.

Jack was staring at her, giving her his full attention, his expression intense. 'But you want someone to put you first sometimes. I overheard you saying it on the phone when we first met… I didn't join the dots until yesterday.'

'I… you did?' Belle's insides did a tiny pirouette.

'No one's ever put you first – not since your mam. Not Annie, Kenzy, Robina, Ted or your da…' Jack said.

'He thought I didn't need him.' Belle screwed up her face, still shocked by their conversation.

'That's the other side of the story…' Jack agreed.

Belle nodded. 'That and asking for what you want.' She swallowed, her heart in her throat. 'You were right about that too.'

'Tell *me* what you want, Belle – I know I've guessed, but say the words, ask.' Jack took a step forwards. The fairy lights in the hall were sparkling around them, giving everything a magical glow.

She licked her lips. 'You're right. I want...' She swallowed because opening up, saying what she needed, still wasn't easy. 'I want someone to put me first. I want to matter...'

Jack looked into the sitting room where the party was in full swing. 'You matter, Belle. Just look at what you did. You brought the village together. Gave my grandmother everything on her Christmas list. She's got a new lease of life, friends, her family. Perhaps even a chance at love...' he added, when Tavish leaned down to drop a gentle kiss on the top of Edina's head.

Belle took a moment to look around the assembled crowd, at the children running and playing, at Rowan and Isla talking and admiring the tree, at Tara beaming as she helped Matt with a tray of drinks. She felt her stomach flip over and her insides warm. Perhaps Jack was right. She nibbled her lip. 'But do I matter to you?' she asked, her heart in her throat.

'Oh, you matter,' Jack said, giving her another of those lopsided smiles. 'That's my side of the story – you matter to me.' He pulled a red envelope out of his pocket and handed it to her, taking another step forwards until they were almost toe to toe. 'I wrote a Christmas list,' he said softly.

'What?' Belle gaped at him.

'Read it.' He watched as she ripped the envelope open and tugged out a crisp white piece of paper.

Belle scanned the words. 'Dear Santa,' she read, fighting tears. 'All I want for Christmas is Belle.' She laughed and let the letter fall to the floor as she reached up, meeting Jack as he leaned down to kiss her. Then she was in his arms and he swept her up, swinging her around as Christmas music began to play loudly in the other room. Belle's head and heart were filled with so many happy emotions; so much had changed in the last few weeks. She wrapped her arms tightly around Jack's shoulders, laughing when he dipped her and then deepened the kiss. She had everything on her Christmas list now – and so much more…

A Letter from Donna

I want to say a huge thank you for choosing to read *Christmas in the Scottish Highlands*. If you enjoyed it, and want to keep up to date with all my latest releases, just sign up at the following link. Your email address will never be shared and you can unsubscribe at any time.

www.bookouture.com/donna-ashcroft

Christmas in the Scottish Highlands took me to a new village in the beautiful Scottish Highlands. I love the Scottish landscape – it's magical, especially when it snows, and is the perfect backdrop for a Christmas story. I really enjoyed meeting all the new quirky characters in Christmas Village – from Edina and Tavish to Bob the donkey! I hope you enjoyed visiting and following Belle and Jack as they tried to give Edina everything on her Christmas list – from pink hair to a reunited family. The two of them had a lot to overcome in the story before they were ready to let love into their lives, and I hope you loved their journey as much as I adored writing it.

If you did, it would be wonderful if you could please leave a short review. Not only do I want to know what you thought, it might encourage a new reader to pick up my book for the first time.

I really love hearing from my readers – so please say hi on my Facebook page, through Twitter, on Instagram, or via my beautiful website.

Thanks,
Donna Ashcroft x

      DonnaAshcroftAuthor

      @Donnashc

      donnaashcroftauthor

      www.donna-writes.co.uk

Acknowledgements

Thanks firstly to Nick Cook. I've always wanted to be a writer, and wrote books from the age of twelve, but I only really got started properly when I had my children. I joined Tring Writers' Circle and Nick used to teach us every other week. His lessons were so inspiring and I learned so much. He really gave me the tools and confidence to move forwards on my writing journey. He also gave me some great advice when I was made redundant and I still have a printout of the email.

Thank you to the bloggers who review my books and have supported me so much since I was published (these are just a few, and apologies if I have inadvertently missed anyone): A Little Book Problem, Audio Killed the Bookmark, Berit Talks Books, B for Bookreview, Bookish Jottings, Bookworm 86, Captured on Film, Caroline's Book Reviews, Chat About Books, Corinne Rodrigues, Booknista, I Am Indeed, Ceri's Lil Blog, Books, Life and Everything, Page-Turners Book Reviews by Caroline, Robin Loves Reading, Shaz's Book Blog, Sibzzreads, Splashes Into Books, Star Crossed Reviews, Stardust Book Reviews, The Book Decoder, and The Writing Garnet. Without the support of bloggers, I wouldn't be where I am today, and I truly appreciate the time you put into reading and reviewing.

I wouldn't be writing this without Natasha Harding, my editor at Bookouture, who believes in me and helps to shape my books for the better. You'll notice her gorgeous son, Lennie, has a cameo in this book. Thank you also to the amazing team at Bookouture. I'd love to name everyone, but a shout-out to Hamzah Hussain, Peta Nightingale, Saidah Graham, Alexandra Holmes, Alex Crow, Claire Gatzen, Rachel Rowlands, Celine Kelly, Noelle Holten, Kim Nash, Sarah Hardy, and everyone else who has worked on this book (nope, it's not all me!). Thanks also to all the other Bookouture authors for your support.

To Jules Wake – who is always on hand when I'm having a writerly meltdown – thank you for the walks, plot discussions, and for helping me to keep my sanity intact. To Chris, Erren and Charlie, for the support and incredible book bunting! To my amazing friends and supporters: Jackie Campbell, Julie Anderson, Paul Campbell, Kirsty Campbell, Leigh Anderson, Andy Ayres, Alison Philips, Claire Hornbuckle, Anne Winckworth, Jan Dunham, Tricia Osborne, Anita Chapman, Sue Moseley, Maria Rixon, Soo Cieszynska, Hester Thorpe, Ian Wilfred, Danel Munday (and all the others who have been so brilliant).

To Louise Patten, who has a real donkey called Bob who is exactly like the one in this book. Thank you for the inspiration!

Thanks to my mum and John, newly married! To my dad, Peter, Christelle, Lucie, Mathis, Joseph, Lynda, Louis, Auntie Rita, Auntie Gillian, Tanya, James, Rosie, Ava, Philip, Sonia, Stephanie and Muriel.

Finally, to the readers who have supported me throughout my journey, buying my books, posting about them, and writing such lovely reviews – a huge and heartfelt thank you. I wouldn't be here without you xx